OUR
HAUNTED
SHORES

OUR
HAUNTED
SHORES

Tales from the Coasts
of the British Isles

Edited by
EMILY ALDER,
JIMMY PACKHAM &
JOAN PASSEY

This collection first published in 2022 by
The British Library
96 Euston Road
London NW1 2DB

Selection, introduction and notes © 2022 Emily
Alder, Joan Passey and Jimmy Packham
Volume copyright © 2022 The British Library Board

'Where the Tides Ebb and Flow' © 1910 The Estate of Lord Dunsany,
reprinted with the permission of Curtis Brown Group, Ltd.

Cataloguing in Publication Data
A catalogue record for this publication is available from the British Library

ISBN 978 0 7123 5421 9
e-ISBN 978 0 7123 6759 2

Frontispiece illustration by W. Graham Robertson from 'The Sea Fit' in the
Algernon Blackwood collection *Pan's Garden* (Macmillan, 1912)
Cover design by Mauricio Villamayor with illustration by Sandra Gómez
Text design and typesetting by Tetragon, London
Printed in England by CPI Group (UK) Ltd, Croydon, CRO 4YY

Contents

INTRODUCTION

"No person", remarks Mr. Parker in Jane Austen's satirical (and unfin-ished) novel *Sanditon* (*c*.1817), "could be really in a state of secure and permanent Health without spending at least six weeks by the Sea every year." What could be less likely to prompt a shiver of unease than sun-bleached memories of this kind of beach holiday: lounging on the sand, building (and stomping over) sandcastles, paddling in the cool waters of the sea, meandering along piers and into penny arcades, probing into the mysterious shallows of rock pools...? But what exactly are those creatures crawling over the rocks? And who is this who is coming along the beach behind us?

Historically, emerging conceptions of the beach as a site of pleas-urable recreation is, strangely enough, roughly commensurate with the emergence of the gothic tradition across the final decades of the eighteenth and the first few decades of the nineteenth centuries. Since then, gothic and weird literature has found much about beaches, coasts, and shorelines that might unsettle readers. Indeed, one of the assump-tions underpinning this anthology is that coastal regions occupy a vital place within the gothic and weird traditions of the British Isles. The importance of shoreline spaces to these genres is largely overlooked in favour of the more familiar (and perhaps more immediately disquiet-ing) settings such as castles, abbeys, woodlands, and sublime mountain ranges. But you do not have to read very far into these literatures to find yourself on the shifting sands of some uncanny shoreline—from Ann Radcliffe through to M. R. James, H. P. Lovecraft, and Susan Hill, to a more recent outpouring of weird coastal fiction by writers including Helen Oyeyemi, Andrew Michael Hurley, Lucy Wood, and Evie Wyld.

The most famous haunted coastline in this literature is almost certainly that of Whitby, as figured by Bram Stoker in *Dracula* (1897). It is into Whitby harbour that the *Demeter*—the ship haunted by Dracula—drifts, bringing the Count, and his terror, to England. Here, the coast is the gateway for a supernatural foreign menace and this sequence is rightly considered among the novel's most striking set pieces. But there is a more subdued moment preceding Dracula's arrival that offers perhaps a more compelling account of the coast's weird qualities. As Mina Murray sits in a graveyard that looks out across the North Sea—"the nicest spot in Whitby", she notes—she is met by an elderly gentleman who points out that lots of the graves around her are empty, for the sailors have drowned at sea and their bodies are lost. "My gog", he says, in dialect-heavy speech, "but it'll be a quare scowderment at the Day of Judgment when they come tumblin' up in their death-sarks, all jouped together an' tryin' to drag their tombsteans with them... some of them trimmlin' and ditherin', with their hands that dozzened an' slippy from lyin' in the sea that they can't even keep their grup o' them." That is, come the Apocalypse, the drowned sailors will return from the sea to reclaim their gravestones—and thereby their identities. This moment speaks to tensions between surfaces and depths: the empty graves belie the memorial inscriptions above them, and Mina's picturesque view of the sea gives way to an image of its depths filled with human corpses. It is suggestive, too, of more everyday horrors, as we are reminded by the old man of the dangers of making a living upon treacherous coastal waters.

As *Dracula* highlights, the coasts of the British Isles occupy a conspicuous position culturally and politically. Across the gothic and weird fiction produced by British and Irish writers, we find anxieties about the French Revolution sweeping across the English

Channel, fears about the precarity of the British Empire and of reverse colonisation, meditations on the major wars of the twentieth century, and preoccupations throughout on that which may wash up on the shore—monstrous or otherwise. Shorelines can also provide an excellent vantage point from which to reflect on the shared, and frequently turbulent, histories of neighbouring nations. A number of the coastal horror stories in this volume adopt this perspective, foregrounding in particular the archipelagic relations of England, Scotland, Wales, and Ireland.

The tales we selected for this volume help us explore further the fraught and unsettling history Britain and Ireland have with their coastal spaces. The tales display some important preoccupations with particular aspects of the histories of these regions. Bram Stoker's "Crooken Sands", for example, is both an extremely compelling *doppelgänger* narrative and a meditation on English-Scottish relations, especially via the performative version of Scottish identity enacted by the tale's protagonist, which comes to an eerie climax on the treacherous terrain of the titular sands. Similarly, Charlotte Riddell's "The Last of Squire Ennismore" invites us to think about connections between England and Ireland, while also telling a haunting tale of shipwreck, plunder, and the devil. The anonymously published "Narrative of a Fatal Event" explores the dark side of rock-pooling, dredging, and other coastal pursuits of the amateur naturalist of the nineteenth century; the central "fatal event" of this tale, too, gestures toward an unsettling weird ecology, a subtle implication of the troubling agency of the natural world.

A number of tales develop this theme of weird nature and eco-horror in their presentation of monstrous sea creatures—in H. G. Wells' "The Sea Raiders" and the anonymously published "What Was It?"—a tale about the kraken—for example. Other tales figure fairy- or nymph-like human creatures connected to the sea and the shoreline, luring unwitting people (men, usually) to their doom, as we see in "The Strange Student" and H. D. Lowry's "Legends". Arthur Machen's "Out of the Earth" provides an opportunity to see how the weird folkloric beings inhabiting our shores provide a means to consider the more far-reaching violence of global conflict. Here, the coast reminds us of the global networks and communities of which we are a part—and against which we perform great violence. The coast, too, shows itself to be a deeply compelling site on which to tell tales of cosmic horror; this is perhaps hardly surprising, as the coast looks out onto the vast and unsettling expanses of the ocean, which carries all manner of things in its depths and whose tides creep up over the land each day, depositing these treasure—or horrors—onto our shores. We see the cosmic horror of the seaside explored by Algernon Blackwood in "The Sea Fit" and by Robert W. Sneddon in "On the Isle of Blue Men", which pits sea-dwelling Lovecraftian tentacled humanoids against people taking refuge in a lighthouse.

Prose, however, is not the only way to tell stories of haunted shores, and this collection also contains some poems. Charlotte Smith's supremely gothic sonnets offer a meditation on the association of the coast with madness and on the power of the sea to exhume the dead and overwhelm the land. The collection is bookended by two poems—Mary Robinson's "The Haunted Beach" and Christina Rossetti's "A Coast-Nightmare". We have chosen these poets in part because weird and gothic poetry passes relatively unnoticed compared to prose, and poetry is an important medium through which writers, especially women writers, engaged with the supernatural and the coastal. Above all, however, we have chosen to bookend the volume with Robinson and Rossetti because these two texts, unlike our other texts, are not definitively set in any particular coastal region. Rather, they offer ideal reflections on the materials they bookend, conjuring up a wonderful and dreamlike atmosphere of horror and unease—an atmosphere, we hope, that is reflected across all of these selections.

Next time summer comes around and many of us turn our thoughts to placid excursions to the beach, we may spare a thought for the blighted protagonists of these weird tales, who remind us that the coast is rarely—if ever—really clear...

EMILY, JIMMY, JOAN
haunted-shores.com

FURTHER READING

Patrick Barkham, *Coastlines: The Story of Our Shore* (London: Granta, 2015)

John Brannigan, *Archipelagic Modernism: Literature in the Irish and British Isles, 1890–1970* (Edinburgh: Edinburgh UP, 2015)

Alain Corbin, *The Lure of the Sea: The Discovery of the Seaside, 1750–1840*, trans. by Jocelyn Phelps ([1988] London: Penguin, 1995)

Lara Feigel and Alexandra Harris (eds), *Modernism on Sea: Art and Culture at the British Seaside* (Oxford: Peter Lang, 2009)

Ruth Heholt and William Hughes (eds), *Gothic Britain: Dark Places in the Provinces and the Margins of the British Isles* (Cardiff: U of Wales P, 2018)

Matthew Ingleby and Matthew Kerr (eds), *Coastal Cultures of the Long Nineteenth Century* (Edinburgh: Edinburgh UP, 2018)

Charlotte Runcie, *Salt On Your Tongue: Women and the Sea* (Edinburgh: Canongate, 2019)

A NOTE FROM THE PUBLISHER

The original short stories reprinted in the British Library Tales of the Weird series were written and published in a period ranging across the nineteenth and twentieth centuries. There are many elements of these stories which continue to entertain modern readers; however, in some cases there are also uses of language, instances of stereotyping and some attitudes expressed by narrators or characters which may not be endorsed by the publishing standards of today. We acknowledge therefore that some elements in the stories selected for reprinting may continue to make uncomfortable reading for some of our audience. With this series British Library Publishing aims to offer a new readership a chance to read some of the rare material of the British Library's collections in an affordable paperback format, to enjoy their merits and to look back into the worlds of the past two centuries as portrayed by their writers. It is not possible to separate these stories from the history of their writing and as such the following stories are presented as they were originally published with the inclusion of minor edits made for consistency of style and sense, and with pejorative terms of an extremely offensive nature partly obscured. We welcome feedback from our readers, which can be sent to the following address:

British Library Publishing
The British Library
96 Euston Road
London, NWI 2DB
United Kingdom

THE HAUNTED BEACH

Mary Robinson

Mary Robinson (1757–1800) was an author, actor, and high-profile celebrity figure in late eighteenth century English society and its gossip columns. She was born in Bristol into relative wealth, which was lost after her father—a whaler—failed to establish a permanent fishery off the Canadian coast. Robinson found her first success on the stage: she (briefly) won the affections of the Prince of Wales, had the future Lady Hamilton for a maid in her dressing rooms, had numerous affairs, and became an extravagant society figure and fashion icon. Robinson began writing in the 1770s but turned in earnest to a literary career in the 1780s, writing prose, poetry, drama, and political pamphlets and essays. She is important as a figure in the history of English Romanticism, and as an early feminist writer and writer concerned with social justice. And like many Romantics, she broached the Gothic more than once—including in novels like *Vancenza* (1792) and *Hubert de Sevrac* (1796)—at a time when the genre was at its height of popularity.

"The Haunted Beach" (1800) is among Robinson's most wonderfully eerie works. It tells the story of a murdered mariner and a fisherman doomed to haunt a beach—yet exact forms of relation between the characters are difficult to gauge. It is an elusive tale, but suited perfectly to its liminal shoreline setting, where the beach figures as a kind of purgatory between life and death. Strangest of all, however, is the suggestion made by a biographer in 1801 that the poem reworks something Robinson herself experienced, when one night she saw two fishermen bring onto the shore, and abandon, a corpse, which remained unburied for several days until Robinson decided to intervene.

Upon a lonely desert beach
Where the white foam was scattered,
A little shed upreared its head,
Though lofty barks were shattered.
The sea-weeds gathering near the door
A sombre path displayed;
And, all around, the deafening roar
Re-echoed on the chalky shore,
By the green billows made.

Above a jutting cliff was seen
Where sea-birds hovered, craving;
And all around the crags were bound
With weeds—for ever waving.
And here and there, a cavern wide
Its shadowy jaws displayed;
And near the sands, at ebb of tide,
A shivered mast was seen to ride
Where the green billows strayed.

And often, while the moaning wind
Stole o'er the summer ocean,
The moonlight scene was all serene,
The waters scarce in motion;
Then, while the smoothly slanting sand
The tall cliff wrapped in shade,

The fisherman beheld a band
Of spectres gliding hand in hand—
Where the green billows played.

And pale their faces were as snow,
And sullenly they wandered;
And to the skies with hollow eyes
They looked as though they pondered.
And sometimes, from their hammock shroud,
They dismal howlings made,
And while the blast blew strong and loud
The clear moon marked the ghastly crowd,
Where the green billows played!

And then above the haunted hut
The curlews screaming hovered;
And the low door, with furious roar,
The frothy breakers covered.
For in the fisherman's lone shed
A murdered man was laid,
With ten wide gashes in his head,
And deep was made his sandy bed
Where the green billows played.

A shipwrecked mariner was he,
Doomed from his home to sever,
Who swore to be through wind and sea
Firm and undaunted ever!
And when the wave resistless rolled,
About his arm he made

A packet rich of Spanish gold,
And, like a British sailor bold,
Plunged where the billows played!

The spectre band, his messmates brave,
Sunk in the yawning ocean,
While to the mast he lashed him fast,
And braved the storm's commotion.
The winter moon upon the sand
A silvery carpet made,
And marked the sailor reach the land,
And marked his murderer wash his hand
Where the green billows played.

And since that hour the fisherman
Has toiled and toiled in vain;
For all the night the moony light
Gleams on the spectered main!
And when the skies are veiled in gloom,
The murderer's liquid way
Bounds o'er the deeply yawning tomb,
And flashing fires the sands illume,
Where the green billows play!

Full thirty years his task has been,
Day after day more weary;
For Heaven designed his guilty mind
Should dwell on prospects dreary.
Bound by a strong and mystic chain,
He has not power to stray;

But destined misery to sustain,
He wastes, in solitude and pain,
A loathsome life away.

TWO SONNETS

Charlotte Smith

Charlotte Smith (1749–1806) was an English Romantic poet and novelist. She was prolific and diverse, writing ten novels, four children's books, translations, natural history texts, educational books, and poems, most famously the *Elegiac Sonnets* (1784), thought to have birthed a revival of the English sonnet tradition. She moved across genres, with novels of sensibility, sentimental fiction, and plots which defined the emergence of the Gothic at the end of the eighteenth century. She included Ann Radcliffe, Samuel Taylor Coleridge, Robert Southey, and Erasmus Darwin amongst her friends. Despite prose outweighing her poetry in both quantity and fame, she identified primarily as a poet, which lent her an air of respectability both professionally and socially after a tempestuous early life, including an arranged marriage to a violent man and a stay in debtors' prison. Despite popularity the public later turned on Smith's somewhat controversial and politically strident writings, and she later became involved in radical circles.

The coast haunts Smith's works, with perhaps the most famous example being the posthumously published *Beachy Head* (1806). In this blank verse poem Smith uses the coastline to travel through time, unveiling the histories stratified in the rockface. Her earlier works take a less naturalist view, and the two selected here are emblematic of her sublime coastal environments. For Smith the coast becomes a space for articulating psychic distress, a liminal space between life and death, sanity and insanity, fiction and unreality. Coasts are leaky places—literalised as she imagines flooded coffins bursting forth from the cliff face. There is no rest for the dead here. But these scenes are not approached with dread, but rather a chilling fascination: Smith does not fear "the solitary wretch" but wishes to be him, to carve out a feminine sanctuary in the crags of rock. In Smith's works coasts are places of both terrifying descent, and potential liberation.

ON BEING CAUTIONED AGAINST WALKING
ON AN HEADLAND OVERLOOKING THE SEA
BECAUSE IT WAS FREQUENTED BY A LUNATIC

Is there a solitary wretch who hies
    To the tall cliff, with starting pace or slow,
And, measuring, views with wild and hollow eyes
    Its distance from the waves that chide below;
Who, as the sea-born gale with frequent sighs
    Chills his cold bed upon the mountain turf,
With hoarse, half-uttered lamentation, lies
    Murmuring responses to the dashing surf?
In moody sadness, on the giddy brink,
    I see him more with envy than with fear;
He has no *nice felicities* that shrink
    From giant horrors; wildly wandering here,
He seems (uncursed with reason) not to know
The depth or the duration of his woe.

SONNET: XLIV

Press'd by the Moon, mute arbitress of tides,
   While the loud equinox its pow'r combines,
   The sea no more its swelling surge confines,
But o'er the shrinking land sublimely rides.
The wild blasts, rising from the Western cave,
   Drives the huge billows from their heaving bed;
   Tears from their grassy tombs the village dead,
And breaks the silent sabbath of the grave!
With shells and seaweed mingled, on the shore,
   Lo! their bones whiten in the frequent wave;
   But vain to them the winds and waters rave;
They hear the warring elements no more:
While I am doom'd—by life's long storm opprest,
To gaze with envy, on their gloomy rest.

NARRATIVE OF A FATAL EVENT

Anon.

A tale of an excursion into the Scottish Highlands gone terribly wrong, "Narrative of a Fatal Event" was published in 1818 in *Blackwood's Magazine*, an important venue for sensation and horror fiction in the nineteenth century. It was not at all uncommon for works to appear anonymously in periodicals in this period—there are numerous reasons for wishing to hold back your name, especially if you're publishing a lurid yarn. And while the author of the "Narrative" remains anonymous, there are a couple of contenders for its authorship: for a long time Walter Scott was assumed to be the author of the work, though critical preference now seems to be leaning towards the lesser known William Laidlaw, a figure closely associated with Scott.

This short story follows two young university graduates on a post-graduation jolly around the Highlands. But the story is also a haunting confession by the guilt-ridden narrator and the titular "fatal event" provides the work's weird and unsettling centrepiece, inflected as it is by the eerie description of tangles of sea-weed, the subdued suggestion of an oddly animate nature, and the horror of a body buoyed and jostled by the waves. This story also gives an insight into an important aspect of the shoreline in the nineteenth century: as a site of scientific enquiry. The young boys of the story present themselves as amateur naturalists engaged in rock-pooling and dredging, popular activities in the period (Charles Darwin writes of the importance to his scientific education of rock-pooling during his student days). Their boating expedition is framed as a "mimic voyage of discovery", too, tying them into more expansive kinds of seafaring. Neither the events of the tale nor their narration offer an especially positive commentary on such endeavours.

[The following melancholy relation has been sent us without a signature or references. It is contrary to our general role to insert any communication under such circumstances, but we are unwilling to give any additional pain, and besides, there is something in the querulous tone of it, that seems to plead for indulgence, &c. and we would be glad to have it in our power to "administer to a mind diseased."]

If it could alleviate in the smallest degree the intense sufferings that have preyed upon my mind, and blasted my hope, during a period now of almost seven and thirty years, I would account the pain I may feel, during the time I am attempting to narrate the following occurrence, of no more consequence than the shower of sleet that drives in my face while I am walking home from the parish church to my parlour fire.

I already remarked, it is within a few months of being thirty-seven years since I left the university of Glasgow in company with a young person of my own age, and from the same part of the country. I shall speak of him by the name of Campbell; it can interest few but myself now, to say that it is not his real name. We had been intimately acquainted for years before we came together to the college, and a predilection for the same studies, a strong bias for general literature, and more especially for those courses of inquiry, which are the amusement rather than the task of minds given to the pursuit of knowledge, had, in the course of four swift years, bound us together in one of those friendships which young men are apt to persuade themselves can never possibly be dissolved, while no sooner are they separated for a time, than every event they meet with in the course of common life tends insensibly to obliterate this youthful union; as the summer showers so imperceptibly melt the wreath of snow upon the mountain, that the evening on which the last speck disappears passes unnoticed.

But our friendship was not destined to be subjected to this slow and wasting process: it was suddenly and fearfully broken off. It is now seven and thirty years, next June, since the event I allude to; and I still flatter myself, that had I had the courage to have saved Campbell's life when probably it was in my power, our mutual regard would have suffered no diminution, wherever our future lots might have been cast.

The teachers of youth in the university of the western capital of the kingdom, had fallen, about that time, into the great and presumptuous error of letting their pupils loose in a desert and boundless field, as if the truth could be found every where by searching the wilderness; and error was only to be stumbled upon by chance, and immediately detected and avoided. Wiser surely it had been to consider truth and error as at least equally obvious to the youthful mind, and therefore to rein in the minds of their pupils, and oblige them to conform to the safe and long established modes of reasoning and thinking.

One lamentable consequence of this presumptuous system was, the effect it had upon the young men of my own age, in arousing in our minds a disregard for the standards of our faith in religion; for instead of studying nature by the help of revelation, we reversed the order of induction, and pretending to follow the works of the Deity, as our principal guide, endeavoured to illustrate the revealed will of God by the analogy of nature. This may appear somewhat foreign to the subject, but a similar train of thought always mingles with my recollections, and it is not the least cause of my unceasing regret, that I should, in the pride and rashness of youthful enthusiasm, have encouraged Campbell, and even often led the way in these danger-ous speculations. It was our last year at Principal ——'s* class: and alas! I have to endure the remembrance that my friend was snatched to a premature death, while he was yet an unbeliever in some of the most sublime mysteries of our holy faith.

As I said already, Campbell and I, after a winter of hard study, proposed to ourselves, and set out on, a journey of six weeks, in in order to indulge our predilection for natural history, among the mountains and isles of the Highlands.

We had one morning ascended a high mountain in Knapdale. Many objects were either new to us or unobserved before, or we saw them under new views. Poor Campbell's spirits seemed to rise, and his mind to take wilder flights, in proportion as he looked to the barometer that he carried, and observed the sinking of the mercury. "This *Cannach*," said he, "that blooms here on the mountains of Scotland, unseen, save by the deer, and the ptarmigan, is not it more delicately beautiful than the *gloriosa* of Siam, or the rose of Cashmere; and if, as philosophers assert, there is an analogy through all the works of nature, and the meaner animals proceed from the parent as slumbering embryos, and the more perfect are produced nearly as they afterwards exist, why do we meet here in this cold and stormy region with the *Festuca vivipara*, which has flowers and seeds in the warmer valleys below? Does this puny grass adapt its economy to its circumstances, and finding that the cold and the winds render its flowers abortive, does it resolve to continue its species by these buds and little plants, which it is observed to shake off, when they can provide for themselves?" These and similar speculations enlivened our botanical labours.

---

* Last year of attendance on the course of Theology.

The day was calm, the sky resplendent, and a view of the sea and the islands, from the point of Cantyre, on the south to Tiree and Coll on the N. West, (the most picturesque and singular portion of our native country) was pourtrayed on the expanse before us. The scene had its full effect upon the mind of my friend, fitted alike to concentrate itself upon the most minute, and expand itself to grasp the most magnificent, objects in nature; he had not been more charmed with the most diminutive plants than now, when he took a rapid review of the vast ocean, with all its mighty movements of tides and currents; of the joint and contending influence of the sun and moon; of the agency of a mass of matter, inert in itself, revolving at a distance, and with a velocity alike inconceivable, and even moving, as by a mysterious cord, the vast pivot around which it rolled; and of the progressive power of man, originally fixed below his tree, and comparatively ignorant, listless, and blind, who had formed unto himself new senses, and new powers and instruments of thought, until he at last weighed the sun as in a balance, and seemed to have gained a view of the infinitude of space, and was lost in the fearful extent of his own discoveries.

We descended towards the shore of what is called the Sound of Jura; through many a dell and bosky wood, sometimes loitering as we stopped to examine the objects of our study, sometimes gaily walking over the barren moor.

The sea-shore presented us with a new field of inquiry, and a new class of objects many curious and beautiful species of *fuci* grow on these shores, and of several of the smaller and finer kinds we were enabled to acquire specimens, with the view of enriching our common herbarium. "On the summit of Knockmordhu," said Campbell, "we were talking of the wonderful adaptation of plants, but is there not something in the economy of these algæ, that shews a wise and intelligent provision, as clearly as does the conformation of any part of the human body? How comes it that the invisible seed of the lichens should be of the same specific weight, or lighter than the air, so that the most precipitous rock that the wind blows upon is furnished with them in abundance? And their sister tribe, these *fuci*, that thrive only within reach of the wave, the Seeds of these are almost equally minute, that they too may be fitted to lodge in the asperities of the rock, and they are of the same weight of the sea water, and float about in it continually; so that every dash of the spray is full of them, and they fix upon every fragment that is detached from the cliff."

As the ebbing tide began to discover to us the black side of the rocky islets, we procured a boat at a small hamlet that overhung a little bay, and went on a mimic voyage of discovery. While we returned again to the main land, the warmth of the day, and the beautiful transparency of the water, which, as the whole extent of the west coast is rocky shore, is highly remarkable, tempted Campbell to propose that we should amuse ourselves with swimming. Owing to a horror I had acquired when a boy, from an exaggerated description of the danger of the convulsive grasp of a person drowning, or *dead grip* as it is called, I always felt an involuntary repugnance to practise this exercise in company with others. However, we now indulged in it, so long that I began to feel tired, and was swimming towards the rocky shore, which was at no great distance. Campbell, who had now forgot his philosophical reveries, in the pleasure of a varied and refreshing amusement, was sporting in all the gaiety of exuberant spirits, when I heard a sudden cry of fear. I turned, and saw him struggling violently, as if in the act of sinking. I immediately swam towards him. He had been seized with cramp, which suspends all power of regular exertion, while at the same time it commonly deprives its victim of presence of mind; and as poor Campbell alternately sunk and rose, his wild looks as I approached him, and convulsed cries for assistance, struck me with a sudden and involuntary panic, and I hesitated to grasp the extended hand of my drowning friend. After a moment's struggle he sunk, exclaiming, My God! with a look at me of such an expression, that it has ten thousand times driven me to wish my memory was a blank. A dreadful alarm now struck my heart, like the stab of a dagger, and with almost a similar sensation of pain; I rushed to the place where he disappeared, the boiling of the water, caused by his descending body, prevented a distinct view, but on looking down, I thought I saw three or four corpses, struggling with each other, while, at the same moment, I heard a loud and melancholy cry from the bushes on the steep bank that overhung the shore. As the boiling of the water settled, I was partly relieved from extreme horror; but I had the misery to see Campbell again; for the water was as clear as the air. He stood upright at the bottom among the large sea-weeds,—he even reached up his arms and exerted himself, as if endeavouring fruitlessly to climb to the surface. I looked in despair towards the shore, and all around. The feeling of hopeless loneliness was dreadful. I again distinctly heard the same melancholy cry. A superstitious dread came over me as before, for a few seconds; but I observed an old grey goat, which had advanced to the jutting point of a rock; he had perhaps been alarmed from the unusual appearance in the sea below, and was blasting for his companions. I now recollected the boat, and swam to the shore, while every moment I imagined I saw before me the extended hand of my friend which I should never more grasp. I rowed back more than half distracted. The water, when Campbell had sunk, was between twelve and fourteen feet deep, and, as I said before, remarkably transparent. Some people are capable of sustaining life under water far longer than others, and poor Campbell was of an extremely vigorous constitution. I saw him again more distinctly, and his appearance was in the utmost degree affecting. He seemed to be yet alive, for he sat upright, and grasped with one hand the stem of a large tangle; the broad frond of which waved sometimes over him as it was moved by the tide, while he moved convulsively his other arm and one of his legs.* I remember well, I cried out in agony, O if I had a rope! With great exertion, and by leaning over the boat with my arm and face under water, I tried to arouse his attention, by touching his hands with the oar. I was convinced that, had there been length of rope in the boat, I could have saved him. He evidently was not quite insensible, for upon repeatedly touching his hand, he let go his hold of the tangle, and after feebly and ineffectually grasping at the oar, I saw him once more stretch up his hand, as if conscious that some person was endeavouring to assist him. He then fell slowly on his back, and lay calm, and still, among the sea-weed.

Unconnected ravings, and frantic cries, could alone express the unsufferable anguish I endured.—His stretched out hand!—I often, often see it still! yet it is nearly thirty-seven years ago. But the heart that would not save his friend, that saw him about to perish, yet kept aloof in his last extremity, perhaps deserves that suffering which time seems rather to increase than alleviate.

It is in vain that I reason with myself,—that I say, "all this is too true,—I hesitated to save him,—I kept aloof from him,—I answered not his last cry for help,—I refused his outstretched hand, and saw him engulphed in the cruel waters,"—but yet surely this did not spring from selfish or considerate care for my own safety. Before and since I have hazarded my life, with alertness and enthusiasm, to rescue others,—no cold calculating prudence kept me back; it was

---

* This appearance might arise from the refraction of the agitated water, as well as from the excited imagination of the narrator.

an instinctive and involuntary impulse, originating from a strong early impression, and on finding myself suddenly placed in circumstances which had been long dreaded in imagination!

But all this reasoning avails nothing. I still recollect the inestimable endowments and amiable disposition of my early and only friend,—memory still dwells upon our taking leave of the city,—our passage of the Clyde,—our researches and walks in the woodlands and sequestered glens of Cowal,—our moonlight sail on Lochfine,—our ascent of the mountain,—the splendid view of the sea and islands,—and our conversation on the summit,—the first cry of alarm,—the outstretched hand and upbraiding look,—the appearance of the sinking body,—the bleating of the goat,—my friend's dying efforts among the sea-weed!

It is nearly seven and thirty years now; yet, day or night, I may almost say, a waking hour has not passed in which I have not felt part of the suffering that I witnessed convulsing the body of the agonies of a strangely protracted death. Why then, will the reader say, does the writer of this melancholy story now communicate his miseries to the public? This natural question I will endeavour to answer. The body of Campbell was found, but the distracting particulars of his fate were unknown. They were treasured in my own bosom, with the same secrecy with which a catholic bigot conceals the *discipline*, or whip of wire, which, in execution of his private penance, is so often dyed in his blood. I avoided every allusion to the subject, when the ordinary general inquiries had been answered, and it was too painful a subject for any one to press upon me for particulars. It was soon forgotten by all but me; and a long period has passed away, if not of secret guilt, at least of secret remorse. Accident led me about a month since, to disclose the painful state of my mind to a friend in my neighbourhood, who pretends to some philosophy and knowledge of the human heart. I hardly knew how I was surprised into the communication of feelings which I had kept so long secret. The discourse happened to turn upon such moods of the mind as that under which I have suffered. I was forced into my narrative almost involuntarily, and might apply to myself the well-known lines:

> Forthwith this frame of mine was wrenched
>   With a strange agony,
> Which forc'd me to begin my tale,
>   And then it left me free.

My friend listened to the detail of my feelings with much sympathy. "I do not," he said, when my horrid narrative was closed, "attempt by reasoning to eradicate from your mind feelings so painfully disproportioned to the degree of blame which justly attaches to your conduct. I do not remind you, that your involuntary panic palsied you as much as the unfortunate sufferer's cramp, and that you were in the moment as little able to give him effectual assistance, as he was to keep afloat without it. I might add in your apology, that the instinct of self-preservation is uncommonly active in cases where we ourselves are exposed to the same sort of danger with that in which we see others perishing. I once witnessed a number of swimmers amusing themselves in the entrance of Leith harbour, when one was seized with the cramp and went down. In one instant the pier was crowded with naked figures, who had fled to the shore to escape the supposed danger; and in the next as many persons, who were walking on the pier, had thrown off part of their clothes and plunged in to assist the perishing man. The different effect upon the bystanders, and on those who shared the danger, is to be derived from their relative circumstances, and from no superior benevolence of the former, or selfishness of the latter. Your own understanding must have often suggested these rational grounds of consolation, though the strong impression made on your imagination by circumstances so deplorable, has prevented your receiving benefit from them. The question is, how this disease of the mind (for such it is) can be effectually removed?"

I looked anxiously in his face, as if in expectation of the relief he spoke of, "I was once," said he, "when a boy, in the company of an old military officer, who had been, in his youth, employed in the service of apprehending some outlaws, guilty of the most deliberate cruelties. The narrative told by one so nearly concerned with it, and having all those minute and circumstantial particulars, which seize forcibly on the imagination, placed the shocking scene as it were before my very eyes. My fancy was uncommonly lively at that period of my life, and it was strongly affected. The tale cost me a sleepless night, with fervour and tremor on the nerves. My father, a man of uncommonly solid sense, discovered, with some difficulty, the cause of my indisposition. Instead of banishing the subject which had so much agitated me, he entered upon the discussion, shewed me the volume of the state trials which contained the case of the outlaws, and, by enlarging repeatedly upon the narrative, rendered it familiar to my imagination, and of consequence more indifferent to it. I would advise you, my friend, to follow a similar course. It is the secrecy of your sufferings which goes far to prolong them. Have you never observed, that the mere circumstance of a fact, however indifferent in itself, being known to one, and one only, gives it an importance in the eyes of him who possesses the secret, and renders it of much more frequent occurrence as the progress of his thoughts, than it could have been from any direct interest which it possesses. Shake these fetters therefore from your mind, and mention this event to one or two of our common friends; hear them, as you now hear me, treat your remorse, relatively to its extent and duration, as a mere disease of the mind, the consequence of the impressive circumstances of that melancholy event over which you have suffered your fancy to brood in solemn silence and secrecy. Hearing it thus spoken of by others, their view of the case will end by becoming familiar and habitual to you, and you will then get rid of the agonies which have hitherto operated like a night-mare to hag-ride your imagination."

Such was my friend's counsel, which I heard in silence, inclined to believe his deductions, yet feeling abhorrent to make the communications he advised, I had been once surprised into such a confession, but to tell my tale again deliberately, and face to face,—to avow myself guilty of something approaching at once to cowardice and to murder,—I felt myself incapable of the resolution necessary to the disclosure. As a middle course I send you this narrative; my name will be unknown, for the event passed in a distant country from that in which I now live. I shall hear, perhaps, the unfortunate survivor censured, or excused; the wholesome effect may be produced in my mind which my friend expects from the narrative becoming the theme of public discussion; and to him who can best pity and apologise for my criminal weakness, I may perhaps find courage to whisper, "the unhappy object of your compassion is now before you."

TWEEDSIDE.

1844

THE STRANGE STUDENT

Anon.

"A Strange Student" was published anonymously in the second issue of *Hood's Magazine and Comic Miscellany* in February 1844. The magazine was launched by the humourist and poet Thomas Hood, who edited the magazine between 1844 and his death in 1845 (after which it was briefly taken on by Charles Rowcroft for another four years). As Hood produced much, but not all, of the content for the magazine, he is a possible contender for authorship of this folkloric tale of love-struck young men and dazzling nymphs of the seashore—though the story is not included in his posthumous collected *Works*.

In its focus on two students from the University of Edinburgh and their perambulations around the wooded promontories of Argyllshire, the tale might put us back in mind of the previous tale in this collection, "Narrative of a Fatal Event" (1818); and its interest in fairy lore anticipates the fairy-dotted shores of the tales included here by James Bowker and Sophia Morrison. But there are perhaps other literary points of resonance as well: the motivating event of the story—the weird infatuation with "two nymphlike creatures", voyeuristically observed as they frolic on the seashore—has echoes stretching as far back as Odysseus' secretive gazing on Nausicaa and her friends. It reminds us, in an odd way, of the seashore as a site of alluring spectacle. The climax of the tale once more imagines a morbid intermingling of the human with the detritus of the shoreline—and reminds all young lovers of the folly of committing oneself so fully to another, of rapturously exclaiming "where she goes I must go..."

W hen I studied at Edinburgh one of my special comrades and classfellows was a young Highlander—a Divinity student, who bore the high Celtic cognomen of Torquil Maclellan.

Now this young man was a character; that is, he had many points of peculiarity in his disposition and habits of thinking and acting which marked him out from among his fellows with more distinctness than the generality of men stand out withal from their kind. These points I shall endeavour to bring before you.

He was young, about nineteen, I think—slight but well made, and very gentlemanlike. He had soft curly black hair, indications of black whiskers, hazel eyes, and a clear white complexion, with a brown bloom on either cheek, where, by-the-bye, the cheek-bones stood out with a discernible but not unpleasing prominence. The expression of his countenance struck me always as eminently Celtic. There was in it a mixture of the pensive and the mild, the fierce and the shy; there would be a bold haughty stare, which would dissolve in a moment into a timid, bashful, almost silly, smile.

He was not at all a clever student, but got along with the rest pretty well by strong efforts, for it was evident he had no enthusiasm for learning. His whole ambition, he told me often, was to dream away his life the humble and contented pastor of some sunny Highland valley. But he had enthusiasm for poetry and the most poetical superstitions of his country. In these subjects his whole spirit was wrapt, so that he walked the world hardly like one of ourselves, but rather like one of those beings of another order, of whom he had exhaustless legends, and in whom fervently he believed. Oh, often have I listened for hours to his tales, each wilder and more original than the one it followed, of second sight, fairies, enchantments, ghosts, wraiths, water-kelpies, banshees, and seraphs, descending and holding converse with holy men, far secluded in lonely valleys among the hills! In these he placed implicit credence, and would have been grievously offended had I doubted them; and for each he had an authority within his own knowledge. A grand-uncle of his had the second-sight, and foresaw and foretold many remarkable events. His mother's third cousin, who was a chief, had a wailing night-spirit that announced death in the family, and which had been heard by his own father on three several occasions: and an aunt had frequent interviews with the enemy of mankind, who came in the shape of a small dark man, and mocked her while at prayer.

Torquil was a poet, but from his bashful disposition I could get sight of but few of his productions; and what I did see were quite in the Ossianic strain—ghosts riding on meteors, and delicate mountain maids with their hair floating abroad on the night-wind, recognising in them the misty forms of their lovers, slain in distant fields. Some were in the Gaelic language, others in measured English prose, but all unfinished; and he guarded them with so much scrupulous jealousy, that there was no securing a copy of any of them.

He was quite a solitary; society was a burden to him, he shunned it in every possible way, and when forced into it his sheepish awkwardness was as painful to others as it was to himself. He had formed a most exalted idea of the female character, and, when in the company of ladies, was so overwhelmed with the sort of ethereal halo wherewith his imagination had invested them, as to be utterly unable to address them in conversation. His greatest pleasures appeared to be to walk alone about the country of a sunny day, or about the lonely streets of the city on a moonlight night; or to sit for hours alone by his fire, looking into it between the bars. Thus have I found him often in his chamber, with his back turned upon his books, his candle long burnt out, and his head bending over the fire, into the glow of which his eyes were intently gazing, while ever and anon a smile of delight or a look of compassion or sorrow would pass over his face at the events of the ideal world that was moving around him. He would always sigh deeply when his reveries were thus broken in upon; but if I had come to listen to his dreams, a new pleasure would re-animate his countenance. He appeared to have no friends or acquaintances, either in the university or in the town. I alone was in his confidence; how this came about I cannot account for, save from the fact that I too, when young, had my whims, and was generally considered a sort of eccentric, half-cracked being, and "like," says the proverb, "draws to like;" probably, it might have arisen from our mutually understanding and appreciating each other's characters.

But, be that as it may, I certainly have had few friends to whom I have been more attached or whose loss I have mourned so deeply.

In temper he was the mildest of creatures, and the gentlest in manners. No one could be more at the command of his emotions than poor Torquil, or more variable in spirits—now he was all mirth and cheerfulness—within an hour he seemed a very picture of melancholy. He was strongly imbued with religion—the pure Calvinism of the North; but had interwoven with it a strange texture of superstitious Mythology, and firmly believed in an intermediate state without all the bliss of Paradise, and with but little of the pains of the other place—which was allotted to that class of half-fallen spirits, who have sported by moonlight in the imagination of his countrymen, from time immemorial.

No person, one would think, could be more apt than he to fall deeply in love, or, when he fell, to be more completely lost in the enchantment of the passion. He seemed cut out for its very victim, and yet, strange to say, he appeared always entirely proof to it; and while I, as in duty bound, was sighing away in a manner becoming my years, and creditable to my discretion, he, though he certainly did not laugh at me, appeared quite callous and devoid of sympathy, and altogether at a loss to perceive the precise nature or *modus operandi* of my pangs. I used to speak to him about this, and, while expatiating in glowing terms on the more glowing eyes and lips of Miss A., the golden tresses of Miss F., (ah, there's a sigh even now!) and the swimming carriage and magnificent voice of Miss S., would take him to task on the subject in expressions now of envy, now of pity.

"Ah!" he would say, "don't hurry me—it is coming yet, I know; and, I fear—for if ever that passion drove a man mad, I am such a man—it will be my death."

There is a certain village on the coast of Argyllshire much frequented as a watering-place, or summer residence, by the Cotton, Sugar, and Iron Lords of Glasgow and Paisley. South-west from it the coast has a singularly bold aspect, consisting of steep rounded promontories in succession, enclosing small narrow bays. These promontories are covered with wood, among which, where there can be found horizontal space enough, there are perched one or two villas of a castellated appearance, to make them harmonise with the rude bluff nature of the scenery. Along the foot of these projecting steeps runs the shore road, generally at about a hundred feet above the water level, often overhung by trees or rocks, and with another wood beneath it; down through which several little pathways lead over the rocks to quiet little bits of hidden beach, most pleasant for bathing. I have travelled much since those days, and to several out-of-the-way places in sunny climates, but a more beautiful walk for a summer's day I have not seen than this lonely road, winding round among rock and wood, with the smooth sea sleeping below, and a fair prospect of fertile low-land basking in the sun beyond it.

To a cottage near this village my father used to remove every summer, and hither I invited my friend Torquil, to pass with us a week or two of June.

He came, and appeared to enjoy himself mightily. The weather was beautiful—clear sunny days and starry nights, and daily and nightly he was out alone, following his own fancy, up among the hills, down that romantic shore road, or out in our small boat upon the waveless sea. At first, for a day or two, I was often with him; after that I hardly saw him at all, and about this I began to be a little piqued, though I said nothing, but went fishing, rambling, and sailing by myself.

But one afternoon, rather late, indeed about an hour before sunset, when the heat of summer was no more to be felt, though all the brightness remained; when the perfume of the flowers, plants, and blossoms, that had been burnt dry at noon, was just beginning to steal freshly forth, aided by the balmy dewiness of evening, that was soon to fall completely over the scene—when a small pale crescentic shadow, which you know to be the moon, was faintly visible aloft in the sky—but the bright sparkle of Hesperus was not yet discernible; at this season, I was slowly returning toward the village, from a walk of several hours, down the winding shore road. Just as I was about to round an abrupt turn, I was awakened from a reverie by the sound of clear cheerful voices talking a little in advance of me. I looked up, and, to my amazement, beheld my friend Torquil strolling leisurely along with a young lady, while a second was walking a little in the rear, apparently twisting a sort of garland with wild flowers. I say to my amazement, for I knew his invulnerability, his power of looking

45

unscathed on the brightest beauty, as well as his bashfulness and total incapacity for female society; yet here he was walking along, talking and smiling with an utter absence of all *mauvaise honte*, to one who, though certainly strange looking, was still a most lovely and lady-like creature.

He was so rapt—so completely to appearance under the spell of his companion's presence—that he did not observe me as I fell respectfully to one side of the road to let them pass. His features were animated by an expression totally new to them, as he looked with an ardent smile down into her face, for she was small and slight—it was an expression of admiration and love, amounting to worship, like what one might fancy on the countenance of a fanatical devotee about to sacrifice himself to his divinity, and it was blended with the shy, tameless, wild-deer sort of look his strongly Celtic face usually wore. He passed me altogether unconscious of my presence—not so did his companion. You have often observed, reader, how a woman, who is conscious of extreme beauty, and withal of a coquettish turn, glances at a stranger, into whose neighbourhood she may for a little be thrown. She gives you a sudden momentary look full in the face or side-long—enquiring, half admiring, and somewhat sweet and kind—next instant it is withdrawn from you, and succeeded by an appearance of ordinary influence—and not all you could say or do, were you foolish enough to try, would ever recall to you that delicious glance—no, it has done its work in her opinion, and one is enough to settle your business, they are too precious to be thrown away. Such a glance full flashing and instantaneous did this lady cast upon me, and in another moment she was lavishing in smiles all her sweetness upon my fascinated friend.

I never in all my life saw a being like her—smallness was the only drawback from the perfection of her beauty; for I hold with the ancients that stature, if not bulk, is a decided constituent of that quality. She was slight and little, yet through the light texture of her dress as she walked, the eye, aided by the fancy, could make out the complete symmetry of her most graceful figure. Her foot was exceedingly small—disproportionately so it would have seemed did not the sight move from it to the slender, beautifully shaped, and the flowerstalk-like springy ankle it supported. Her face, again, in its extreme and ripe loveliness, betokened the perfection of womanhood, albeit the slight elastic undulating form might have looked the girl—and it had even in a greater degree the peculiar expression which I have called Celtic, and described as animating the face of Torquil—indeed so strong was this expression, that it seemed almost to border on that of insanity. She wore a dress of some silken stuff of a beautiful green colour, not quite in the fashion, nor yet in that prior to it, yet deviating from them only in those particulars in which they seemed to have as usual left pure and classic grace behind them. A small green velvet bonnet, with lining of a lighter shade of the same colour, was allowed to fall back upon her neck, exposing her face and the top of her yellow head to the full glow of the low-fallen sun, as if she little dreaded or cared for aught but the ripening effect of its rays upon the mingled roses of her face, neck, and brow. A shawl of deep green tint was thrown with much elegance, plaidwise, about her shoulders—her shoes were of green leather, and she wore a snood or narrow band of some glittering cloth of the same hue round her head, as if to bind her golden tresses. Her whole person was glistening with gold and precious stones—every part of her dress, that afforded any excuse for a jewel, bore many and dazzling ones, especially the band over her forehead, that round her waist, her wrists, and her fingers, and the emerald seemed to be of all the most especial favourite. Moreover there hung with careless grace from her waist down round the skirt of her dress a very light and slender garland of little wildflowers, similar to that the other young lady behind appeared to be twining.

This latter person I had no time to observe, so occupied were my eyes and thoughts with the other, the immediate companion of my friend. I had merely time to notice cursorily that she too was slight and small, and was dressed in a style somewhat similar, before they were all out of sight from me behind the rock at the corner of the road. Her face I did not see.

As I walked along the way homeward, my mind was agitated by a thousand doubts and conjectures—who or what these ladies could be, or how my strange, shy, solitary friend had managed to procure or accomplish an introduction to their acquaintance. The conclusion I came to was, that the first was the daughter of some of the princely merchants who had villas in the neighbourhood, and *insane*; for on no other supposition could I account for the singular outlandish strangeness of her looks and dress; and that the second was either a hired keeper or companion, or some kind sister who performed out of affection that office.

I was on thorns till I got an opportunity of talking with Torquil on the subject, which was not till next day at noon; for not till then did he come home to our cottage. He asked me to take a walk with him down the shore road, and as we went he talked in glowing terms of this his first mistress.

"Alas! Peregrine!" said he, "it is come upon me at last, and I am lost. I am become but a secondary being, a poor insignificant satellite to that bright orb you saw. I have now no separate existence from her—where she goes I must go, and if she put me from her I must die."

"Tuts! nonsense man!" said I, "wait awhile and you will wonder—laugh—at your present ecstasies; I have an idea how you feel, but let me tell you, from actual experience, there is nothing makes a man feel so cheap as when returned to his sober senses he looks back upon the vagaries and antics he has been made to play by that most powerful, most unstable, and most ridiculous of the passions, love."

"Ah! you talk only as far as you know—my passion you can never understand—its object is not like the daughters of this earth, she is an ethereal being, a creature as much superior to womankind as is yonder blue empyrean to this thick air."

"Just so I thought of my own Laura, till I found her lunching on cold roast pork and bottled porter. But how the deuce did you get acquainted with her let me ask?"

"I will tell you," said he, "the first day after my arrival here I had wandered away down this road to about a mile beyond the last of the villas—that with the tower and clock attached, and, leaving the road, went down the rocks under the trees to the water's edge. It was about noon, and I had thoughts of bathing; at all events the spot looked so romantic that I was inclined to explore it. But, when about halfway down, I was arrested by the sight of two nymphlike creatures, who with mirth were laving the snow of their unclad feet in the little waves that washed a small nook of white sandy beach, and picking their tottering, but most graceful steps, among the sharp pebbles and shells—for some moments I watched them unseen—I ought not in honour, but I could not help it, I was fascinated. At length they left the beach, and ran quickly up the rocks in the opposite direction from where I was,—suddenly one of them, with a small suppressed scream, fell,—I sprang from where I was concealed, bounded across the bushy rocks, and in a minute more had raised her in my arms. One of those small white feet was bleeding, and a few drops were on a sharp slaty point of the rock that had grazed it as it flew over. I came back afterwards, and broke off that bit of stone, and here it is."

49

As he spoke he drew from the bosom of his waistcoat a small fragment of stone, marked with a deep red stain. When I had looked at it here placed it.

"At her own request I helped her companion to bear her up to the road behind a turn of which a small open green carriage, with two cream-coloured ponies, was waiting. She would not let me leave her, and we drove down about three miles farther to where her home is—"

"Ah," said I, "and where is it, and what sort of folks are her friends?"

"You have walked down, have you not, to a place where you lose sight of the sea, where the road goes round behind a small rather low-lying and wood-covered promontory,—here we dismounted, and entering the wood by a narrow-tangled path, came at length to a stone wall, ivy-covered, and concealed by small trees and thick brushwood. A small green door in the wall opened, and we entered a garden,—it is in a most singular taste,—there is no appearance of art, all the flowers and bushes seem to spring naturally and spontaneously, and it is only when you can perceive no weed, nor any plant devoid of its beauty or its fragrance, that you acknowledge the hand of art has been there. The walks are grass-carpeted, and bordered with the most beautiful flowers, native to our country, and many of the richest tints and odour that I have hitherto been a stranger to. Through this, by many a winding, we went past many a flowery arbour and many a fantastic fountain, and statue of woodnymph or satyr in marble or bronze, till we reached her home. It is an extensive dwelling of one story, facing the south-west, and with an open area of green-sward in front, shut in all round by fruit trees of all descriptions. It is on the plan of a cottage, and the front and roof, which is thatched with heath, are covered with flowering creepers, ivy, and wood-ling—the walls completely, and the roof partially. But how can I make you know the splendour, the luxury of the interior, where everything that could be contrived by the most voluptuarian Sybarite, or executed by the slaves of the lamp, is offered to the ravished senses; where every organ meets everywhere with some new and not hitherto dreamed of gratification."

"Bless my soul!" cried I, "I have been here every summer for this eight years past, and never before heard of a villa down this road farther than Mr. M——'s, the cotton broker; and such a Paradise, too, and so secret, I'm afraid you have found your way to the Cumnor, and stumbled on the Amy Robsart of some great man. You'd better mind your eye, Torquil, or you will get into trouble, as sure as fate."

"No," cried he, with an enthusiastic smile, "the lady of my life is mistress of the mansion, and owns no lord of any kind. There is none within those bounds, save in her service, or by her invitation."

"It is strange," said I, "that I did not find out this demesne. I know perfectly the low jutting land you mean. Now I last year went down there and entered the wood, but in place of a stone wall, I came to a rocky ledge, about twelve feet high, and shelving outwards over me so as to be inaccessible without a ladder, or without climbing a tree, and dropping from a branch—a proceeding from which, had I been inclined to it, I would have been deterred by the sight of a very respectable adder uncoiling itself among the bushes."

Here we had a long dispute, about whether I had been to the same place or not, or whether his stone wall did not fill up a gap in the rocky ledge I spoke of; and I resolved to make every inquiry in a quiet way at the village, whether anybody knew of the existence of the villa, or whether any servant from it was in the habit of coming there to make purchases of necessaries. At last I proposed to him, that as the day was fine, we might walk down together, and he could at least show me the wall with its door. With some reluctance he consented, and we went down the road together; but we had scarcely gone a hundred yards, when one of those bright insects, called in the language of the country witch-butterflies, caught my eye, and giving chase up the rocks beside the road, my foot missed a point I was stepping to, and falling, I hurt my side so severely, as to be glad to crawl home as speedily as with his assistance I could. I was confined to bed, or to the house, for more than a week after.

Whilst I was so confined, Torquil appeared to be revelling in the society of this, his charmer, about whom he seemed to be love-mad. She, her villa, her youthful friends, their music,—so much beyond anything we had ever heard together in church, theatre, or concert-room—the viands, the wines, the sporting, and the dances, formed the sole subjects of the conversation the few hours he was with me; whilst, at other times, my mind was in a continual ferment about what could be the common-sense meaning of all this so romantic affair, and what was likely to be the upshot.

At length, when I had got so far well as to be able to sit up dressed in my room—though I could not walk much without pain—one evening Torquil came in, and after sitting a little, rose, and pressing my hand between his two, while the tears stood in his eyes, bade me "good night," and left me. I was wondering what could be the matter, and I began to associate his present demeanour with his mysterious love in green, when a servant entering, gave me a letter. I opened it, and the hand at once, before I had looked at the signature, told me it was from Torquil.

He told me he had left me, and that I should never see him more; that he was not going home to his father's house in the Highlands, nor to Edinburgh, but to a very distant country, from which, if he should ever return, it would be many years thereafter. He was deeply sorry, it said, to part from me—he had been very happy with me; but he was going to be happier now—very happy, indeed, and very powerful; possessed of a power which he would continually exert for *my* welfare. He had taken this method of parting with me to avoid the deep pain of a parting,—in words—a bidding farewell—to both of us; and wished me every success and happiness in this and another world.

When I read this, springing from my seat, I spoke unconsciously aloud—

"At length it has occurred, and Torquil has committed the folly I feared—he has made a runaway match, and allied himself to that girl, who I am now convinced is insane—but hardly more so than he!"

All the evening and night I was in a state of the utmost anxiety, and next day feeling much stronger I took a staff and set out, the weather being warm and beautiful, to seek this secluded villa, and make enquiries to ascertain what had become of my friend.

After a long walk I reached the spot where the road left the shore, and went behind the peninsula of land; I looked around me, and was now sure, from particulars Torquil had mentioned in our former dispute, that this was the place both of us meant. Leaving the highway I entered the wood between it and the sea, and soon came to the ledge of rock I had before remarked. Moving cautiously along beneath it I at length reached a spot where it appeared accessible. Still there was no appearance of any artificial wall; I mounted over this portion with more ease than I had expected, but found no difference on the one side from the other. There was the same wood of low trees which appeared likely never to reach much beyond their present dwarfish stature, and between and around them there was an abundance of brambles, furze, stinging-nettles, and other brushwood.

Through this I made my way doubtfully with the end of my stick, and at length reached an open space, where I perceived a bare, grassy hillock, quite rounded and regular in shape. I now began, in spite of me, to entertain somewhat strange ideas, which were increased to inexpressible awe and feeling of insecurity—of mysterious danger—when moving round it I saw, on its south west side, an open level space, with a very large thorn-tree in the midst, and close by it one of those scathed circles on the grass denominated *fairy wings*. I could not withstand the feelings that took possession of me, but taking to my heels fled through the wood. In a minute or two I heard the murmur of waves, and reached the line of rocks that formed the shore, over which I resolved to scramble till I should find my way back to the road without again traversing that enchanted wood.

But here as I was moving along, stepping from one point to another, my progress was arrested by a sort of half-covered wide-mouthed cave, that had a floor of sand and pebbles stretching up from the sea-brink to about twenty feet back under the rocks. Just as I was thinking of stepping over this at a narrow part my eyes were attracted by a figure laid at length on the sand, with the head and shoulders washed by the tiny waves of the ebbing tide, and the face downwards.

Struck with new dread and curiosity, I made my way down over the rough points and angles of the rocks, and coming close to the body could at once perceive, by the dress, though drenched with wet and stained with sand, that it was my poor friend Torquil.

I raised the body, and though the features were a little disfigured, apparently by having lain against the pebbles, yet I directly knew them; his black hair, his eyes, nose, and mouth were foul with sand, and among the locks some glutinous sea-weed had got entangled and hung drooping into the water.

Reader, what were now my thoughts? I cannot tell—they changed every instant—I felt as if in a dream, only I knew I was awake. Amazement, grief, superstitious awe, terror—terror for my own safety—flew through my mind, and I was constrained, leaning against the side of that lonely and fatal cave with the body in my arms, to pray aloud to Heaven for succour and protection.

When I had become somewhat composed, I set about dragging the body up the rocks, out of the way of crabs and other fish. With some trouble I carried it to a grassy spot, where covering the face and upper part of the body with the handkerchiefs from my pocket and neck, which I secured down with stones; and spreading over the whole broken-down branches which I saw about, I left the spot, and made the best of my way to the village.

I had no sooner reached it than I was compelled to take once more to my bed; the trial had been too much for me. But I gave directions to a party of men, who set out that same day by water, and brought the remains round in our boat.

In Scotland there are no inquests, but the Sheriff-Substitute and Procurator-Fiscal, as I believe the officers are called, made an investigation immediately into the case; but on hearing the surgeon's report who had examined the body, and questioning such witnesses as they thought fit to put on oath, came to the conclusion that the death had been accidental, by drowning.

I sent to his father in the Highlands the letter of farewell he had written me, with an account of the circumstances preceding his death. In about four days he himself came on horseback across the country, but his son had been buried in the village churchyard, and he could only see his grave. He came and saw me, and a poor broken-hearted old man he seemed; but he was not allowed to stay or talk much to me, for by that time I was in a state of fever.

Reader,—on inquiry I found there was no villa of any kind south of Mr. M——'s, the one with the small tower and clock. Also, that the point of land is called "Ardshire, or the Fairy's Promontory."

PEREGRINE.

WHAT WAS IT?

Anon.

"What Was It?" is another anonymous story and appeared in Charles Dickens's successful literary magazine *All The Year Round*. Published in 1866, this story of a giant marine creature, "neither rock, nor wreck, nor whale, not serpent", sits between Tennyson's poem "The Kraken" (1830) and H. G. Wells's "The Sea Raiders" (1896). The tale taps into widespread popular interest in stories of sea monster sightings, and like many of its kind is framed as if it were an account of a real event. It is reported second-hand by a narrator whose uncle had witnessed the animal while visiting Shetland for work decades previously. Surprised that no one is taking advantage of an abundance of fish visible from the shore, the uncle is initially sceptical of "a low dark object... the precise nature of which was wholly indiscernible".

The creature is only ever partially glimpsed, its true size and shape concealed by mist and waves, or heard at night through the water. Such evocative glimpses and elusiveness align this creature with the mysterious depths in which it abides, and which it is in some ways bodying forth. The story itself focuses as much on the creature's disruptive—and circumstantial—effect on the local fishing community as on the animal itself: it deters the fishermen from launching their boats and becomes embroiled in the love triangle playing out between the tale's three main characters.

M any years ago—not much less, I am concerned to say, than fourscore—it fell, in the line of professional duty, to the lot of my uncle—great-uncle, you understand—then a young officer of engineers, to visit, of all spots in the earth, the Shetland Isles. His journey, as stated in his note-book, from which this remarkable incident is taken, was connected with the intended restoration of Fort Charlotte—a work of Cromwell's day, intended for the protection of the port and town of Lerwick, but which came to considerable sorrow in the succeeding century, when a Dutch frigate, storm-stayed, devoted an autumn evening to knocking it about the ears of the half-dozen old gentlemen in infirm health who constituted the garrison.

On the evening that preceded his departure from Chatham, my uncle appears to have given a little supper of adieu, at which were present Captains Clavering and Dumpsey, Messieurs Chips, Bounce, and The Tourist.

Whether the last three gentlemen belonged to the service or not cannot be ascertained. The army-lists of that period have been searched in vain for their names, and we are driven to the conjecture that the sportiveness of intimate friendship may have reduced what was originally "Carpenter" to Chips, and supplied the other two gentlemen with titles adapted to their personal merits or peculiarities.

From my relative's memoranda of the overnight's conversation, it would seem to have taken, at times, a warning and apprehensive tone; at other times, to have been jocular, if not reckless. The wet blanket of the party was Dumpsey, whose expressions of condolence could hardly have been more solemn had my uncle been condemned to suffer at daybreak, with all the agreeable formalities at that time incident to high treason!

Chips appears to have followed the lead of Captain Dumpsey, and (if we may assign to him certain appalling incidents of the North Seas, to which my uncle has appended, as authority, "Ch.") with considerable effect. Mr. Bounce seems to have propounded more cheerful views, with especial allusion to the exciting sport his friend was likely to enjoy in those remote isles; while The Tourist has, to all appearance, limited himself to the duty of imparting to my uncle such local information as he was able to afford. In fact, so far as can be guessed, the conversation must have proceeded something in this fashion:

"Tell you what, old fellow," Dumpsey may have said, "going up to this place isn't exactly a hop across Cheapside. If there's any little matter of—of property, in which I can be serviceable as administrator, legatee, and so forth—after your—in the event of your remaining permanently within the Arctic circle—now, say so."

"Prut!—Pshaw!" probably said my uncle.

"The kraken fishery has been bad this year, they tell me," said Chips, quietly. "Otherwise, your friend might have secured a specimen or two of the bottle-nosed whale and moored them as breakwaters in the Irish Channel."

"He did nearly as well," returned the unabashed Bounce. "Bill was bobbing one day for coalfish in rather deepish water—thousand fathoms or so—when there came a tug that all but pulled his boat under. Bill took several turns round a cleat, and, holding on, made signals to his sloop for assistance. Meanwhile, his boat, towed by the thing he had hooked, set off on a little excursion to the Faro Islands; but a fresh breeze springing up, the sloop contrived to overhaul him, and secure the prize. What do you think it was? You'd never guess. A fine young sea-serpent, on his way to the fiords, fresh run, and covered with sea-lice as big as Scotch muttons!"

"I should, I confess, much like to learn, from rational sources," said Captain Clavering, "whether these accounts of mysterious monsters, seen, at long intervals, in the North Seas, have any foundation of truth."

My uncle was disposed to believe they had. It was far from improbable that those wild and unfrequented sea-plains had become the final resort of those mighty specimens of animal life, which it seemed intended by their Creator should gradually disappear altogether. Indifference, the fear of ridicule and disbelief, the want of education, preventing a clear and detailed account—such, no doubt, had been among the causes tending to keep this matter in uncertainty. It was not long since that a portion of sea-serpent, cast upon the Shetland shores, had been sent to London, and submitted to the inspection of a distinguished naturalist, who (the speaker believed) pronounced it a basking shark.

My relative's voyage must have been made under auspicious circumstances, since, notwithstanding a brief detention at Aberdeen, a heavy tossing in the miscalled "roost" of Sumburgh, and a dense fog as they approached Lerwick, the good ship dropped anchor in the last-named port on the tenth day.

There were no inns, there are none *now* in Shetland, and my uncle took lodgings in the house of Mrs. Monilees, than whom, he observes, no woman ever less deserved her name. Living must have been cheap in those days, for Mrs. Monilees boarded, lodged, and washed her guest, for eighteenpence a day, and declared she made a handsome profit of him; the only "lee" of which my uncle ever suspected her.

Fort Charlotte was not a work of any remarkable extent, and my uncle's survey and report of all the Dutch had left of her, were very soon completed. His orders being to await an answering communication, which could scarcely be expected to arrive in less than a fortnight, abundant leisure was afforded for making excursions in the neighbourhood, and he resolved that the first should be directed to the lovely bay and ruined castle of Scalloway.

It was then the custom—if it is not still—to walk out upon the moorland, catch the first pony you fancied, take him whither you would, and turn him loose when you'd done with him. Arming himself, therefore, with a bridle and pad, my uncle stepped upon the moor, and speedily captured a likely-looking shelty that had an air of pace. The pony seemed perfectly aware what was wanted of him; and, having hastily rubbed noses with a friend—as if requesting him to mention at home that he had been pressed by an obtrusive traveller, but hoped to have done with him, and be back to supper—at once trotted off without guidance towards Scalloway.

The day was fine overhead, but certain misty wreaths—the skirts, as my uncle conjectured, of an adjacent sea-fog—kept sweeping up the valley, crystallising pilgrim and steed with a saltish fluid, and melting away into the blue.

It was on the lifting of one of these gauzy screens, that my uncle found that he had turned an angle in the road, and was within sight of the village of Scalloway, with its dismantled keep, memorial of the oppression of evil Pate Stewart, Earl of Orkney, hanged a century before, but still (as The Tourist would tell us, were he here) the Black Beast of Orkney and Shetland.

On a fine clear summer's day the coast scenery of this part is singularly beautiful. From the heights overlooking the picturesque harbour may be traced the blue outline of many of the hundred

isles forming the Shetland Archipelago, while countless holms*
and islets, green with velvety sward, stud the rippling waters. Far to
the westward—nearly twenty miles, I think—heaves up out of the
ocean depths the mighty Fughloe, now Foula, Island—Agricola's
"Ultima Thule"—whose threatening bounds the most daring mariner
approaches with reluctance.

As my uncle expected, a mist was hanging to seaward, and shut
out all the nearer holms and headlands. He therefore devoted the first
half-hour to a visit to the castle, being accompanied in his progress by
four young ladies, carrying baskets of woollen-work—the produce of
island-industry—of which, he was sternly informed, it was the custom
of every traveller of distinction to purchase about a ton.

The mist had, by this time, cleared considerably. Not a sail of any
kind was visible on the calm blue sea, but so many coasting and fishing
craft lay at anchor in the roadstead, as to have all the appearance of a
wind-bound fleet. Excepting when a small boat moved occasionally
between ship and shore, complete inactivity appeared to prevail;
and this was the more remarkable, since the herring-season was
near its close, and my uncle was aware that, on the opposite—the
eastern—shore, every hour of propitious weather was being turned
to the best account.

Here, however, though there were many sailors and fishermen about the beach and quay—lounging, sleeping, or chatting in
groups—there was clearly neither preparation, nor thought of it.
What made this state of things still more unaccountable was that the
bay, even to my uncle's inexperienced eye, was absolutely alive with
"shoals" of herring and mackerel, clouds of sea-fowl pursuing them
and feasting at their will.

---

* The "holm," at low tide, is connected with the main.

The goodwives, if, having their work in their hands, they did not partake of their husbands' idleness, certainly abetted it, since it seemed as if four-fifths of them had assembled on the shore and the little quay.

Curious to elucidate the mystery, my uncle drew near to a man who had just come ashore from a herring-smack, and seemed to be its master, and, with some difficulty, for the seagoing Shetlanders are neither polished nor communicative, drew him into conversation.

Would it be possible, he presently asked, to visit Fughloe; and on what terms could a smack—the skipper's, for instance—be chartered for the purpose?

"Fughloe!" repeated the man, with a grin on his bronzed features, "why—fifty pounds."

"Fifty *what*?" shouted my uncle. "For a four hours' sail?"

"You won't get one of us for less," said the man, sullenly, and probably in a different dialect from that into which my uncle has rendered it. "And *I* wouldn't tempt you to try it."

"You have done so well with the cod and the herrings this season, that money's no object, I suppose?"

The man's face grew dark.

"We have done *bad*," he said; "and we're doing worser."

"With miles of fish yonder waiting to jump into your nets?"

"Waiting to do *what*? Why, sir, *they* knows it just as well as we, perhaps better," was the oracular reply.

"Know what?"

"Eh! don't *you* know?" said the man, turning to my uncle; "so, you're a stranger. Will you come a little way along o' me?" he added, in a tone meant to be civil. My uncle assented.

Passing the remaining cottages, from one of which the skipper procured his telescope, they ascended the nearest height, until they had opened a large portion of the bay towards the west. Then the man stopped, and extended his shaggy blue arm in a direction a little to the south of the now invisible Fughloe.

"The fog's shutting in again," he said; "but you look *there*, steady. *That's what keeps us!*"

My uncle did look steadily along the blue arm and the brown finger, till they ended in fog and sea; but, *in* the latter—*through* the former—he fancied he could distinguish a low dark object belonging to neither, the precise nature of which was wholly indiscernible.

"Now you've got him, sir," said the man. "Take the glass."

My uncle did so; and directed a long and penetrating gaze at the mysterious object.

Twice he put down the glass, and twice—as if unsatisfied with his observation—raised it again to his eye.

"I see the—the islet—clearer now," he said, at last; "but—but—"

"I know what's a-puzzling you, sir," said the skipper. "You noticed, when we was standing below, that it was two hours' flood; and yet that little islet, as you call it, lifts higher and higher."

"True. It was little more than a-wash when I first made it out," said my uncle; "let me see if—" he put the glass to his eye. "Why, as I live, it has heaved up thirty feet at least within this minute! Can any rock—"

"There's three hundred fathom, good, between *that* rock and the bottom, sir," said the man, quietly. "It's a creature!"

"Good Heavens, man!—do you mean to tell me *that object* is a living thing?" exclaimed my uncle, aghast.

For answer, the man pointed towards it.

His fingers trembling with excitement, my uncle could not, for a moment, adjust the glass. When he did so, a further change had taken place, and the dispersing mist afforded him, for the first time, a distinct and uninterrupted view.

At a distance from the nearest point of shore, which my uncle's professional eye estimated at a league and a half, there floated, or rather wallowed, in the sea a shapeless brownish mass, of whose dimensions it was impossible to form any conception whatever; for while at times it seemed to contract to the length of perhaps a hundred feet, with a breadth of half that measure, there were moments when—if the disturbance and displacement of the water might indicate movements of the same animal—its appalling proportions must have been measured by rods, poles, and furlongs!

Through the skipper's glass, which was an excellent one, my uncle observed that its height out of the water had diminished by nearly half; also, that clouds of sea-fowl were whirling and hovering about the weltering mass, though without, so far as he could distinguish, daring to settle upon it.

Fascinated by an object which seemed sent to rebuke his incredulity, in placing before his eyes this realisation of what had been hitherto treated as fantastic dreams, my uncle continued to gaze, rooted to the spot, until the mist, in one of its perpetual changes, shut out the object altogether, when the skipper, touching his hat, made a movement to descend.

In their way back to the village, the seaman told my uncle that, about a week before, the bay of Scalloway, and indeed all the neighbouring estuaries, had become suddenly filled with immense shoals of every description of fish, the take of herrings alone being such as to bid fair to more than compensate for the losses of the season. Three days before, while the bustle was at its height, the wind light from sou'-sou'-west, and smooth sea, a sealing-boat from Papa Stour, approaching Scalloway, had rounded Skelda Ness, and was running across the bay, when one of the crew gave notice of an extraordinary appearance, about a mile distant, on the weather bow. The next moment, a mighty globe of water, apparently many hundred yards in circuit, rose to the height of their sloop's mast, and, breaking off into huge billows, the thunder of which was heard for miles around, created a sea which, distant as was the vessel from the source of commotion, tossed her like an egg-shell.

Traditions of volcanic action are not unknown to the Shetland seamen. Imagining that a phenomenon of this kind was occurring, they at once bore up, and, having the wind free, rapidly increased their distance from the danger, while, in every direction, boats, partaking of their alarm, were seen scudding into port. The appalled seamen glanced back to seaward. The momentary storm had ceased, and the spray and mist raised by the breaking water subsiding, gave to view an enormous object rising, in a somewhat irregular form, many feet above the surface, and—unless the terror of the crew led them to exaggerate—not less than half a mile in extent.

"A rock thrown up," was their first idea. One look through the glass dispelled it. The object, whatever it might be, lived, moved, was rolling round—or, at all events, swinging—with a heavy lateral movement, like a vessel deeply laden, the outline changing every moment; while, at intervals, a mountainous wave, as if created by some gigantic "wallow," would topple over the smoother sea.

Dusk was closing in when the sealing-boat reached the quay. They had been closer to the monstrous visitor than any, except one small craft—young Peter Magnus's—which had had to stand out to sea, but was now seen approaching. When she arrived, nearly the whole population was assembled, and assailed her crew with eager question. Peter looked grave and disturbed ("'Tis a young fellow, I'm afeerd, without much heart," said the skipper), and seemed by no means sorry to set foot on shore.

"It's neither rock, nor wreck, nor whale, nor serpent, nor anything we know of *here*," was all that could be got from Peter, but one of his hands, who had taken a steadier look at the creature, declared that it made intelligent movements; also, that, in rolling, it displayed its flanks, which were reddish brown, and covered with bunches as big as botheys, and things like stunted trees! Pressed as to its size, he thought it might be three-quarters to a mile round, but *there was more below*!

"Not many of us fishermen turned in that night," the skipper went on to say. "We were up and down to the beach continually; for, the night being still, we could *hear* the beast, and from its surging, and a thundering noise that might be his blowing, we thought he might be shifting his berth. And so he was; for at daybreak he worked to the east'ard, and has lain moored ever since where you saw. But we still hear him, and the swell he makes comes right up to our boats in the harbour. Why don't we venture out a mile or so? *This* is why. Because, if he's a quarter so big as they say—and, sir, I'm afeerd to tell you what that *is*—supposin' he made up his mind to go down, he'd suck down a seventy-four, if she were within a mile of him. We're losing our bread, but we must bide his pleasure, or rather, God's, that sent him," concluded the honest skipper, "come what will on it."

"There was one chance for us," he presently added. "The Sapphire, surveying ship, is expected every day, and some think the captain wouldn't mind touching him up with his carronades; but when he sees what 'tis, I don't think he'll consider it his dooty!"

They had reached the village during this conversation, and were approaching a group of persons engaged apparently in some dispute, when a young man burst out from the party, and, in a discomposed manner, was walking away. The skipper stopped him.

"Well, Peter, my lad; what's wrong *now*?"

"I think she's mad!" was Peter's doubtful answer, as he brushed back his hair impatiently from his hot, excited brow. He had handsome but effeminate features, and seemed about twenty.

The skipper spoke a word or two with him apart, patted his shoulder, as if enforcing some advice, and rejoined my uncle.

"Young Magnus, my sister's son," he said. "A sweethearts' quarrel, sir, that's all. But she *do* try him sure! All, Leasha, Leasha!" he continued, shaking his head at a young woman who sat at work upon the gunwale of a boat, and appeared the centre of an admiring circle of both sexes, who stood, sat, or sprawled about her, as their fancy prompted. She was very handsome, haughty-looking for her station, and, at this moment, out of humour.

Though she could not hear the skipper's exclamation, she understood the gesture that accompanied it, and, smoothing her brow, appeared to stand on the defensive.

Young Magnus, who had returned to the circle, stepped forward.

"Now, Leasha," he said, "will you dare to say before my uncle what you did to me—yes, to *me*?" repeated the young man, striking his breast passionately.

The word was ill chosen. Leasha's spirit rose.

"Dare!" she said, in a suppressed voice. "You shall see," she said. "But remember, Mr. Edmonston," addressing my uncle's companion, "this has nothing to do with such as *you*. I said that, among Scalloway men, we had both children and cowards. I said that, because a wrecked hull, or a raft of Norway timber, or at worst a helpless dying monster of some sort is floating on our shores, we are not ashamed to skulk and starve in port. Not a boat will put out to take up the fish within half a mile of this beach"—she stamped her bare and sinewy but well-formed foot upon it—"nor even venture near enough to discover what it is that has scared away your courage and reason. Shame on all such, I say, and shame again."

"You don't know what you are talking of, Leasha," said Edmonston. "We do. If there were not danger, I should not be *here*. I might be willing to risk my life, but not my ship, which, while God spares her, must be my son's and grandson's bread. You speak at random, girl, and Peter Magnus is no more to blame than the rest of us; less, perhaps," said the good-natured skipper, "for his boat is but a kittle thing. A 'wreck,' child? Who ever saw a rig with *nine masts*! 'Norway rafts?' Psha! Call it a sea-thing, you're nearer to the truth; but he's a bold seaman, and a precious fool to boot, that puts his craft near enough to ask whence he hails."

"*I* would do it if I were a man," cried the girl, beating her foot upon the ground. "And—and I will not say what I should think of the bold man that did it *now*."

Young Magnus coloured to the temples, for the challenge was directed to him, but made no reply. There had stood, meanwhile, a little aloof from the group, a young fisherman, tall, athletic, and with a countenance that would have been handsome but for a depression of the nose, the result of an injury, and for a somewhat sullen and sinister expression, which was perhaps habitual to him. The words had not left Leasha's lips before he uncoiled his arms, which had been folded on his broad chest, and strode into the circle, saying, quietly,

"*I* will go."

"You'll not be such a fool, Gilbert Suncler (Sinclair)," said Edmonston.

"You'll see," said the other, in his short, sullen manner. "Some of you boys shove her off," pointing to his boat, "while I run up yonder."

He went to a cottage close at hand, and was back almost instantly, carrying something under his fishing-cape, and a gun. His boat was already in the water, and fifty dexterous hands busied in stepping the mast, setting the sails, and stowing the shingle-ballast. She was ready.

"Who's going with you, since you *will* go?" growled Edmonston.

"I've only room for one man living," said Sinclair, in his sinister way. "Now, I don't want to take advantage over Peter Magnus. Him, or none."

The young man stood irresolute for a moment, then, with one glance at Leasha, leaped into the boat. Sinclair pushed off, eagerly.

"You have done well, girl," said Edmonston, sternly. "If either return alive, it will not be Peter Magnus."

"What—what do you mean?" exclaimed the girl, clutching his sleeve as he turned away.

"That Gilbert Sinclair is a treacherous, malignant devil, and at this moment mad with jealous—Stop—"

But Leasha had dashed down the beach.

"Peter! Peter!" she shrieked, "come back! For the love of Heaven— back! I must speak with you!"

"*Too late!*" replied Sinclair, with a grin. "Wait till he brings you what you want to know."

As the last word was uttered there was a splash astern. Magnus had leaped into the water.

"Ha! ha! *Coward!*" roared Sinclair, as his boat shot into the fog.

Evening was now approaching, and my uncle, deeply interested, and resolved to see the adventure out, accepted the skipper's invitation to pass the night at his cottage. After taking some refreshment, they strolled out again upon the shore and quay. The mist was clearing, and the moon had risen. My uncle asked what his host imagined Sinclair proposed to do, expressing his doubts whether he intended anything but bravado.

Edmonston was not so sure of that. Ruffian as he was, with a spice of malice that made him the terror and aversion of the village, Sinclair was a perfect dare-devil in personal courage, and, his blood being now up, he was certain, if he returned at all, to bring back tidings of some description. The man's unlucky passion for Leasha (who was betrothed, Edmonston said, to his nephew) had been the cause of much uneasiness to the friends of both. "God pardon me if I misjudge the man," concluded Edmonston; "but if ever murder looked out of man's eye, it did from his when Peter jumped into his boat today."

By eleven o'clock the haze had lifted so much that the skipper proposed to ascend the height, and try if anything could be seen. The night was still as death; and, as they rose the hill, the soft rippling murmur of the sea barely reached their ears.

"I never knew him so quiet as *this*," remarked Edmonston; "I take it, he's—"

Before he could finish, a sound, compounded of rush and roar, so fearful and appalling that it can be likened to nothing but the sudden bursting of a dam which confined a pent-up sea, swooped from seaward, and seemed to shake the very rock on which they stood. There was a bellow of cavernous thunder, which seemed to reverberate through the distant isles; and, far out, a broad white curtain appeared to rise, blend with the dispersing fog, and move majestically towards the land.

"It's the surf! 'He has sounded,'" whispered Edmonston. "Listen—now!"

Perfect silence had succeeded the tumultuous roar, and again they heard nothing but the sough of the sea lapping the crags below. But, after the lapse of perhaps a minute, the hush was invaded by a soft sibilating murmur, increasing to a mighty roar; and, with a crash like thunder, a billow—fifteen feet in height—fell headlong upon the rocky shore. It was followed by two or three more, each smaller than the preceding; and once again silence resumed her sway.

At daybreak it was seen that the terrible Sentinel of Scalloway had returned to his fathomless deeps.

And where was Sinclair? He was seen no more; but, weeks afterwards, a home-bound boat, passing near the spot where the monster had lain, nearly came in contact with some floating wreck. From certain singular appearances, some of which seemed to indicate that the wreck had been but recently released from the bottom, the crew were induced to take it in tow, and bring it into port. There it was at once identified as the forward portion of Gilbert Sinclair's boat, torn—or as Scalloway men insist to this day, *bitten*—clean off, just forward of the mast; the grooves of one colossal tooth—the size of a tree—being distinctly visible!

There are persons, it is true, who have endeavoured to lessen the mysterious interest of my uncle's story, by suggesting a different explanation; hinting, for example, that the object might have been composed of nothing more extraordinary than the entangled hulls of two large vessels, wrecked in collision; and that Sinclair, suspecting this, and endeavouring to reduce them to manageable proportions through the agency of gunpowder, had destroyed himself with them.

But, if so, where were the portions of wreck? We have also the support of no less a person than the author of Waverley, who, in his notes to the Pirate, mentions the incident, and its effect upon the hardy seamen of Scalloway; while my uncle himself, at a subsequent visit to that port, smoked a pipe with Mr. Magnus in the very boat—then converted into an arbour—that had been bitten in two by the sea-monster. So that, with him, I frankly ask—if it was not a kraken—*What was it?*

ONE DAY AT ARLE

Frances Hodgson Burnett

Frances Hodgson Burnett (1849–1924) was a prolific author of drama and prose, now famous primarily for the novels *Little Lord Fauntleroy* (1886) and *The Secret Garden* (1911). While these classic works have established her to posterity as a writer for children, "One Day at Arle" shows her skill at darker stories speaking to adult lives. It is set in a small fishing community and is told as much through dialogue, in local dialect, as through omniscient narration. In keeping with Burnett's realistic style, it is not a ghost story, but it tells an unsettling tale of the mortal peril facing a man on the seashore, his symbolic reward for having divided his wife from her preferred lover in her youth. In this way, the story adopts a characteristic Gothic narrative trajectory in which suppressed secrets from the past resurface to disrupt the present.

"One Day at Arle" begins with a marriage in crisis, as Meg Lonas confronts her unhappy husband, Seth, about his misdeeds and declares she will leave him; for consolation, Seth turns to work on the boat Mary Anne with his fellow fishermen. As in so many tales of haunted coasts, this littoral zone becomes a liminal space and the narrative plays wonderfully with our sense of time passing—achingly, agonisingly—over its climactic action. The tide itself is personified as a child, chasing waves and playing with shells and weed, but never loses its sinister inexorability: the tides will always be "creeping—creeping—creeping".

One day at Arle—a tiny scattered fishing hamlet on the northwestern English coast—there stood at the door of one of the cottages near the shore a woman leaning against the lintel-post and looking out: a woman who would have been apt to attract a stranger's eye, too—a woman young and handsome. This was what a first glance would have taken in; a second would have been apt to teach more and leave a less pleasant impression. She was young enough to have been girlish, but she was not girlish in the least. Her tall, lithe, well-knit figure was braced against the door-post with a tense sort of strength; her handsome face was just at this time as dark and hard in expression as if she had been a woman with years of bitter life behind her; her handsome brows were knit, her lips were set; from head to foot she looked unyielding and stern of purpose.

And neither form nor face belied her. The earliest remembrances of the coast people concerning Meg Lonas had not been over-pleasant ones. She had never been a favourite among them. The truth was they had half feared her, even as the silent, dogged, neglected child who used to wander up and down among the rocks and on the beach, working harder for her scant living than the oldest of them. She had never a word for them, and never satisfied their curiosity upon the subject of the treatment she received from the ill-conditioned old grandfather who was her only living relative, and this last peculiarity had rendered her more unpopular than anything else would have done. If she had answered their questions they might have pitied her; but as she chose to meet them with stubborn silence, they managed to show their dislike in many ways, until at last it became a settled point among them that the girl was an outcast in their midst. But even in those days she gave them back wrong for wrong and scorn for scorn; and as she grew older she grew stronger of will, less prone to forgive her many injuries and slights, and more prone to revenge them in an obstinate, bitter fashion. But as she grew older she grew handsomer too, and the fisher boys who had jeered at her in her childhood were anxious enough to gain her good-will.

The women flouted her still, and she defied them openly; the men found it wisest to be humble in their rough style, and her defiance of them was more scornful than her defiance of their mothers and sisters. She would revenge herself upon them, and did, until at last she met a wooer who was tender enough, it seemed, to move her. At least so people said at first; but suddenly the lover disappeared, and two or three months later the whole community was electrified by her sudden marriage with a suitor whom she had been wont to treat worse than all the rest. How she treated him after the marriage nobody knew. She was more defiant and silent than ever, and gossipers gained nothing by asking questions. So at last she was left alone.

It was not the face of a tender wife waiting for a loving husband, the face that was turned toward the sea. If she had hated the man for whom she watched she could not have seemed more unbending. Ever since her visitor had left her (she had had a visitor during the morning) she had stood in the same place, even in the same position, without moving, and when at last the figure of her husband came slouching across the sands homeward she remained motionless still.

And surely his was not the face of a happy husband. Not a handsome face at its dull best, it was doubly unprepossessing then, as, pale and breathless, he passed the stern form in the doorway, his nervous, reluctant eyes avoiding hers.

"Yo'll find yo're dinner aw ready on th' table," she said to him as he passed in.

Everything was neat enough inside. The fireplace was clean and bright, the table was set tidily, and the meal upon it was good enough in its way; but when the man entered he cast an unsteady, uncomprehending glance around, and when he had flung himself into a chair he did not attempt to touch the food, but dropped his face upon his arm on the table with a sound like a little groan.

She must have heard it, but she did not notice it even by a turn of her head, but stood erect and steadfast until he spoke to her. She might have been waiting for his words—perhaps she was.

"Tha canst come in an' say what tha has to say an' be done wi' it," he said at last, in a sullen, worn-out fashion.

She turned round then and faced him, harder to be met in her rigid mood than if she had been a tempest.

"Tha knows what I ha' getten to say," she answered, her tone strained and husky with repressed fierceness. "Aye! tha knows it well enough. I ha' not much need to tell thee owt. He comn here this morning an' he towd me aw I want to know about thee, Seth Lonas—an' more too."

"He comn to me," put in the man.

She advanced towards the table and struck it once with her hand.

"Tha'st towd me a power o' lies," she said. "Tha's lied to me fro' first to last to serve thy own eends, an' tha'st gained 'em—tha'st lied me away fro' th' man as wur aw th' world to me, but th' time's comn now when thy day's o'er an' his is comn agen. Ah! thou bitter villain! Does ta mind how tha comn an' towd me Dan Morgan had gone to th' fair at Lake wi' that lass o' Barnegats? That wur a lie an' that wur th' beginnin'. Does ta mind how tha towd me as he made light o' me when th' lads an' lasses plagued him, an' threeped 'em down as he didna mean to marry no such like lass as me—him as wur ready to dee fur me? That wur a lie an' that wur th' eendin', as tha knew it would be, fur I spurned him fro' me th' very next day, an' wouldna listen when he tried to straighten' out. But he got at th' truth at last when he wur fur fro' here, an' he browt th' truth back to me today, an' theer's th' eend fur thee—husband or no."

The man lay with his head upon his arms until she had finished, and then he looked up all white and shaken and blind.

"Wilt ta listen if I speak to thee?" he asked.

"Aye," she answered, "listen to more lies!"

And she slipped down into a sitting posture on the stone doorstep, and sat there, her great eyes staring out seaward, her hands lying loose upon her knee, and trembling.

There was something more in her mood than resentment. In this simple gesture she had broken down as she had never broken down in her life before. There was passionate grief in her face, a wild sort of despair, such as one might see in a suddenly-wounded, untamed creature. Hers was not a fair nature. I am not telling the story of a gentle, true-souled woman—I am simply relating the incidents of one bitter day whose tragic close was the ending of a rough romance.

Her life had been a long battle against the world's scorn; she had been either on the offensive or the defensive from childhood to womanhood, and then she had caught one glimpse of light and warmth, clung to it yearningly, for one brief hour, and lost it.

Only today she had learned that she had lost it through treachery. She had not dared to believe in her bliss, even during its fairest existence; and so, when light-hearted, handsome Dan Morgan's rival had worked against him with false stories and false proofs, her fierce pride had caught at them, and her revenge had been swift and sharp. But it had fallen back upon her own head now. This very morning handsome Dan had come back again to Arle, and earned his revenge, too, though he had only meant to clear himself when he told her what chance had brought to light. He had come back—her lover, the man who had conquered and sweetened her bitter nature as nothing else on earth had power to do—he had come back and found her what she was—the wife of a man for whom she had never cared, the wife of the man who had played them both false, and robbed her of the one poor gleam of joy she had known. She had been hard and wild enough at first, but just now, when she slipped down upon the door-step with her back turned to the wretched man within—when it came upon her that, traitor as he was, she herself had given him the right to take her bright-faced lover's place, and usurp his tender power—when the fresh sea-breeze blew upon her face and stirred her hair, and the warm, rare sunshine touched her, even breeze and sunshine helped her to the end, so that she broke down into a sharp sob, as any other woman might have done, only that the repressed strength of her poor warped nature made it a sob sharper and deeper than another woman's would have been.

"Yo' mought ha' left me that!" she said. "Yo' mought ha' left it to me! There wur other women as would ha' done yo', there wur no other man on earth as would do me. Yo' knowed what my life had been, an' how it wur hand to hand betwixt other folk an' me. Yo' knowed how much I cared fur him an' what he wur to me. Yo' mought ha' let us be. I nivver harmed yo'. I wouldna harm yo' so sinful cruel now."

"Wilt ta listen?" he asked, labouring as if for breath.

"Aye," she answered him, "I'll listen, fur tha conna hurt me worser. Th' day fur that's past an' gone."

"Well," said he, "listen an' I'll try to tell yo'. I know it's no use, but I mun say a word or two. Happen yo' didna know I loved yo' aw' yo're life—happen yo' didna, but it's true. When yo' wur a little lass gatherin' sea-weed on th' sands I watched yo' when I wur afeared to speak—afeared lest yo'd gi' me a sharp answer, fur yo' wur ready enow wi' 'em, wench. I've watched yo' fur hours when I wur a great lubberly lad, an' when yo' gettin' to be a woman it wur th' same thing. I watched yo' an' did yo' many a turn as yo' knowed nowt about. When yo' wur searchin' fur drift to keep up th' fire after th' owd mon deed an' left yo' alone, happen yo' nivver guessed as it wur me as heaped little piles i' th' nooks o' th' rocks so as yo'd think 'at th' tide had left it theer—happen yo' did n't, but it wur true. I've stayed round th' old house many a neet, feared summat mought harm yo', an' yo' know yo' nivver gave me a good word, Meg. An' then Dan comn an' he made way wi' yo' as he made way wi' aw th' rest—men an' women an' children. He nivver worked an' waited as I did—he nivver thowt an' prayed as I did; everything come easy wi' him—everything allus did come easy wi' him, an' when I seed him so light-hearted an' care-less about what I wur cravin' it run me daft an' blind. Seemt like he couldna cling to it like I did, an' I begun to fight agen it, an' when I heerd about that lass o' Barnegats I towd yo', an' when I seen yo' believed what I didna believe mysen, it run me dafter yet, an' I put more to what he said, an' held back some, an' theer it wur an' theer it stands, an' if I've earnt a curse, lass, I've getten it, fur—fur I thowt yo'd been learnin' to care fur me a bit sin' we wur wed, an' God knows I've tried to treat yo' fair an' kind i' my poor way. It wurna Dan Morgan's way, I know—his wur a better way than mine, th' sun shone on him somehow—but I've done my best an' truest sin'."

"Yo've done yo're worst," she said. "Th' worst yo' could do wur to part us, an' yo' did it. If yo'd been half a mon yo' wouldna ha' been content wi' a woman yo'd trapped with sayin' 'Aye,' an' who cared less for yo' than she did fur th' sand on th' sea-shore. What's what yo've done sin' to what yo' did afore? Yo' conna wipe that out and yo' conna mak' me forget. I hate yo', an' th' worse because I wur beginnin' to be content a bit. I hate mysen. I ought to ha' knowed"—wildly—"he would ha' knowed whether I wur true or false, poor chap—he would ha' knowed."

She rocked herself to and fro for a minute, wringing her hands in a passion of anguish worse than any words, but a minute later she turned on him all at once.

"All's o'er betwixt yo' an' me," she said with fierce heat; "do yo' know that? If yo' wur half a mon yo' would."

He sat up and stared at her humbly and stupidly.

"Eh?" he said at last.

"Theer's not a mon i' Arle as isna more to me now than tha art," she said. "Some on 'em be honest, an' I conna say that o' thee. Tha canst get thee gone or I'll go mysen. Tha knows't me well enow to know I'll ne'er forgie thee for what tha's done. Aye"—with the passionate hand-wringing again—"but that wunnot undo it."

He rose and came to her, trembling like a man with the ague.

"Yo' dunnot mean that theer, Meg," he said slowly. "You dunnot mean it word fur word. Think a bit."

"Aye, but I do," she answered him, setting her white teeth, "word fur word."

"Think again, wench." And this time he staggered and caught hold of the door-post. "Is theer nowt as'll go agen th' wrong? I've lived wi' thee nigh a year, an' I've loved thee twenty—is theer nowt fur me? Aye, lass, dunnot be too hard. Tha was allus harder than most womankind; try an' be a bit softer like to'rds th' mon as risked his soul because he wur a mon an' darena lose thee. Tha laid thy head on my shoulder last neet. Aye, lass—lass, think o' that fur one minnit."

Perhaps she did think of it, for surely she faltered a little—what woman would not have faltered at such a moment?—but the next, the memory of the sunny, half-boyish face she had clung to with so strong a love rushed back upon her and struck her to the heart. She remembered the days when her life had seemed so full that she had feared her own bliss; she remembered the gallant speeches and light-hearted wiles, and all at once she cried out in a fierce impassioned voice: "I'll ne'er forgie thee," she said—"I'll ne'er forgie thee to th' last day o' my life. What fur should I? Tha's broke my heart, thou villain—tha's broke my heart." And the next minute she had pushed past him and rushed into the house.

For a minute or so after she was gone the man stood leaning against the door with a dazed look in his pale face. She meant what she said: he had known her long enough to understand that she never forgave—never forgot. Her unbroken will and stubborn strength had held her to enmities all her life, and he knew she was not to be won by such things as won other women. He knew she was harder than most women, but his dull nature could not teach him how bitter must have been the life that rendered her so. He had never thought of it—he did not think of it now. He was not blaming her, and he was scarcely blaming himself. He had tried to make her happy and had failed. There were two causes for the heavy passion of misery that was ruling him, but neither of them was remorse.

His treachery had betrayed him, and he had lost the woman he had loved and worked for. Soul and body were sluggish alike, but each had its dull pang of weight and wretchedness.

"I've come to th' eend now surely," he said, and, dropping into her seat, he hid his face.

As he sat there a choking lump rose in his throat with a sudden click, and in a minute or so more he was wiping away hot rolling tears with the back of his rough hand.

"I'm forsook somehow," he said—"aye, I'm forsook. I'm not th' soart o' chap to tak' up wi' th' world. She wur all th' world I cared fur, an' she'll ne'er forgie me, for she's a hard un—she is. Aye! but I wur fond o' her! I wonder what she'll do—I do wonder i' my soul what she's gettin' her mind on!"

It did not occur to him to call to her or go and see what she was doing. He had always stood in some dull awe of her, even when she had been kindest, and now it seemed that they were too far apart for any possibility of approach at reconciliation. So he sat and pondered heavily, the sea air blowing upon him fresh and sweet, the sun shining soft and warm upon the house, and the few common flowers in the strip of garden whose narrow shell walks and borders he had laid out for her himself with much clumsy planning and slow labour.

Then he got up and took his rough working-jacket over his arm.

"I mun go down to th' Mary Anne," he said, "an' work a bit, or we'll ne'er get her turned o'er afore th' tide comes in. That boat's a moit o' trouble." And he sighed heavily.

Half-way to the gate he stopped before a cluster of ground honey-suckle, and perhaps for the first time in his life was conscious of a sudden curious admiration for them.

"She's powerful fond o' such loike bits o' things—posies an' such loike," he said. "Thems some as I planted to please her on th' very day as we were wed. I'll tak' one or two. She's main fond on 'em—fur such a hard un."

And when he went out he held in his hand two or three slender stems hung with the tiny pretty humble bells.

He had these very bits of simple blossoms in his hand when he went down to where the Mary Anne lay on the beach for repairs. So his fellow-workmen said when they told the story afterwards, remembering even this trivial incident.

He was in a strange frame of mind, too, they noticed, silent and heavy and absent. He did not work well, but lagged over his labour, stopping every now and then to pass the back of his hand over his brow as if to rouse himself.

"Yo' look as if yo' an' th' missus had had a fallin' out an' yo'n getten th' worst o' th' bargain," one of his comrades said by way of rough jest.

They were fond of joking with him about his love for his handsome, taciturn wife. But he did not laugh this time as he usually did.

"Mind thy own tackle, lad," he said dully, "an' I'll mind mine."

From that time he worked steadily among them until it was nearly time for the tide to rise. The boat they were repairing had been a difficult job to manage, as they could only work between tides, and now being hurried they lingered longer than usual. At the last minute they found it must be moved, and so were detained.

"Better leave her until th' tide ebbs," said one, but the rest were not of the same mind.

"Nay," they argued, "it'll be all to do o'er agen if we do that. Theer's plenty o' time if we look sharp enow. Heave again, lads."

Then it was that with the help of straining and tugging there came a little lurch, and then it was that as the Mary Anne slipped over on her side one of the workers slipped with her, slipped half underneath her with a cry, and lay on the sand, held down by the weight that rested on him.

With his cry there broke out half a dozen others, and the men rushed up to him with frightened faces.

"Are yo' hurt, Seth, lad?" they cried. "Are yo' crushed or owt?"

The poor fellow stirred a little and then looked up at them pale enough.

"Bruised a bit," he answered them, "an' sick a bit, but I dunnot think theer's any bones broke. Look sharp, chaps, an' heave her up. She's a moit o' weight on me."

They went to work again one and all, so relieved by his words that they were doubly strong, but after toiling like giants for a while they were compelled to pause for breath. In falling the boat had so buried herself in the sand that she was harder to move than ever. It had seemed simple enough at first, but it was not so simple, after all. With all their efforts they had scarcely stirred her an inch, and their comrade's position interfered with almost every plan suggested. Then they tried again, but this time with less effect than before, through their fatigue. When they were obliged to pause they looked at each other questioningly, and more than one of them turned a trifle paler, and at last the wisest of them spoke out:—

"Lads," he said, "we conna do this oursens. Run for help, Jem Coulter, an' run wi' thy might, fur it wunnot be so long afore th' tide'll flow."

Up to this time the man on the sands had lain with closed eyes and set teeth, but when he heard this his eyes opened and he looked up.

"Eh!" he said, in that blind, stupid fashion. "What's that theer tha's sayin' Mester?"

"Th' tide," blundered the speaker. "I wur tellin' him to look sharp, that's aw."

The poor fellow moved restlessly.

"Aye! aye!" he said. "Look sharp—he mun do that. I didna think o' th' tide." And he shut his eyes again with a faint groan.

They strove while the messenger was gone; and they strove when he returned with assistance; they strove with might and main, until not a man among them had the strength of a child, and the boldest of them were blanching with a fearful, furtive excitement none dared to show. A crowd had gathered round by this time—men willing and anxious to help, women suggesting new ideas and comforting the wounded man in rough, earnest style; children clinging to their mothers' gowns and looking on terror-stricken. Suddenly, in the midst of one of their mightiest efforts, a sharp childish voice piped out from the edge of an anxious group a brief warning that struck terror to every heart that beat among them.

"Eh! Mesters!" it said, "th' tide's creepin' up a bit."

The men looked round with throbbing pulses, the women looked also, and one of the younger ones broke into a low cry. "Lord, ha' mercy!" she said; "it'll sweep around th' Bend afore long, an'—an'"—and she ended with a terror in her voice which told its own tale without other words.

The truth forced itself upon them all then. Women began to shriek and men to pray, but, strange to say, the man whose life was at stake lay silent, with ashen lips, about which the muscles were tensely drawn.

His dull eyes searched every group in a dead despair that was yet a passion, in all its stillness.

"How long will it be," he asked slowly at last—"th' tide? Twenty minutes?"

"Happen so," was the answer. "An', lad, lad! we conna help thee. We'n tried our best, lad"—with sobs even from the uncouth fellow who spoke. "Theer is na one on us but 'ud leave a limb behind to save thee, but theer is na time—theer is na"—

One deep groan and he lay still again—quite still. God knows what weight of mortal agony and desperate terror crushed him in that dead, helpless pause.

Then his eyes opened as before.

"I've thowt o' deein'," he said with a catch of his breath. "I've thowt o' deein', an' I've wondered how it wur an' what it felt like. I never thowt o' deein' like this here." Another pause and then—

"Which o' yo' lads 'll tell my missus?"

"Ay! poor chap, poor chap!" wailed the women. "Who on 'em will?"

"Howd tha noise, wenches," he said hoarsely. "Yo' daze me. Theer is na time to bring her here. I'd ha' liked to ha' said a word to her. I'd ha' liked to ha' said one word; Jem Coulter"—raising his voice—"canst tha say it fur me?"

"Aye," cried the man, choking as he spoke, "surely, surely." And he knelt down.

"Tell her 'at if it wur bad enow—this here—it wur not so bad as it mought ha' been—fur *me*. I mought ha' fun it worser. Tell her I'd like to ha' said a word if I could—but I couldna. I'd like to ha' heard her say one word, as happen she would ha' said if she'd been here, an' tell her 'at if she had ha' said it th' tide mought ha' comn an' welcome—but she didna, an' theer it stands." And the sob that burst from his breast was like the sob of a death-stricken child. "Happen"—he said next—"happen one o' yo' women-foak con say a bit o' a prayer—yo're not so fur fro' safe sand but yo' can reach it—happen one o' yo' ha' a word or two as yo' could say—such like as yo' teach yo're babbies."

Among these was one who had—thank God, thank God! and so, amid wails and weeping, rough men and little children alike knelt with uncovered heads and hidden eyes while this one woman faltered the prayer that was a prayer for a dying man; and when it was ended, and all rose glancing fearfully at the white line of creeping foam, this dying man for whom they had prayed lay upon his death-bed of sand the quietest of them all—quiet with a strange calm.

"Bring me my jacket," he said, "an' lay it o'er my face. Theer's a bit o' a posie in th' button-hole. I getten it out o' th' missus's garden when I comn away. I'd like to howld it i' my hand if it's theer yet."

And as the long line of white came creeping onward they hurriedly did as he told them—laid the rough garment over his face, and gave him the humble dying flowers to hold, and having done this and lingered to the last moment, one after the other dropped away with awe-stricken souls until the last was gone. And under the arch of sunny sky the little shining waves ran up the beach, chasing each other over the glittering sand, catching at shells and sea-weed, toying with them for a moment, and then leaving them, rippling and curling and whispering, but creeping—creeping—creeping.

They gave his message to the woman he had loved with all the desperate strength of his dull, yet unchanging nature; and when the man who gave it to her saw her wild, white face and hard-set lips, he blundered upon some dim guess as to what that single word might have been, but the sharpest of them never knew the stubborn anguish that, following and growing day by day, crushed her fierce will and shook her heart. She was as hard as ever, they thought; but they were none of them the men or women to guess at the long dormant instinct of womanhood and remorse that the tragedy of this one day of her life had awakened. She had said she would never forgive him, and perhaps her very strength made it long before she did; but surely some subtle chord was touched by those heavy last words, for when, months later, her first love came back, faithful and tender, with his old tale to tell, she would not listen.

"Nay, lad," she said, "I amna a feather to blow wi' th' wind. I've had my share o' trouble wi' men foak, an' I ha' no mind to try again. Him as lies i' th' churchyard loved me i' his way—men foak's way is apt to be a poor un—an' I'm wore out wi' life. Dunnot come here courtin'—tak' a better woman."

But yet, there are those who say that the time will come when he will not plead in vain.

TWO FOLK TALES

James Bowker

In these two short folkloric "goblin tales", James Bowker offers a vision of the north-west coast of England—of Morecambe Bay—as haunted by fairy sprites and a version of the common "wanderer" figure, accompanied here by a spectral animal familiar. The fate of the strange pilgrim in "The White Dobbie" might put us in mind of the guilty fisherman of Mary Robinson's "Haunted Beach" (the first text in this volume); and the fairy world in "The Enchanted Fisherman" recalls the numerous fairy-beings haunting the shores of Gothic fiction—most frequently in Ann Radcliffe's novels.

A request in *Notes and Queries* on 23 October 1891 gives a hint of the difficulties involved in compiling a full bibliography and biography for Bowker: "Can any of your readers inform me... where a complete list of his works can be obtained? Any other information respecting him would be esteemed." On the title page of *Goblin Tales of Lancashire* (1878) Bowker signs himself "F.R.G.S.I."—Fellow of the Royal Geographical Society of Ireland—and another book appears under this authorship in 1884, *Birds of the Bible: Chats with the Children about Bible Birds*. The narratives and folklore included in *Goblin Tales* first appeared between 1874–5 in *Ben Brierley's Journal*, an important and popular periodical for working-class readers around Manchester and Lancashire, and which celebrated, as do Bowker's stories here, Lancashire dialect writing. Bowker published two further works in serial form in *Brierley's*: "Nat Holt's Fortune" (1876) and "Phoebe

Carew: A Tale of the North Coast" (1880). A ghost story of Bowker's, "Eily's Ghost", appeared in Mary Elizabeth Braddon's *Belgravia* Christmas Annual for 1876—a review of which refers to Bowker as "a Lancashire lad", suggestive of his association with regional writings.

The Enchanted Fisherman

There are few views in the north of England more beautiful than that which is seen from Morecambe, as the spectator looks over the beautiful bay, with its crescent coastline of nearly fifty miles in extent. At low water the dazzling sands, streaked by silvery deceptive channels, stretch to the distant glimmering sea, the music of whose heavings comes but faintly on the gentle breeze; but at tide-time a magnificent expanse of rolling waves sweeps away to Peel, and is dotted over with red-sailed fishing boats and coasters. Far to the north the huge heather-covered Furness Fells stand sentinel-like over the waters, and above them, dimly seen through the faint blue haze, tower the grand mountains of the magic lake country. The scene is full of a sweet dreamlike beauty; but there are times when the beautiful is swallowed in the majestic, as the mists come creeping over the sea, obscuring the coasts, and hiding everything save the white caps of the waves gleaming in the darkness, through which the muttering diapasons of the wind, as though in deep distress, sound mysteriously; or when, in winter, the moon is hidden by scudding clouds, and the huge rollers, driven before the breeze, dash themselves to death, as upon the blast come the solemn boom of a signal gun, and the faint cries of those in danger on the deep.

Years ago, however, before the little village of Poulton changed its name, and began to dream of becoming a watering-place, with terraces and hotels, instead of the picturesque, tumble-down huts of the fishermen, against which, from time immemorial, the spray

95

had been dashed by the salt breezes, the only people who gazed upon the lovely prospect were, with the exception of an occasional traveller, the families of the toilers of the sea, and the rough-looking men themselves. These hardy fellows, accustomed to a wild life, and whose days from childhood had been spent on or by the sea, loved the deep with as much tenderness as a strong man feels towards a weak and wayward maiden, for they were familiar with its every mood, with the soothing wash of its wavelets when the sunbeams kissed the foam-bells, as they died on the white sands, and with the noise of the thunder of the breakers chased up the beach by the roaring gales.

One evening a number of these men were seated in the cosy kitchen of the John-o'-Gaunt, listening to "Owd England" as he narrated some of his strange experiences.

"I moind," said he, "when I was nobbut a bit of a lad, Tum Grisdale bein' dreawnt; an' now as we're tawkin' abeaut th' dangers o' th' sonds, yo'll mebbi hearken to th' tale. Poor Tum was th' best cockler i' Hest Bank, an' as ust to th' sands as a choilt is to th' face o' its mother; but for o that he wir dreawnt on 'em after o. I can co to moind yet—for young as I wor I're owd enough to think a bit when owt quare happent, an' th' seet o' th' deead bodies th' next ebb wir wi' me day an' neet fur lung afterwart—th' day when Tum an' his missis an' th' two lasses seet eawt o' seein' some relations o' th' missis's soide, as livt i' th' Furness country yon, th' owd mon an' th' dowters i' th' shandray, an' th' missis ridin' upo' th' cowt at th' soide. It wir a gradely bonnie afternoon, at th' back eend o' th' year. Th' day as they should o come back wir varra misty; an' abaat th' edge o' dark, just as here an' theear a leet wir beginnin' to twinkle i' th' windows, an' th' stars to peep aat, th' noise ov a cart comin' crunchin' o'er th' beach tuk mi feyther to th' door. 'Why, yon's owd Tum Grisdale cart back ageean,' he cried eawt. An' he dartit eawt o' th' dur, an' me after, as fast as I could. A creawd o' folk an' childer soon gathert reawnt, wonderin' what wir up; but neawt could bi larnt, for though th' lasses as seet eawt, as breet an' bonnie as posies o gillivers, wir theear i' th' shandray, they wir too freetent an' dazed, an' too wake wi' th' weet an' cowd, to say a whord. One thing, however, wir sewer enough, th' owd folk hedn't come back; an' altho' th' toide then hed covert th' track, an' wir shinin' i' th' moonleet, wheear th' mist could bi sin through, just as if it hedn't mony a Hest Bank mon's life to answer for, a lot o' young cocklers wir for startin' off theear an' then i' search on 'em. Th' owder an' mooar expayrienced, heawiver, wodn't hear on it. Two lives i' one day wir quoite enough, they said; so they o waitit till th' ebb, an' then startit, me, loile as i'wir, among th' rest, for mi feyther wir too tekken up i' talking to send me whoam. It wir a sad outin', but it wir loively compaart wi' t comin' back, for when we tornt toart Hest Bank, th' strungest o' th' lads carriet owd Tum an' his missis, for we hedn't getten far o'er th' sonds afooar we feawnt th' poor owd lass, an' not far off, i' th' deep channel, owd Tum hissel. They wir buriet i' th' owd church-yart, an' one o' th' lasses wir laid aside on 'em, th' freet hevin' bin too mich for her. When t' tother sister recovert a bit, an' could bide to talk abaat it, hoo said as they geet lost i' th' mist, an' th' owd mon left 'em i' th' shandray while he walkt a bit to foind th' channel. When he didn't come back they geet freetent, but t' owd woman wodn't stir fray th' spot till they heeart t' watters comin', an' then they went a bit fur, but could find nowt o' Tum, though they thowt neaw an' then they could heear him sheautin' to 'em. Th' sheawts, heawiver, geet fainter an' fainter, an' at last stopt o' together. Givin' thersels up for lost, they left th' reins to th' mare an' t' cowt. Th' poor owd lass wir quoite daz't at th' absence o' Tum; an' as th' cowt wir swimmin' across th' channel hoo lost her howd, an' wir carriet away. Th' lasses knew neawt no mooar, th' wench olus said, till th' fowk run deawn to th' cart uppo' th' beach. Hor as wir left, hoo wir olus quare at after; an' hoo uset to walk alung t' bay at o heawers just at th' toide toime, yo' known, an' it wir pitiful t' heear her when th' woint wir a bit sriller nor usal, sayin' as hoo could heear her owd fayther's voice as he sheauted when hee'd wander't fray 'em an' couldn't foint way to 'em through t' mist. Hoo afterwarts went to sarvice at Lankister, to a place as th' paason fun' for her, i' th' idea o' th' change dooin' her good; but it worn't lung afooar th' news come as hoo wir i' th' 'sylum, an' I heeart as hoo deed theear some toime after."

No sooner had the grey-headed old fisherman finished his story than one of the auditors said, "Hoo met weel fancy hoo heeart th' voice ov her fayther, for monnie a neet, an' monnie another hev I heeart that cry mysen. Yo' may stare, bud theear's mooar saands to be heeard i' th' bay nor some o' yo' lads known on; an' I'm no choilt to be freetent o' bein' i' th' dark. Why nobbut th' neet afooar last I heeart a peal o' bells ringin' under th' watter." There was a moment of surprise, for Roger Heathcote was not a likely man to be a victim to his own fancies, or to be influenced by the superstitions which clung to his fellows. Like the rest of his companions, he had spent the greatest portion of his life away from land; and either because he possessed keener powers of observation than they, or loved nature more, and therefore watched her more closely, he had gradually added to his store of knowledge, until he had become the recognised authority on all matters connected with the dangerous calling by which the men-folk of the little colony earned daily bread for their families. As he was by no means addicted to yarns, looks of wonder came over the faces of the listeners; and in deference to the wishes of Old England, who pressed him as to what he had heard and seen, Roger narrated the adventure embodied in this story.

*

The fisherman's little boat was dancing lightly on the rippling waters of the bay.

The night was perfectly calm, the moon shining faintly through a thin mist which rested on the face of the deep. It was nearly midnight, and Roger was thinking of making for home, when he heard the sweet sounds of a peal of bells. Not without astonishment, he endeavoured to ascertain from what quarter the noises came, and, strange and unlikely as it seemed, it appeared that the chimes rang up through the water, upon which, with dreamy motion, his boat was gliding. Bending over the side of the skiff he again heard with singular distinctness the music of the bells pealing in weird beauty. For some time he remained in this attitude, intently listening to the magical music, and when he arose, the mist had cleared off, and the moon was throwing her lovely light upon the waters, and over the distant fells. Instead, however, of beholding a coast with every inch of which he was acquainted, Roger gazed upon a district of which he knew nothing. There were mountains, but they were not those whose rugged outlines were so vividly impressed upon his memory. There was a beach, but it was not the one where his little cottage stood with its light in the window and its background of wind-bent trees. The estuary into which his boat was gliding was not that of the Kent, with its ash and oak-covered crags. Everything seemed unreal, even the streaming moonlight having an unusual whiteness, and Roger rapidly hoisted his little sails, but they only flapped idly against the mast, as the boat, in obedience to an invisible and unknown agency, drifted along the mysterious looking river. As the fisherman gazed in helpless wonder, gradually the water narrowed, and in a short time a cove was gained, the boat grating upon the gleaming sand. Roger at once jumped upon the bank, and no sooner had he done so, than a number of little figures clad in green ran towards him from beneath a clump of trees, the foremost of them singing—

> To the home of elf and fay,
>> To the land of nodding flowers,
> To the land of Ever Day
>> Where all things own the Fay Queen's powers,
>>> Mortal come away!

and the remainder dancing in circles on the grass, and joining in the refrain—

> To the home of elf and fay,
> To the land of Ever Day,
>> Mortal come away!

The song finished, the little fellow who had taken the solo, tripped daintily to Roger, and, with a mock bow, grasped one of the fingers of the fisherman's hand, and stepped away as though anxious to lead him from the water.

Assuming that he had come upon a colony of Greenies, and feeling assured that such tiny beings could not injure him, even if anxious to do so, Roger walked on with his conductor, the band dancing in a progressing circle in front of them, until a wood was reached, when the dancers broke up the ring and advanced in single file between the trees. The light grew more and more dim, and when the cavalcade reached the entrance to a cavern, Roger could hardly discern the Greenies. Clinging to the little hand of his guide, however, the undaunted fisherman entered the cave, and groped his way down a flight of mossy steps. Suddenly he found himself in a beautiful glade, in which hundreds of little figures closely resembling his escort, and wearing dainty red caps, were disporting themselves and singing—

> Moonbeams kissing odorous bowers
> Light our home amid the flowers;
>
> While our beauteous King and Queen
> Watch us dance on rings of green.
>   Rings of green, rings of green,
>   Dance, dance, dance, on rings of green.

No sooner had the fisherman entered the glade than the whole party crowded round him, but as they did so a strain of enchanting music was heard, and the little beings hopped away again, and whirled round in a fantastic waltz. Roger himself was so powerfully influenced by the melody that he flung himself into the midst of the dancers, who welcomed him with musical cries, and he capered about until sheer fatigue forced him to sink to rest upon a flowery bank. Here, after watching for a while the graceful gambols of the Greenies, and soothed by the weird music, the sensuous odours, and the dreamy light, he fell into a deep sleep. When he awoke from his slumber the fairies had vanished, and the fisherman felt very hungry. No sooner, however, had he wished for something to eat than on the ground before him there appeared a goodly array of delicacies, of which, without more ado, Roger partook.

"I'm in luck's way here," he said to himself; "It's not every day of the week I see a full table like this. I should like to know where I am, though." As the wish passed his lips he saw before him a beautiful little being, who said in a sweet low voice—

> In the land of nodding flowers,
> Where all things own the Fay Queen's powers!

The fisherman no sooner saw the exquisite face of the dainty Greenie than he forgot altogether the rosy-cheeked wife at home, and fell hopelessly over head and ears in love with the sweet vision. Gazing into her beautiful eyes he blurted out, "I don't care where it is if you are there." With a smile the queen, for it was indeed the queen, seated herself at his side. "Dost thou, Mortal, bow to my power?" asked she. "Ay, indeed, do I to the forgetfulness of everything but thy bonny face," answered Roger; upon which the queen burst into a hearty fit of laughter, so musical, however, that for the life of him the fisherman could not feel angry with her. "If the king were to hear thee talking thus thou wouldst pay dearly for thy presumption," said the Fay, as she rose and tripped away to the shadow of the trees. The enraptured Roger endeavoured to overtake her before she reached the oaks, but without success; and though he wandered through the wood for hours, he did not again catch a glimpse of her. He gained an appetite by the freak however, and no sooner had he wished for food again than dishes of rich viands appeared before him.

"I wish I could get money at this rate," said the fisherman, and the words had hardly left his lips when piles of gold ranged themselves within his reach. Roger rapidly filled his pockets with the glittering coins, and even took the shoes from off his feet, and filled them also, and then slung them round his neck by the strings.

"Now, if I could but get to my boat," thought he, "my fortune would be made," and accordingly he began to make his way in what he believed to be the direction of the river. He had not proceeded very far, however, when he emerged upon an open space surrounded by tall foxgloves, in all the beautiful bells of which dreamy-eyed little beings were swinging lazily as the quiet zephyr rocked their perfumed dwellings. Some of the Greenies were quite baby fairies not so large as Roger's hand, but none of them seemed alarmed at the presence of a mortal. A score of larger ones were hard at work upon the sward stitching together moth and butterfly wings for a cloak for their Queen, who, seated upon a mushroom, was smiling approvingly as she witnessed the industry of her subjects. Roger felt a sudden pang as he observed her, for although he was glad once more to behold the marvellous beauty of her face, he was jealous of a dainty dwarf in a burnished suit of beetles' wing cases and with a fantastic peaked cap in which a red feather was coquettishly stuck, for this personage he suspected was the King, and forgetting his desire to escape with the gold, and at once yielding to his feelings, he flung himself on the luxuriant grass near the little being whose weird loveliness had thrown so strange a glamour over him, and without any thought or fear as to the consequences he at once bent himself and kissed one of her dainty sandalled feet. No sooner had he performed this rash act of devotion than numberless blows fell upon him from all sides, but he was unable to see any of the beings by whom he was struck. Instinctively the fisherman flung his huge fists about wildly, but without hitting any of the invisible Greenies, whose tantalising blows continued to fall upon him. At length, however, wearying of the fruitless contest, he roared out, "I wish I were safe in my boat in the bay," and almost instantaneously he found himself in the little skiff, which was stranded high and dry upon the Poulton beach. The shoes which he had so recently filled with glittering pieces of gold and suspended round his neck were again upon his feet, his pockets were as empty as they were when he had put out to sea some hours before, and somewhat dubious and very disgusted, in a few minutes he had crept off to bed.

*

When the strange tale of the fisherman's wonderful adventure with the hill folk was ended, the unbelievers did not hesitate to insinuate that Roger had not been out in the bay at all, and that the land of nodding flowers might be found by anyone who stayed as long and chalked up as large a score at the John-o'-Gaunt as he had done on the night when he heard the submerged bells and had so unusual a catch.

Others, however, being less sceptical, many were the little boats that afterwards went on unsuccessful voyages in search of the mysterious estuary and the colony of Greenies, and a year afterwards, when a sudden gale swept over the restless face of the deep and cast Roger's boat bottom upwards upon the sandy beach, many believed that the fisherman had again found the land of Ever Day.

The White Dobbie

Many years ago, long before the lovely Furness district was invaded by the genius of steam, the villagers along the coast from Bardsea to Rampside were haunted by a wandering being whose errand, the purpose of which could never be learned, used to bring him at night along the lonely roads and past the straggling cottages. This pilgrim was a wearied, emaciated-looking man, on whose worn and wan face the sorrows of life had left deep traces, and in whose feverish, hungry-looking eyes, mystery and terror seemed to lurk. Nobody knew the order of his coming or going, for he neither addressed anyone, nor replied if spoken to, but disregarded alike the "good neet" of the tramp who knew him not, and the startled cry of the belated villager who came suddenly upon him at a turn of the road. Never stopping even for a minute to gaze through the panes whence streamed the ruddy glow of the wood fires, and to envy the dwellers in the cosy cottages, he kept on his way, as though his mission was one of life and death, and, therefore, would not brook delay.

On wild wintry nights, however, when the salt wind whirled the foam across the bay, and dashed the blinding snow into heaps upon the window-sills and against the cottage doors, and darkness and storm spread their sombre wings over the coast, then was it certain that the mysterious being would be seen, for observation had taught the villagers and the dwellers in solitary houses along the lonely roads between the fishing hamlets that in storm and darkness the weird voyager was most likely to appear.

At such times, when the sound of footsteps, muffled by the snow, was heard between the soughs and moans of the wailing wind, the women cried, "Heaven save us; 'tis th' White Dobbie," as, convulsively clutching their little ones closer to their broad bosoms, they crept nearer to the blazing log upon the hearth, and gazed furtively and nervously at the little diamond-paned window, past which the restless wanderer was making his way, his companion running along a little way in advance, for not of the mysterious man alone were the honest people afraid. In front of him there invariably ran a ghastly-looking, scraggy white hare, with bloodshot eyes. No sooner however did anyone look at this spectral animal than it fled to the wanderer, and jumping into his capacious pocket, was lost to sight.

Verily of an unearthly stock was this white hare, for upon its approach and long before it neared a village, the chained dogs, by some strange instinct conscious of its coming, trembled in terror, and frantically endeavoured to snap their bonds; unfastened ones fled no man knew whither; and if one happened to be trotting alongside its belated master as he trudged homeward and chanced to meet the ghastly Dobbie with its blood-red eyes, with a scream of pain almost human in its keen intensity, away home scampered the terrified animal, madly dashing over hedge and ditch as though bewitched and fiend-chased.

For many years the lonely wanderer had traversed the roads, and for many years had the hare trotted in front of him; lads who were cradled upon their mother's knee when first they heard the awe-inspiring footfalls had grown up into hearty wide-chested men, and men who were ruddy fishers when the pilgrim first startled the dwellers in Furness had long passed away into the silent land; but none of them ever had known the wayfarer to utter a syllable. At length, however, the time came when the solemn silence was to be broken.

One night when the breeze, tired of whispering its weird messages to the bare branches, and chasing the withered leaves along the lanes, had begun to moan a hushed prelude to the music of a storm, through the mist that had crept over the bay, and which obscured even the white-crested wavelets at the foot of the hill on which stood the sacred old church, there came at measured intervals the melancholy monotone of the Bardsea passing bell for the dead.

Dismally upon the ears of the dwellers in the straggling hamlet fell the announcement of the presence of death, and even the woman who had for years been bell-ringer and sexton, felt a thrill of fear as she stood in the tower but dimly lighted by a candle in a horn lantern, and high above her head the message of warning rang out; for, although accustomed to the task, it was not often that her services were required at night. Now and again she gazed slowly round the chamber, upon the mouldering walls of which fantastic shadows danced, and she muttered broken fragments of prayers in a loud and terrified voice, for as the door had been closed in order that the feeble light in the lantern might not be extinguished by the gusts of wind, isolated as she was from the little world upon the hillside, she felt in an unwonted manner the utter loneliness of the place and its dread surroundings.

Suddenly she uttered a shrill shriek, for she heard a hissing whisper at her ear and felt an icy breath upon her cheek. She dared not turn round, for she saw that the door opening upon the churchyard remained closed as before, and that occasionally passing within the range of her fixed stare, a white hare with blood-red eyes gambolled round the belfry.

"T' Dobbie!" sighed she, as the dim light began to flicker and the hare suddenly vanished.

As she stood almost paralysed, again came the terrible whisper, and this time she heard the question—

"Who for this time?"

The horrified woman was unable to answer, and yet powerless to resist the strange fascination which forced her to follow the direction of the sound; and when the question was put a second time, in an agony of fear she gazed into the wild eyes of the being at her elbow, her parched tongue cleaving to her open mouth. From the pocket of the dread visitor the ghastly animal gazed at the ringer, who mechanically jerked the bell-rope, and the poor woman was fast losing her senses, when suddenly the door was burst open, and a couple of villagers, who had been alarmed by the irregular ringing, entered the tower. They at once started back as they saw the strange group—the wanderer with sad, inquiring look, and pallid face, the phantom hare with its firelit eyes, and the old ringer standing as though in a trance. No sooner, however, did one of the intruders gaze at the animal than it slipped out of sight down into the pocket of its companion and keeper, and the wanderer himself hastily glided between the astonished men, and out into the darkness of the graveyard.

On many other gloomy nights afterwards the ringer was accosted in the same manner, but although the unnatural being and the spectral hare continued for some winters to pass from village to village and from graveyard to graveyard, a thick cloud of mystery always hung over and about them, and no one ever knew what terrible sin the never-resting man had been doomed to expiate by so lonely and lasting a pilgrimage.

Whence he came and whither he went remained unknown; but long as he continued to patrol the coast the hollow sound of his hasty footsteps never lost its terror to the cottagers; and even after years had passed over without the usual visits, allusions to the weird pilgrim and his dread companion failed not to cause a shudder, for it was believed that the hare was the spirit of a basely-murdered friend, and that the restless voyager was the miserable assassin doomed to a wearisome, lifelong wandering.

THE LAST OF
SQUIRE ENNISMORE

Charlotte Riddell

In "The Last of Squire Ennismore" (1888), Charlotte Riddell (1832–1906) offers an extremely effective weird tale that makes brief but canny (or, indeed, uncanny) usage of a footprint in the sand—a trope that, we might propose, is the ur-spectre haunting the fiction of the British Isles since it first sent Robinson Crusoe into his petrified funk in 1719.

Riddell was born Charlotte Eliza Lawson Cowan to an English mother and Irish father in Carrickfergus, in what is now Northern Ireland; she moved to England in 1855, where she began a writing career to help alleviate financial difficulties encountered first after the death of her father and then again after her husband's death. Riddell—publishing as Mrs. J. H. Riddell, V. M. Starling, and F. G. Trafford—was a remarkably prolific writer, producing over thirty novels and many more short stories. She remains best known to us as a writer of ghost stories—most notably *Weird Stories* (1882)—and of London city life.

"Squire Ennismore" can be read productively as a tale negotiating Anglo-Irish relations: the story-within-the-story is told to a character known to us only as "the Englishman" as he sits above the fictional Ardwinsagh Bay on the west coast of Ireland—the site of the eerie events befalling the titular squire. It is also a tale of shipwreck, debauched carousing, and of having to pay one's debts—and of finding oneself stuck with both the devil and the deep blue sea. Among the tale's numerous striking descriptions is that of Ennismore's haunted house, which seems to pitch and roll like a ship caught in a tempest and about to be wrecked on the shore. It's as if the house has become possessed by the coastal tragedy that sets the plot in motion.

"Did I see it myself? No, sir; I did not see it; and my father before me did not see it; or his father before him, and he was Phil Regan, just the same as myself. But it is true, for all that; just as true as that you are looking at the very place where the whole thing happened. My great-grandfather (and he did not die till he was ninety-eight) used to tell, many and many's the time, how he met the stranger, night after night, walking lonesome-like about the sands where most of the wreckage came ashore."

"And the old house, then, stood behind that belt of Scotch firs?"

"Yes; a fine house it was, too. Hearing so much talk about it when a boy, my father said, made him often feel as if he knew every room in the building, though it had all fallen to ruin before he was born. None of the family ever lived in it after the Squire went away. Nobody else could be got to stop in the place. There used to be awful noises, as if something was being pitched from the top of the great staircase down into the hall; and then there would be a sound as if a hundred people were clinking glasses and talking all together at once. And then it seemed as if barrels were rolling in the cellars; and there would be screeches, and howls, and laughing, fit to make your blood run cold. They say there is gold hid away in those cellars; but not one has ever ventured to find it. The very children won't come here to play; and when the men are ploughing the field behind, nothing will make them stay in it, once the day begins to change. When the night is coming on, and the tide creeps in on the sand, more than one thinks he has seen mighty queer things on the shore there."

"But what is it really they think they see? When I asked my land-lord to tell me the story from beginning to end, he said he could not remember it; and, at any rate, the whole rigmarole was nonsense, put together to please strangers."

"And what is he but a stranger himself? And how should he know about the doings of real quality like the Ennismores? For they were gentry, every one of them—good old stock; and as for wickedness, you might have searched Ireland through and not found their match. It is a sure thing, though, that if Riley can't tell you the story, I can; for, as I said, my own people were in it, of a manner of speaking. So, if your honour will rest yourself off your feet, on that bit of a bank, I'll set down my creel and give you the whole pedigree of how Squire Ennismore went away from Ardwinsagh."

It was a lovely day, in the early part of June; and, as the Englishman cast himself on a low ridge of sand, he looked over Ardwinsagh Bay with a feeling of ineffable content. To his left lay the Purple Headland; to his right, a long range of breakers, that went straight out into the Atlantic till they were lost from sight; in front lay the Bay of Ardwinsagh, with its bluish-green water sparkling in the summer sunlight, and here and there breaking over some sunken rock, against which the waves spent themselves in foam.

"You see how the currents set, sir? That is what makes it danger-ous, for them as doesn't know the coast, to bathe here at any time, or walk when the tide is flowing. Look how the sea is creeping in now, like a race-horse at the finish. It leaves that tongue of sand bare to the last, and then, before you could look round, it has you up to the middle. That is why I made bold to speak to you; for it is not alone on the account of Squire Ennismore the bay has a bad name. But it is about him and the old house you want to hear. The last mortal being that tried to live in it, my great-grandfather said, was a creature, by name Molly Leary; and she had neither kith nor kin, and begged for her bite and sup, sheltering herself at night in a turf cabin she had built at the back of a ditch. You may be sure she thought herself a made woman when the agent said, 'Yes: she might try if she could stop in the house; there was peat and bog-wood,' he told her, 'and half-a-crown a week for the winter, and a golden guinea once Easter came,' when the house was to be put in order for the family; and his wife gave Molly some warm clothes and a blanket or two; and she was well set up.

"You may be sure she didn't choose the worst room to sleep in; and for a while all went quiet, till one night she was wakened by feeling the bedstead lifted by the four corners, and shaken like a carpet. It was a heavy four-post bedstead, with a solid top: and her life seemed to go out of her with the fear. If it had been a ship in a storm off the Headland, it couldn't have pitched worse; and then, all of a sudden, it was dropped with such a bang as nearly drove the heart into her mouth.

"But that, she said, was nothing to the screaming and laughing, and hustling and rushing that filled the house. If a hundred people had been running hard along the passages and tumbling downstairs, they could not have made a greater noise.

"Molly never was able to tell how she got clear of the place; but a man coming late home from Ballycloyne Fair found the creature crouched under the old thorn there, with very little on her—saving your honour's presence. She had a bad fever, and talked about strange things, and never was the same woman after."

"But what was the beginning of all this? When did the house first get the name of being haunted?"

"After the old Squire went away: that was what I purposed telling you. He did not come here to live regularly till he had got well on in years. He was near seventy at the time I am talking about; but he held himself as upright as ever, and rode as hard as the youngest; and could have drunk a whole roomful under the table, and walked up to bed as unconcerned as you please at the end of the night.

"He was a terrible man. You couldn't lay your tongue to a wickedness he had not been in the fore-front of—drinking, duelling, gambling—all manner of sins had been meat and drink to him since he was a boy almost. But at last he did something in London so bad, so beyond the beyonds, that he thought he had best come home and live among people who did not know so much about his goings on as the English. It was said he wanted to try and stay in this world for ever; and that he had got some secret drops that kept him well and hearty. There was something wonderful queer about him, anyhow.

"He could hold foot with the youngest; and he was strong, and had a fine fresh colour in his face; and his eyes were like a hawk's; and there was not a break in his voice—and him near upon threescore and ten!

"At long and at last it came to be the March before he was seventy—the worst March ever known in all these parts—such blowing, sleeting, snowing, had not been experienced in the memory of man; when one blusterous night some foreign vessel went to bits on the Purple Headland. They say it was an awful sound to hear the death-cry that went up high above the noise of the wind; and it was as bad a sight to see the shore there strewed with corpses of all sorts and sizes, from the little cabin-boy to the grizzled seaman.

"They never knew who they were or where they came from, but some of the men had crosses, and beads, and such like, so the priest said they belonged to him, and they were all buried decently in the chapel graveyard.

"There was not much wreckage of value drifted on shore. Most of what is lost about the Head stays there; but one thing did come into the bay—a queer thing—a puncheon of brandy.

"The Squire claimed it; it was his right to have all that came on his land, and he owned this sea-shore from the Head to the breakers—every foot—so, in course, he had the brandy; and there was sore ill-will because he gave his men nothing—not even a glass of whiskey.

"Well, to make a long story short, that was the most wonderful liquor anybody ever tasted. The gentry came from far and near to take share, and it was cards and dice, and drinking and story-telling night after night—week in, week out. Even on Sundays, God forgive them! the officers would drive over from Ballycloyne, and sit emptying tumbler after tumbler till Monday morning came, for it made beautiful punch.

"But all at once people quit coming—a word went round that the liquor was not all it ought to be. Nobody could say what ailed it, but it got about that in some way men found it did not suit them.

"For one thing, they were losing money very fast.

"They could not make head against the Squire's luck, and a hint was dropped the puncheon ought to have been towed out to sea, and sunk in fifty fathoms of water.

"It was getting to the end of April, and fine, warm weather for the time of year, when first one, and then another, and then another still, began to take notice of a stranger who walked the shore alone at night. He was a dark man, the same colour as the drowned crew lying in the chapel graveyard, and had rings in his ears, and wore a strange kind of hat, and cut wonderful antics as he walked, and had an ambling sort of gait, curious to look at. Many tried to talk to him, but he only shook his head; so, as nobody could make out where he came from or what he wanted, they made sure he was the spirit of some poor wretch who was tossing about the Head, longing for a snug corner in holy ground.

"The priest went and tried to get some sense out of him.

"'Is it Christian burial you're wanting?' asked his reverence; but the creature only shook his head.

"'Is it word sent to the wives and daughters you've left orphans and widows, you'd like?' but no; it wasn't that.

"'Is it for sin committed you're doomed to walk this way? Would masses comfort ye? There's a heathen,' said his reverence; 'did you ever hear tell of a Christian that shook his head when masses were mentioned?'

"'Perhaps he doesn't understand English, Father,' says one of the officers who was there; 'try him with Latin.'

"No sooner said than done. The priest started off with such a string of aves and paters that the stranger fairly took to his heels and ran.

"'He is an evil spirit,' explained the priest, when he had stopped, tired out, 'and I have exorcised him.'

"But next night my gentleman was back again, as unconcerned as ever.

"'And he'll just have to stay,' said his reverence, 'for I've got lumbago in the small of my back, and pains in all my joints—never to speak of a hoarseness with standing there shouting; and I don't believe he understood a sentence I said.'

"Well, this went on for awhile, and people got that frightened of the man, or appearance of a man, they would not go near the sands; till in the end Squire Ennismore, who had always scoffed at the talk, took it into his head he would go down one night, and see into the rights of the matter himself. He, maybe, was feeling lonesome, because, as I told your honour before, people had left off coming to the house, and there was nobody for him to drink with.

"Out he goes, then, as bold as brass; and there were a few followed him. The man came forward at sight of the Squire and took off his hat with a foreign flourish. Not to be behind in civility, the Squire lifted his.

"'I have come, sir,' he said, speaking very loud, to try to make him understand, 'to know if you are looking for anything, and whether I can assist you to find it.'

"The man looked at the Squire as if he had taken the greatest liking to him, and took off his hat again.

"'Is it the vessel that was wrecked you are distressed about?'

"There came no answer, only a forbye mournful shake of the head.

"'Well, *I* haven't your ship, you know; it went all to bits months ago; and as for the sailors, they are snug and sound enough in consecrated ground.'

"The man stood and looked at the Squire with a queer sort of smile on his face.

"'What *do* you want?' asked Mr. Ennismore, in a bit of a passion. 'If anything belonging to you went down with the vessel it's about the Head you ought to be looking for it, not here—unless, indeed, it's after the brandy you're fretting.'

"Now, the Squire had tried him in English and French, and was now speaking a language you'd have thought nobody could understand; but, faith, it seemed natural as kissing to the stranger.

"'Oh! that's where you are from, is it?' said the Squire. 'Why couldn't you have told me so at once? I can't give you the brandy, because it's mostly drunk; but come along, and you shall have as stiff a glass of punch as ever crossed your lips.' And without more to-do off they went, as sociable as you please, jabbering together in some outlandish tongue that made moderate folks' jaws ache to hear.

"That was the first night they conversed together, but it wasn't the last. The stranger must have been the height of good company, for the Squire never tired of him. Every evening, regularly, he came up to the house, always dressed the same, always smiling and polite, and then the Squire called for brandy and hot water, and they drank and played cards till cock-crow, talking and laughing into the small hours.

"This went on for weeks and weeks, nobody knowing where the man came from, or where he went; only two things the old house-keeper did know—that the puncheon was nearly empty, and that the Squire's flesh was wasting off him; and she felt so uneasy she went to the priest, but he could give her no manner of comfort.

"She got so concerned at last that she felt bound to listen at the dining-room door; but they always talked in that foreign gibberish, and whether it was blessing or cursing they were at she couldn't tell.

"Well, the upshot of it came one night in July—on the eve of the Squire's birthday—there wasn't a drop of spirit left in the puncheon—no, not as much as would drown a fly. They had drunk the whole lot clean up—and the old woman stood trembling, expecting every minute to hear the bell ring for more brandy, for where was she to get more if they wanted any?

"All at once the Squire and the stranger came out into the hall. It was a full moon, and light as day.

"'I'll go home with you tonight by way of a change,' says the Squire.

"'Will you so?' asked the other.

"'That I will,' answered the Squire.

"'It is your own choice, you know.'

"'Yes; it is my own choice: let us go.'

"So they went. And the housekeeper ran up to the window on the great staircase and watched the way they took. Her niece lived there as housemaid, and she came and watched too; and, after a while, the butler as well. They all turned their faces this way, and looked after their master walking beside the strange man along these very sands. Well, they saw them walk out and out to the very ebb-line—but they didn't stop there—they went on, and on, and on, and on, till the water took them to their knees, and then to their waists, and then to their arm-pits, and then to their heads; but long before that the women and the butler were running out on the shore as fast as they could, shouting for help."

"Well?" said the Englishman.

"Living or dead, Squire Ennismore never came back again. Next morning, when the tide ebbed again, one walking over the sand saw the print of a cloven foot—that he tracked to the water's edge. Then everybody knew where the Squire had gone, and with whom."

"And no more search was made?"

"Where would have been the use searching?"

"Not much, I suppose. It's a strange story, anyhow."

"But true, your honour—every word of it."

"Oh! I have no doubt of that," was the satisfactory reply.

LEGENDS

H. D. Lowry

Henry Dawson Lowry (1869–1906) was a short story writer, novel-ist, poet, and journalist, born in Truro in Cornwall. He studied in Cornwall then Oxford, and, in the same year he started his chemistry degree, his short stories on the strange wonders of Cornwall were accepted for publication in the *National Observer*. Later Lowry joined the staff of the *Pall Mall Gazette*, and across his career wrote for *Black and White*, *Ludgate Magazine*, and the *Morning Post*. He published in the *Daily Express* under the name "The Impenitent". Despite a prolific publishing career Lowry never enjoyed much fame in his life, and was somewhat overshadowed by his illustrious cousin, the author Catherine Amy Dawson Scott (1865–1935) who founded PEN, the global writer's association which thrives to this day. Dawson Scott even completed *Wheal Darkness* (1927), the Cornish Gothic novel left incomplete upon Lowry's death, and absorbed some aspects of his work into her own novel, *The Haunting* (1921).

"Legends" comes from Lowry's 1893 *Wreckers and Methodists*, a col-lection of tales about the odd and the eerie in the county of Cornwall. Like much of Lowry's work it is concerned with the uncanny paradox of the representation of the Cornish people as both criminal and reserved, savage and solemn, wreckers and methodists. There is a vein of preternatural punishment that runs through Lowry's tales, and this is particularly apparent in this odd little story of something that could be a woman's corpse, could be a revenant, could be a sea creature. The idea of being doomed to inevitably return to the sea upon one's death, or as a punishment for a crime, is one that haunts maritime fictions. This one in particular taps into the profound and devastating familiarity the Cornish would have had with maritime disaster and bodies on their shores.

This is the story told of John Lenine, the man that lay dying as I went forth from my cottage one Sunday at evening to preach at Porth; this the story I pondered as I came down the coomb towards the village, set upon taking the path that leads by the cliffs to that next coomb in which the chapel stands. For I had seen but yesterday how for some the torture of hell begins with the death-bed: and what I had seen remained with me, active in my mind.

Men talk still of that terrible winter that bound the fields with frost, and afterwards hid them for weeks with deep snow, at the beginning of the century. For six weeks the frost never lifted, even on our Cornish coast, where we are wont to have roses in our gardens at Christmas-time. Then came a space of warm and rainless weather, so that by the end of February month the wells were low as in the hottest summer, and the birds (albeit decimated by the frost) would have been building had there been leafage anywhere revealed to their active quest. But with the opening of March, after a windless night of terrible coldness, the wind rose and the snow began to fall—to drive, rather, in a sharp, cutting powder out of the East. For two days it fell continuously; for two days that wild wind harried it, so that the drifts in some places were of incredible deepness, while whole fields elsewhere had scarce a trace of snow. Only the sheep were smothered where they had gathered for shelter under the lee of the hedges. For the wind, driving the snow across the fields, could carry it no further than the hedges; but beating against them, raised it eddying into the air, so that great drifts were formed where it fell and was piled up in the lewth.

'Tis of the first night only I have to speak, when the wind swept the sea of its ships, and strewed all coasts with torn bodies of men. Upon that night a great vessel came ashore in the bay and quickly went to pieces on the rocks. The story is horrible enough. Let me say, then, that no tradition lays the wreck to the account of the villagers. No ship could live in such a wind and sea as raged that night, and the *Bonne Marie* was lured to her destruction by no treacherous light. Soon after dawn, when the villagers had dug a way out of their snowed-up dwellings, news came to them of the wreck, and in an hour the cliffs and beach were thronged with treasure-seekers. But John Lenine had spent that night upon the cliffs, and in the morning was not of the crowd. He was a young man then, and a splendid sailor. He was strong, and rudely handsome. He would have been sure of liking had he not also been morose and "clubbish" to a degree. He had gone down to the sea in hope of finding plunder; he saw the ship come in under the cliffs and break up quickly as the great waves ground her sides against the rocks. Then, in the first glimmering of dawn, he set himself to watch for what the sea might cast up. Little enough he found; but presently, as the sky paled, he marked a figure that lay helplessly on a small flat ledge on the seaward side of a steep and weed-grown rock. In a moment he had gained the rock, and was looking down on the ledge, where lay a dead woman just beyond reach of the waves. She was young, and had been beautiful. She must have died of exposure after the sea at full tide had flung her up to that ledge of the rocks.

Lenine descended carefully, and raised the body in his arms, climbing desperately with his limp burden until he had gained the summit of the rock. Then he stood for a moment looking down at the body. He held it by the wrist, so that it partly trailed on the rock, partly hung loose from his grasp. He looked around him, then let the woman fall again on the wet weed while he knelt to rifle her clothing. There was nothing of value in the pocket of her dress, but on her hand was a ring of shining precious stones. For a space he strove to shift this ring, but his fingers were stiff with cold and he could not move it, though he had small reverence in his haste for that fallen temple of God, the woman's body. Then he lost all patience. He raised the lax arm and put the finger into his mouth, clenching his teeth upon it passionately. By fair means or foul he would have the ring. But the finger of the dead woman turned and twisted in his mouth, grinding of itself betwixt his teeth, and the whole body, rising once and falling, writhed horribly, as a snake writhes when you have trodden upon it. Lenine started backwards with a shriek of horror, drawing himself up at full height against the cliff as he thrust the dreadful body from him. For memory afterwards he had sight of the woman's eyes, that slowly opened, regarding him, as the body writhed and slid over the wet weed back into the sea. Then, presently, he turned and struggled through the snowdrifts to the village.

Of the years that followed report is more vague, if not less terrible; for John Lenine left the village soon after the wreck of the *Bonne Marie*. For fifty years God let him live, and when after thirty years he came back none dared to ask how he had spent the interval. There was a wife came with him, a young girl that spoke to him tremulously in a foreign tongue. She was a child almost; white, and frail, and delicately made, with dark eyes ever pleading piteously for a little tenderness in this hard life. He may have loved the child well enough, but—from this very fact, perhaps—he was only a terror to her. She died soon, and was laid in the churchyard on the slope of the coomb-side. Then, before his time, did this man enter into the blackness of darkness reserved to him assuredly for ever. By day he wandered over the waste-lands with his gun. At night he drank sullenly in his own house, or broke with terrifying boisterous mirth upon the sedate crowd that assembled nightly until ten o'clock at *The Lighthouse*. Men knew his utter misery, yet saw in him no object for their pity. For twenty years a damned soul had lived among us in Trelorne; and now, as night settled down on the sea, he was to go forth alone to the judgment.

Of this man, then, were my thoughts as I passed through the village and made my way up the steep pathway that leads out on to the cliffs. On my right, as I neared the top of the ascent, the great white beach (that even then brought the gentry by scores each summer to Trelorne) stretched in a semicircle three miles long. All was vague and cold in the growing darkness, but not so vague but that I saw beyond a doubt a thing that had been wonderful without the horror that followed.

There is no landing at Trelorne save for fishing boats, that are beached at high water and drawn up on to the tract of blown sand at the head of the coomb. Yet at the water's edge, in the very shadow of the cliff, a great ship lay at anchor, and with all sails set. There was not the smallest breeze that night, yet her sails were bellied out as if she moved steadily before a strong wind. And still she lay motionless at anchor. Great as my wonder was, I remembered my ignorance of the sea, and trusted that my wonder did but result therefrom. Others, at any rate, would have observed the appearance, and I, if it were lawful cause for wonder, might tell my tale when I had come back to the village. I must hasten now for the service at Porth.

I turned again towards the waste-lands, and upon the instant was aware of a man's figure that moved towards me silently through the twilight. I know not what benumbing horror fell upon me, but at the sight I stood stone still, and turned deadly cold. The man moved towards me, silently, slowly. Then, as he passed—I standing shuddering aside—his eyes were raised to meet mine. The face I looked upon was the face of the man Lenine, and I knew it as I looked for the face of a man that went forth hopeless to meet the penalty of seventy sinful years. His eyes were fixed upon me, mocking still, as on that last night when I had sought to show to him God's mercy and forgiveness; and thus he passed down the pathway to the beach. I watched him, petrified, and saw his figure disappear as the sands turned grey in the twilight. Then, at sound of a step behind me, I turned, to meet Dr. Williams, who came awe-stricken across the waste.

I could not speak for a moment. The words stuck in my throat. At last I found a voice.

"John Lenine—?" I gasped.

"Is just dead," he answered solemnly.

And through the mists I marked that ghostly ship moving with all sail set out into the darkness of the sea.

A GHOST OF THE SEA

Francis Prevost

Harry Francis Prevost Battersby (1862–1949) was a novelist, poet, journalist, and psychical investigator, appearing in print as H. F. P. Battersby or Francis Prevost. He trained at Sandhurst and served in the Royal Irish Rifles, before moving into war journalism, reporting to the *Morning Post* on the Boer War, where he was wounded. He wrote novels, collections of short fiction, plays, psychical texts, and poems. He translated Tolstoy, reported on sporting events, and his work frequently explored the psychology of forbidden love. He was particularly fascinated by the "etheric realm" and the possibilities of astral projection, the subject of the research text *Man Outside Himself* (1942).

"A Ghost of the Sea" is born out of Prevost's fascination with the paranormal. The fictional tale is written like a parapsychical report, taking Cornwall as its scene. Like H. D. Lowry's "Legends", also featured in this collection, this story draws on Cornwall as a site of paranormal interest in the nineteenth century, frequented by known psychical researchers like Elliott O'Donnell (known as "Mr. Ghosts" in the US). Yet, Prevost labours that this could have taken place at "any sea-board town". The coast becomes a generic locus of psychical activity, of paranormal disturbance. What matters is the proximity to the sea and the specific liminality of the coastline. In Cornwall, the protagonist is told the story of another coast—an eerie tale of Eastbourne. Oral stories of weary maritime and coastal travellers recur in gothic fiction, with Samuel Taylor Coleridge's *Rime of the Ancient Mariner* (1798–1817) being a potential origin point. There is something about the water that lends itself to these narratives, harking back to seamen's superstitions, to the folklore of coastal life. Maybe we have included some tales here you will share with a fellow traveller on your next haunting coastal jaunt.

I

One touches the spiritual in letters with uncertain fingers. Destiny is involved enough for most of us without invoking the super-known; and these breathless visitors leave a trail across human incident which spoils it for almost any purpose of comparison. Yet a ghost interests. Interests the common man, because he is a creature who doubts, and who would like to illumine the dim possibilities of death and judgment by a single proved apparition. He is bored by Moses and the prophets, but he craves something with wings. We may leave him to his illusions. Spook-aided conduct is barren in the end as all extrinsic morality, and this story is written neither to convince nor to startle. It is told by a student in human ailment for any equally interested, without comment on the possible reality of its terrible vision. Though no believer in spirits, I confess myself unable to explain what I relate on any theory, known to me, of alienation or telepathy which could over-ride such an accumulation of coincidence, and the reader must remember this confession as he proceeds.

The scene lay in northern Cornwall. It was not contingent to the story, but it made an effective setting. The events recorded here might have happened at any sea-board town as well as in that desolate valley of the West, which split the parapets of the red cliffs with a shifting wedge of sand. The dull roar of its waves hung always in the air, through which the shrill screaming of sea-birds stretched like sharp threads of colour. A thin brown stream wandered in the sand, as a traveller with tired feet. But every month, when the moon filled and the tide thrust its white face past the head, that film of grey river rose and bulged a belly of silver from shore to shore; leaving a fringe of sea-froth along the marshes, and tossing its sea treasures up against the hillocks of blown sand, tagged with sharp grasses, which hid the hollow of the combe.

A square white cottage on the south side, under the cliffs, seemed rather to enforce the desolate remoteness of the place, as though in that terrible quarantine only such men could live as were a peril to their kind. North and south, unbroken for miles, stood the sheer front of perilous cliffs, rent and twisted and scarred with fire, a veritable rampart of death; and even across this narrow haven was driven, for most hours of the tide, a seething fence of broken foam.

Landward were the lonely moors of Lyonnesse, swept by the wind's drag-net all the winter, savage and dark and bare; beneath them once the wrecker had made his den, and flashed false lights across the sea; and still, though he had gone, and only the merlin dropped now upon his prey from his floating anchorage in the air, death stayed between that oily current and the splintered fangs of stone—stayed and feasted.

I had been walking since morning, by the sheep-track along the cliff, half a midsummer day, and was dry even in spirit. Otherwise, probably, I should have passed by very much on the other side of that dreary staring sea-lodge, whose white walls wavered in the glare of heated sand. Instead, I ploughed ankle deep through the hot light dust, and noticed, as I neared the cliff, the figure of a man stretched lazily beneath it, whom I recognised, on closer inspection, as an old acquaintance, a man of the most social mind, who seemed completely inappropriate to such a place. He rose at my hail, and accepting the claim with a sweep of his hat, came towards me.

At closer quarters I seemed to lose the man I had known; the gait, lounge, and stoop were the same, but the face and hands were become like the veins of a withered leaf, and turned to the transparent brownness of a woodland stream.

It was almost horrible. I asked what he was doing there.

He eyed me guardedly, as if measuring my perception.

"Doing," he said, "nothing. What are you?"

"Walking; Cornwall, Devon, and a bit of Dorset; a coasting trip."

"And you've put in here for water?"

"For liquid of some sort; what have you?"

"Milk, whisky—"

"Good?"

"Smugglers! been robbing the Queen's revenue and defrauding thirsty throats for the last forty years. I unearthed it from an old safe my host had boarded up, warm as first love and mild as new milk; and, he being an honest soul and wearing a blue ribbon, I have had to lap it up myself."

As we walked towards the cottage he told me something of the place; of the man and woman with whom he lodged, who were sea-thieves become Methodist and agricultural; of that deadly coast, and the waste uplands about it; with weird tales and fears which gave a bleaker colour to the moorland light and almost to its people; but he told me nothing about himself. Yet of all wrecks, derelict on that shore, his was the strangest.

Six months earlier Dick Melton's face was among the well-known of London. He was an authority in equity cases, the best teller of a dangerous story in Mayfair, and could sing a vulgar song urbanely. His future and his fortune were assured, and he was about to marry. Then, suddenly, he disappeared. It was given out that something—that ominous "something"—had happened, and that silence would be the kindest tribute to his memory.

We had met more than occasionally, and I had liked him. There was something distinctively straight and sane in his thought and his talk. He admitted the divine right of no subject to silence, but of almost all things, not base or foul, to some sort of respect. We had talked everything over with open hands, from the foundations of faith to the latest scandal, and were still good friends, without finding, I believe, a single point of complete agreement.

I had met Dick Melton last on the evening after he had won a long and intricate case and was in a vortex of congratulation. He was usually fond of praise, and of receiving it graciously, but that night he turned his back to it with an unmistakable "vanity of vanities" in a dulled eye. I noticed it then, I remembered it now, and wanted the reason. Doubtless the cause of that and of his exile were the same.

Yet I could make no guess. Moral delinquencies are not lived down by men of energy and talent in out-of-the-way places, and defaulting of a grosser sort leaves no uncertain track. Opium occurred to me, but a second glance at Melton's eyes dispelled that suggestion, and I knew of no other vice, too disreputable for our standards, which could lead a man into the wilderness or leave him there so completely his own master.

We did justice to the smuggler's whisky, and sat down under the cliff for a pipe, but Melton would not smoke, and, remembering what an epicure in tobacco he had once been, I asked why.

He shrugged his shoulders.

"Well," he said vaguely, "I've dropped it."

"Didn't suit you?"

"No," he answered, "it didn't suit me here."

Here evidently made the difference. What was it? sea air, or piety, or failing health?

He did not say; he seemed disinclined for speech, especially about himself; but while I spoke of London he warmed somewhat, as a Londoner will, and when I rose to go—

"Look here," he said, "you can't get to Stanna before midnight, if that is where you would stop; rest the night here, if you will risk our fare; my heart is dry for a little talk."

So I stayed, and, till the folk with whom he lodged came home from their work and spread supper, I told him all he cared to hear of the world he had forsaken. His interest was pathetic; sometimes keen and strained, then dropping back to a flat dead smile, as though he had suddenly pressed his face against some barrier he had forgot. He had been a politician with a grasp of foreign intrigue unusual in an Englishman, but now it was only of his friends that he asked news: he could neglect the fate of empires.

After supper I suggested a stroll by the sea, but Melton seeming nervously disinclined to leave the cottage, we sat under its great chimney through which the twilight stars could be seen before they shone in the open sky. He supposed I should be tired, and left me early; but I was surprised later, hearing the front door slam, to see him walking swiftly down towards the water. I lay for some hours awake, but he did not return.

II

The next morning, after breakfast, when I had lighted my pipe before starting, Melton asked abruptly:

"Can you tell me anything of Miss Exmoor?"

I may have looked my surprise, for he added:

"I was to have married her; perhaps you know that? It was broken off and I came here. I was to blame; I did it; did it badly too. But she never wrote me a word: girls don't, perhaps; it's less to them."

"No, no," I said, "it's more to them. That's why! They can't."

"A very curious *why*," he sighed. "Can you tell me anything?"

There was a great deal I could not; he may have seen it in my face. I dropped him a few bare facts, thinking even they should have been disguised.

"She is still unmarried," I concluded.

"Yes, I supposed that." He hesitated a moment. "Will you tell me what is said of her?"

"Good or bad?"

"Anything. She flirts?"

"So they say."

"Yes, so they said; what woman does not who can? Is that all?"

"That is all, I believe, but it may be a good deal."

"It was, you mean?"

"So I understood."

He looked hard into my eyes as if to strain the sentence from any malice they might have added.

"Are you in a hurry?" he went on presently; "if not, and it would not bore you, I should like to tell you why I am here. Yesterday I thought myself indifferent. I have thought so for six months, and really it amounts to very little what view the world takes of me in the end. Perhaps your presence has weakened me, for today I wish, when it is all over, to be understood. It is a bad business at the best, but even the worst—especially the worst—want justice; aye, and interest, kindness, almost love. I think, too, it might help her to be honest if she knew why I was false: oh! I don't mean now, later, when I'm done with. Will you hear me?"

I replied by unslinging my knapsack. I was very willing to hear him.

"If you don't mind the sun," he said, "shall we go across to the dunes? I never warm now, there seems to be ice in my blood, but the sun helps me to speak."

We went across the river and through the yellow drift-sand to the wandering hillocks along the shore, tufted with snake-grass and the blue sea-holly. He spread himself on their steaming whiteness, feeling for the heat like a lizard.

"Curious," he said, as he lay with his open fingers pressed against the sand, "till you came I was content to be missed on any terms; now—I'm not.

"When I left you all I had the choice of saying why I went, and being thought a fool, or of holding my tongue and seeming a knave. I chose that; it's the simpler choice for a lawyer, but it was bitter enough at first. Then I came here and forgot it all, or supposed I had; it's easier to renounce the world than one fancies, but it's harder to renounce oneself. We want to be taken at our own figuring even when dust, in 'marble's language, Latin pure, discreet,' you know; that's the victory for most of us over the grave!"

He paused a moment, the bitterness passed from his face, and he smiled at me sadly.

"It's not all posthumous vanity," he said; "at present, from my tale, I should be judged merely a common liar; but later on, when I'm past the gain of anyone's pity, what I tell you may be credited, credited *to* me, and perhaps those who have trusted me may be less ashamed. Will you report it?"

I promised I would do that and more.

"There is no more," he said. Then he drew himself up on to his elbow, and began abruptly:

"I was in Egypt three years ago; you may remember. There was a difficulty about some Canal Bonds, and I represented clients a good deal interested. Well, that doesn't concern us. I stayed in Cairo, at Shepheard's; I met a girl there who was good enough to take a deeper interest in me than I deserved. Her father was something in the Government reconstruction department; something big; and she and her mother were waiting till a house should be ready for them. The story is too long to tell. In the end we vowed the usual eternities, and I repented of them in a week—no! in about three. She was one of those girls who think that everything this side of a certain temptation is virtue, and they include a good deal; a perplexing amount to a man who confounds it with propriety, and who imagines that a woman who begins with a wink will stop nowhere; but she often stops very suddenly." He looked nervously, as he spoke, towards the sea. "I'm speaking for myself: I made that mistake. I behaved badly, but she only liked me the better, because she thought me too staid before, and supposed that *she* had made the difference; and a woman likes to make a difference, even for the worse—if she loves you."

I doubted the point, but did not debate it: there is, perhaps, no moral postulate true for all the sex, or false for some member of it. But I dislike all *ex uno* generalities.

Melton shifted his position to a fresh patch of hot sand, and spread out his arms.

"I had to leave for home rather abruptly," he went on, "and we arranged nothing but to write. I thought she would forget me in a month or two, and hoped it fervently; but she did not. She wrote every week for half a year; then came a break, and whilst I was wondering what had caused it she appeared in London. She had persuaded her mother that she required change; but it was on a change of name that she was thinking, and she had come for it to me.

"It was early in the season; I met her at a crush before I knew she was in town, and she told me she had been living for that moment. I never saw her again. I think she must have heard shortly after that I was engaged to Miss Exmoor, but she never reproached me even through the post. She spent the summer quietly, I believe, with some country friends, and left in the autumn for Egypt.

"That was May. In September I was at Eastbourne. It was towards the end of the month, the one fine month of last year, if you remember. Miss Exmoor was staying there with some friends, and I joined her for a week after some climbing in the Pyrenees. I was as fit as a man could be, and my time and mind full of two big cases to come on before Christmas. Would you consider me," he said, turning sharply round, "a likely subject for hallucinations or any other sort of nervous mania?"

"No," I replied; "no man less so."

"So I supposed," he said; "you thought me over sane at times. Well, we used to walk every evening after dinner on the parade, and one night I had strolled with Miss Exmoor the length of that brick-paved walk towards the Head. Coming back, I noticed a curious yellow streak of light in the water near the shore. It moved as we moved like a ray of the moon; only it was no ray, but a misty brightness, and there was no moon to make it. I stopped and pointed it out to my companion, or rather, I tried to, for she could see nothing, and rallied me jestingly on after-dinner apparitions.

"I am a trifle short-sighted, you know, and do not see quite clearly in the dusk, so I put up my eye-glass to discover what the thing could be... It was the body of a woman floating—within the water near the shore, floating—"

"Do you mean to say," I broke in, "that your glass defined what had seemed a blur of light to the shape of a woman?"

"That is what it did," he said; "the shape appeared to float in the water as a cloud floats in the air, for it was bent somewhat with the movement of the sea; and slid through it swiftly like a fish, but without apparent effort."

"Do you know what this little business of your eye-glass means as an argument?" I asked.

"I know now, of course; then—I knew nothing. I felt a choking coldness round me, like the coils of a snake, that throttled me numb; it seemed as if my blood were running out at my feet. Men jest about fear; they never would if they had felt it. I forget what I said or did at the moment: laughed the thing off somehow, managed anyhow to dupe my companion, and got her indoors. The rest of the evening was like a fevered dream. The rosy lamps, the murmur of women's voices, the flicker of their jewels, the quick notes of music, the long wail of a song, a certain blatant red screen, all seemed blended in a misty tank of green water, through which the body of that woman went. I endured it to the end, but before the last good-night I was on the beach, hurrying down to the sea. It was there to meet me, rocking indolently to and fro, beautiful, terrible, the graceful figure of a girl, faintly luminous, and the pale colour of its loosened hair. I don't think I doubted for a moment what it was: there was an instant flash of recognition in its eyes, the lips smiled; I had kissed them all too often under the hard Cairene moon not to know them then. I cannot remember now what I said, or how I acted; so much has happened since, and I was in no state to observe. I questioned it, commanded, implored, but no answer came back, though its eyes seemed to show I could be heard.

"The next day I was in town. Morning brought new confidence, and I told myself that this was business for the doctors. I saw Hadley Burroughs—do you know him?"

"Yes."

"He is as good as can be had, isn't he?"

"For the eyes, yes."

"I asked him to look at mine, but I told him nothing of what I had seen. He said they were in perfect order, and fit for anything. I went on from him to Spencer."

"Sir Evan?"

"Yes; he takes that kind of failure, you know. I told him my trouble as far as I cared to, and sat down under his glasses. He found incipient optic neuritis; you know what that is?"

"No, in Evan Spencer's patients I do not. I believe it is something in his ophthalmoscope. Anyhow it is catching, for no one who consults him escapes it."

"I see, something bogus? So it struck me at the time; but he thought it could be cured if I would consent to take sufficient trouble. I explained that the trouble was with me already, and promised absolute obedience. But it came to nothing. He said I must have change, go to the sea, and so forth. To the sea, forsooth! but I went—for one night. I told myself the whole thing was irrational; but I found it easier to say so in town than on the beach, and came back.

"Then I tried to 'devil' the thing myself; bought a dozen books on diseases of the brain, nervous apparitions, partial mania, blunders of the eye, and so forth; all very interesting, but telling me nothing I did not know and everything I did not want, so I shut up the books, and waited for something to happen. But nothing did. I seemed absolutely sound and sane. I even persuaded myself the appearance had been some passing derangement, and went down one afternoon to Brighton to test a new stretch of sea."

"Why?"

"To get clear of association. I thought I had succeeded, for though

I stayed all that evening on the front I saw nothing. I went back to my hotel on wings. But the evening after, the thing was there, floating in the water at my feet."

"The next night?" I inquired.

"Yes, the second. I went after that to several other places, and it was always on the second night that it appeared."

"That seems as though the salt air had something to do with it."

"Does it? I told myself a dozen things of the sort, and believed none of them. In fact, I believed nothing. The appearance of the mental image of one's late sweetheart is not, in black and white, so very terrible; only, unhappily, it was not in black and white, not indeed in anything commonly conceivable, nor was it a mental image. I had never seen, nor, indeed, so thought of her; in spite of the inducements of her evening dresses. It was my consolation to believe they were still aiding her flirtations, for I told myself that no woman who flirts could well achieve a spiritual duplicate. And as the practical solution of my trouble was apparently to avoid the sea, I determined to adopt it. But even that failed me.

"I had returned from a 'week end' in the country, and found a letter waiting me from Egypt. It was from a friend there, and mentioned the death of Miss... I can't give you her real name, but the one I used will do—of Miss Charmian, on the last arrived P. and O. It was believed she had fallen overboard. She was accustomed, it seemed, to sit upon the taffrail, in spite of cautions, and was last seen there one evening. No splash had been heard and no cry, though the night was an oil calm, and many passengers were on deck.

"That letter altered all things for me, and ended them; it was my order of dismissal from this company of strolling players, in which I hoped to take the big parts. I made out from it that Miss... Charmian must have been drowned when the boat was a couple of days from Port Said, the night before I had seen at Eastbourne that ghostly body in the sea."

"That was surmise?"

"It was at first, but I confirmed it. She was missed about twenty-five hours before I saw her."

"Her!"

"Yes, that closed the pleadings: I had known it was she all along, but between 'her' dancing, laughing, flirting as I supposed, and 'her'—dead was all the difference."

"How?"

"Ah! one was nothing, some trick of thought-photography we're not in touch with; at least, so I told myself; but the other was all. She desired me, despaired of me, died for me! that was herself!"

"Did it frighten you?"

"No, I think not. It stunned me. I felt it was the end. It stamped itself red and broad across my brain, as a signet crushes out the wax, so that every thought afterwards must show some part of the pattern. I fought it for a month, with that shadow of death between me and my fellows, and an empty chair beside me at every feast, but only for a month. Then I made my bow to the big audience I loved so well, to the woman I worshipped, and came down here."

He shivered as he spoke. I wiped the heat and, possibly, the fear from my face, and looked out over the sea.

"What do you make of it?" he asked presently.

"Not much," I said; "the eye-glass beats me, and the coincidence of that appearance with her death, you being a complete stranger to the fact, would be astounding as coincidence. Of course a doctor says everything of the sort must be eyes or brain. There may be something wrong with the sight which causes you to see the thing which is not;

that is fairly common; people see spectral cats, or donkeys, and so forth, but we consider them sane so long as they know what they are looking at, and don't desire to stroke or ride them. Or a man's eyes may be all right, and the mischief further in, making him fancy things that are not; that is mania of a sort also common enough, but its victim may be perfectly sane otherwise, and is called so if he is conscious of his delusions, but when he begins to mew to the cat or cut sticks for the donkey, we shut him up."

"I see, and are those the only two causes of trouble?"

"Oh, no, the causes are many, but they work out at the top in much the same way."

"Yes, but if my eyes are amiss, how does my glass help them? If the trouble is inside, nothing outside can define it."

"No, I admit that."

"And if my brain is the traitor, why should it go wrong that very day, the first on which some other theory becomes possible? Doesn't that stagger you?"

"It certainly stretches the tether of chances."

"Besides, if this thing were an illusion, wouldn't memory come in somewhere? Shouldn't I be likely to re-see the woman as I was used to see her? Don't delusions make their bricks for the most part of remembered straw, and, further, would not one's previous notions of beauty and canons of taste count for something?"

"Probably."

"But they don't! I see the woman as God made her; I see her changed from the colour of life, not to the white of death, but to the hue of some imprisoned light I could not match in the rainbow. Is that likely as an illusion? And is it not less so that so unhuman, so bizarre a creature should at once impose itself on one as resist-lessly beautiful?"

"I think there is not so much in that," I said; "one often sees in dreams what seems to be outside experience, and all sorts of strange admirations are possible in trance."

"But this is no trance," he said.

"Perhaps not, but it might be."

"Trance! do I seem entranced?"

"No, not now, but the motion of the sea at night might have an hypnotic effect?"

He laughed.

"What are you going to do here?" I asked.

"To do? I'm done with doing. What view do you think the high court of common talk would hold of a man who loved to distraction a floating ghost of the sea? There's only one alternative to the head that wears a crush hat in such cases—you must be mad, or it must be ignorant; I needn't tell you which it takes. Do! no, I remain. I don't know what you doctors call this," holding up a lean bloodless hand, "but I shan't run to much more of it."

No man knows another's trouble; even the heart often knows of its own bitterness only the scald and strain. I said what I could, not of comfort, none was possible, but of pity, which I felt from my soul.

"But you don't believe me," he mourned.

"Give me time," I pleaded; "we're on such broken ground in these matters at present, that one doubts every footprint. I've never found cause to believe in spirits, and my conversion at such short notice would be worth very little. Have you seen nothing more?"

"More," he said slowly; "I wonder sometimes if there *can* be more. I have seen the sea grow white with the faces of the dead, as the shallows grow white in storm. For the sea is full of the dead, of the faces of the dead that are drowned; some mere trails and wisps of things with eyes, some fearfully imperfect, some beautiful. They tear to and fro like caged beasts within the waves, not heeding each other, but staring into the air, and their faces are not as ours, but sharp as the stript passions of men."

"How have you seen these things?" I inquired.

"Bit by bit; first a shadow, then a light, then a face; some come and go, some stay; many, perhaps, I do not see, for there is often a stirring in the sea which I cannot understand."

"Do you see them by day?"

"I have seen them faintly, not often."

"You think they are there always?"

"Certainly."

"Did it strike you that these further visions somewhat discounted the reality of the first?"

"No, why? If there is one ghost in the sea, there must be many; its dead are many."

"Yes, but why should you see them by degrees? That looks like sympathetic extension along whatever diseased nerve or fibre produced the first appearance."

"The eye sees what it has learnt to see," he said absently, "almost what it is told to see. The lens only brings the picture in to the plate, and the plate is sensitised by our brains; we see what we have the wit to see. Look!" He waved his hat, and a cloud of startled birds rose suddenly at the edge of the sea, and swirled to and fro in dispersing sheets of shaded whiteness. "What have you seen?"

"Birds," I said.

"Aye, but what! Did you see the dunlins wheel from white to grey, or the pigmy curlews by their bills and tail-coverts, or the redshank by his stripes, the sea-pie's bill, or the peewit's crest? You saw none of these! Why? They were there, I saw them all."

"I understand," I said; "but men have pointed out to me blue fishes in broad daylight crawling over their boots."

"Oh, come!" he interrupted, "my argument was that things of real existence might be invisible till we learnt to see them."

"Yes," I said, "I understand."

III

We lunched together in the cottage on bacon, porridge, broad beans, and potatoes—cold, the fire having expired, and Melton being too indifferent to re-light it. And I could remember when he would have refused an ortolan that lacked quince in the cooking.

While we ate, he proposed I should prolong my stay a couple of days.

"Though there is nothing to see here but me," he added plaintively.

"That will be enough," I replied.

"I believe," he hazarded with a smile, "you are the same old broker in curios as ever, and I am the last."

We sat in the rough porch while I smoked a pipe, and afterwards climbed out along the jagged ledges of rocks to the edge of the sea. It stretched from us four thousand miles to the cities of the New World, and rose for the first quarter mile in a foaming flight of white steps, which rose steep in storm and fell thunderously, so that the noise of them far inland was like the sullen roar of guns.

The tide was running now, and went past us straining and plunging towards the shore. The sun dropped red into a ditch of clouds, and burnt the watery sky above him to a fierce strong glow, which turned the sea in its turn to a flood of purple dye. The colour ran eastward, and we faced about to watch it, in Melton's phrase, "play the fool with everything."

"Listen!" he said abruptly.

I could hear nothing but the rush of the waves.

"The ground swell is rising," he explained; "it is only a whisper now, but it will howl before midnight. Hello! What's that?"

It seemed nothing to my eyes, as I followed the direction of his, but a white angle in a ledge of rock just reached by the sea.

"It's a man's arms," he said.

"Rubbish!" I retorted, "it's a bent quartz vein."

But as I spoke the water pushed it forward.

"Well, it's a quartz vein that will have to be buried," he replied, "so we may as well go for it at once."

I saw, as we came nearer, that he was right. The water in the gulley was rocking a man's body along its narrow trough; the arms were raised, and the hands clasped tightly together above its head in some last wild appeal to a deliverer. They were stiff now as wood, but there was in them an agony more terrible than stared from the eyes; their failure seemed fixed there with a kind of malice.

Melton picked his way along the upper shelf of the cleavage, and tried to lift the body by the neck of its jersey, but the stuff gave way.

"Lend a hand, will you?" he cried, "we must carry it fore and aft between us."

It was no easy matter walking along that knife edge, with the water pulsing over one's boots, and those poor sodden limbs swaying between us, and Melton slipped once into a crevice above his thighs; but we managed to get on easier ground and carried the drowned man up to the border of the dunes.

Melton stooped down, turning the body over in search of some clue to its identity. Used as I am to death, there seemed something callous in his treatment. He peered into the eyes.

"Swede," he hazarded.

"Close them!" I said.

He looked up sharply.

"You don't like it?" he inquired.

"No, I don't! and I prefer to treat the dead with more respect."

He smiled, and his smile was sadder than the dead man's despair, but he drew the lids down quietly, and laid its limbs together. I placed two shells on the eyes, and as I rose, Melton passed his arm into mine and we left the body there, slanting, facing the west, and tinged with the last dull purple light.

"It's only a body," remarked my companion after a pause, musingly, and, I thought, with apology.

"A man's body," I said.

"Man's body or dog's body; there's no odds in bodies."

"I don't agree with you," I replied.

"No, I suppose not, because neither you nor your friends believe in immortality with all your wits; you say man has a soul and a body, but the fact is that man is a soul in a body. Could you see, as I do, the souls of men naked in the sea, you would not trouble about their eye-balls."

I said I considered funeral sentiment merely an extension of tenderness to the most helpless, a loyalty in compassion, but he disagreed; it was fear, he said, fear and doubt, and to change the subject I asked if there had been any wreck to account for the remains.

"There was a boat sunk under the island two days ago, run down; they sent notice of it along the coast, and Tom has been on the lookout I believe; he makes something from these finds."

I had been hungry, but ate little supper; the recovery of corpses does not better one's appetite, and I was bothered by a disquieting resemblance between the horror in the dead man's eyes and a look I had seen once or twice in Melton's.

"Tom," said the latter, to our host during the meal, "there's a body on the south barrows."

"Aye, and how kem it there, sir?" asked the man.

"We hauled it out of the water for you; came down channel, I fancy."

"Rent, sir?"

"No, drowned quiet by the look of it; possibly one of that boat's crew—the *Sea-gull*'s, was it?"

"Aye, aye, vury laike, vury laike. Them that go daun to sea in ships," he murmured, treading vaguely through the verse, as though conceiving that the fitness of things in such accidents demanded scriptural balance.

"Ah, Tom," said Dick Melton sadly, "there are wonders in the deep waters stranger than ever that singer dreamed of."

After supper we sat talking of times past and of things gone for good and bad, till Melton rose suddenly with an air of nervous apprehension, and, begging me to excuse him, went out. The old couple beside the fire watched him and shook their heads. I laid a fore-finger interrogatively to my own.

"Lor! bless you naw, sir," said the wife decisively, "naaght wrang there. A straange gent'man is Mister Malten, but's got's wits and to plenty."

They gossiped together of their lodger, ignoring me, but in acknowledgment, it seemed, of my interest. They had clearly no doubts as to his sanity, and treated his salving of the corpse as proof of an improvement in his economic ideas. Their talk wandered to other such derelicts with unpleasant precision of detail, though they seemed to enjoy it, and showed incidentally a fund of rough pity and pious trust in the benignity of other men's misfortunes.

IV

Melton's forecast had been fulfilled, and one could hear the slow continual thunder of the surf deepen as the tide laid open the river mouth to the sea, and over it the hoarser trumpeting of the bar. The boom of water that breaks on water through a mile of beaten foam is very different from the clash of water that breaks on shore; there is a deadly softness in it that smothers sound, and deadlier strength.

I listened alone for about an hour, while its note crept down among the deepening seas, and then a womanish fear of my own company overcame me, and I went out.

Water was running close to the cottage where in the morning had been a triple bank of sand: I dipped my fingers into it and put them to my mouth; the taste was brackish.

The tide had dammed the river back and forced it out across the fields. I walked on to the little wooden bridge which spanned a dried elbow of the stream, but it was covered by the flood. Clearly Melton had not turned north, so I faced towards the lower margin of the dunes where the dead man lay. I passed it with a shudder, and a little further on found Melton standing by the edge of the dim waste of foam which seemed to slant upwards into the sky; his hands were thrust into his pockets, and he was staring out across the sea. I thought he would start at my touch, but instead I had to shake him.

He looked round at me dully.

"What's up?" he shouted through the pounding of the sea.

"Nothing—nothing!" I called back, "only a bit lonely!"

He caught hold of my arm, and walked me back from the shore.

"Lonely?" he said, when the roar ceased to choke our words, "with all that company!" and he nodded towards the sea; "I wish I could introduce you."

I wished nothing less; that company, even at second-hand, seemed undesirable.

"He is there tonight," he went on; "your friend with the eyes; I wonder what it was they saw. Pious people fancy that the drowning edit a review of their past lives during its last half-second; but that is one of their many kind arrangements which don't always come off. I have been pulled out of the water, drowned as far as any consciousness went, and all I can remember thinking of was a row of poached eggs, which was curious, because one generally sees them in a circle, a shape which might have entitled them to consideration as an intimation of immortality."

He spoke in a drawling nervous way, different from his common speech, which always bit.

"I suppose you expected to find me raving somewhere along the sands to an inapparent audience of little fishes," he continued; "I'm afraid you've missed that exhibition, though I do rave sometimes; that is permitted, you know, to a lover. I've even stood waist-deep in this water to kiss the ripple which seemed to be her mouth, and to see the gold light on her arms run round me. Oh! I've played the fool to perfection and with complete perception. I've felt the wet chill through my clothes, and considered the nuisance of changing them as I waded out to my goddess." He sighed, and then said in an altered way, "come, you're cold; let us go in!"

He turned as we left the bay, flung back his face, and sang out to the rolling seas:

"Good-night!"

"Don't think me mad," he said, "on that account; it's matter of habit and courtesy. It strikes me if all this were pure fancy, I should sometimes hear a reply."

"You never do?"

"Never! No word or whisper have I ever heard, though there's provocation enough, God knows. Surely, if there's any self-persuasion possible in the matter, it might come in there? Why, I've watched her mouth purse round the pet words she used to use, and seen them written in her eyes, and yet heard nothing, though the seas were crying 'Sweet' from shoal to shoal." He turned on the threshold of the door. "Ah, me! and to think that all of it may but be a slackened spirt of blood across my brain."

I stayed there the day following, and have since wished heartily I had not. I was, in fact, somewhat ashamed of myself, and wanted to see my philosophy come back on the spot. It did not come, however.

As the day went on, I began to feel my companion's presence in a curious way. It was not alone that he was there, but as though something were happening about him, a movement which one felt with an unknown sense, but felt as consciously as a draught of air.

I told myself it was ridiculous; that it was not in reason and could not be in nature; but arguments against one's senses are as useless as firelight to a man with an ague; and a glance at the strange transparence of Melton's face did not mend matters; there is nothing in reason nor in nature to make the flesh of a healthy man like brown water, but something had done it.

We sat and talked all day. It seemed futile enough at times to discuss the world's progress with one who had stepped off its path and would never lift a hand to stay or move it more; but it was of interest to him. He reverted only once to the trouble which had brought his sentence of banishment, and it was of a graver sentence that he spoke.

"You ask for how long I am here. You ought to be able to tell me that. I am here for as long as I last."

I interposed something in protest, not very coherent, I imagine, for he said:

"You remind me of the Irishman who was certain when his friend had been sentenced for life, that he would not live half the time. I am here for life, and I shall not live the half; will you forgive me if I ask you a favour on the strength of it? Yes?"

"Go on."

"When my 'Weighed and found wanting' is written, will you come if I send you word? I am not afraid, but just a bit shy of death—this death. It's a stupid request, but I should like to have you here if you could come—to see me off."

I said, with the conventional insincerity men use towards death, that he had many years before him; but that I would come from any quarter of the world when the word reached me of his need.

"I thought you would," he said.

After supper we went out together; he even locked his arm in mine. The night was clear, but wandering clots of cloud, black against the deep night-blue, were floating in from the sea. The stars flickered round them like the points of spears.

Held so close to my companion, I felt, or thought I felt, a dull vibration in him; it was a vibration and not a pulse, but I failed in any way to define it.

"It is so strange," he said as we went along, "if these things are really here and not the bad jokes of my brain, that you cannot see them. Mountain loads of fiery chariots may have required second sight, but it seems incredible that the ring of light out there should be invisible to anyone."

"Where?"

"About half a mile off the point; due west."

"I daresay; but most people can see a moonbeam."

He looked at me with a curious smile.

156

"Seldom one so much refracted," he said; "the moon won't be up for two hours."

I gazed at the strange glow steadily for a full minute; it lay on the water in an irregular plait, as the colour of moonlight, but brighter at its outward edges.

"Look here," I said, wrenching my arm from his, "I didn't stay here to see your ghosts, and if you've any confounded way of making them visible, I hope you'll drop it."

"I have no way," he replied in a low voice, "and I would not for worlds you should learn to see them if I had. Ah, my God, no! one is enough. Come, let us go indoors."

As he spoke the light slowly faded, burnt up again an instant, and disappeared. We parted at the door; he went back to the sea. I tried to sleep. But I did not succeed, and I lay by my open window till the plovers' call came from the shore and the east grew yellow; then I got up and lit a pipe.

Melton came in about two hours later with the early dawn. He seemed utterly exhausted, and staggered. He held out his hand.

"You're not offended, are you?" he said.

I took his hand and pressed it, more sorry for him than could be said. He returned my pressure faintly, and sat down beside me, holding my hand.

Before the sun was hot we had breakfasted in his little room overlooking the grey sea, and I set out once more upon my way.

Nothing reached me from that desolate haven for ten full months. Then, one morning in early spring, a telegram was forwarded me from town with the one word "Come!" I should have understood it without the soft name of the Cornish post-town on the sheet; and started west at once. My absence from home lost me the express, and left me to be dragged over the slow miles at my journey's end into the early hours of the morning. I was able, however, to charter a gig at once, and started by daybreak for the long hilly drive towards the sea.

When we pulled up at the head of that sandy valley, the day was hot and calm, with a faint veil seawards of mist. I pushed on hurriedly to the cottage, and found the two old people sitting in the kitchen, the woman's arms lying limp on the white scrubbed table, the man's by his side.

They looked the picture of palsied fear, lifted their heads together with a jerk as I entered, and said without further greeting:

"He's out!"

The quaint absurdity of it struck me, anxious as I was. The woman's head dropped forward as I turned to go, and she groaned out—

"Eh, I've seen sech things!"

I went rapidly along the lower line of the dunes, and then, finding nothing, turned north across the stream. My ideas were so fixed on a walking figure, that I almost passed unnoticed the body of a man lying flat on the wet sand between the barrows and the ebbing sea. I ran forward, and kneeled beside it; but that which had been Dick Melton was passed for ever beyond reach or need of help.

He had fallen with his face towards the sea, his arms flung out before him. He must have dropped in the thinnest film of the retreating tide, for his sleeves were soaked on the under side. His face was buried between his arms, and I think he had drowned in about half an inch of water, but owing to his exhausted condition nothing but an opinion was possible, and the inquest doctors would only certify to syncope.

I have fancied that, knowing he was near his end, he had flung himself forward into the sea, hoping by a like death to be united to the woman he had once loved so ill; but that he died thus is only surmise, for the very effort may have cost him his life. Yet one wishes to think that those poor lovers, whatever the meaning of his strange vision, in their deaths at least were not divided, for, truly, remorse of love never paid its debt more fully.

He had begged for burial among the sand dunes of the shore, but the law forbade him that and laid him, still within sound of the sea, beside the little church in the combe. It stands, as it has stood for nine centuries, squarely and bravely against the fierce blasts of the storm, among a scanty and prayerless people—the furthest outwork in God's war. And from lichened archways above his grave, Saxon ghouls peer still through the driven mist, after the nights and days of a thousand years; while beneath them, the foam sheet thickens, and the echoes of its thunders drown into silence the imprisoned ghosts of the sea.

CROOKEN SANDS

Bram Stoker

Bram Stoker (1847–1912) surely needs little by way of introduction. Stoker was born in a coastal suburb in the north of Dublin, holidayed frequently in Cruden Bay in Aberdeenshire, visited Whitby in 1890, and returns repeatedly in his fiction to the significance of coasts and coastal waters. We have already gestured in our Introduction to the importance the coast plays in his most famous novel, *Dracula* (1897), and it is prominent in other novels such as *The Watter's Mou'* (1895) and *The Mystery of the Sea* (1902). Even his unhinged Midlands-set final novel, *The Lair of the White Worm* (1911), takes its readers (and gigantic worm woman) on a brief excursion down the Mersey and out through the Liverpool docks into the Irish Sea.

"Crooken Sands" was first published in the 1894 Christmas edition of *The Illustrated Sporting and Dramatic News* and it was later gathered together with other short tales of Stoker's by his widow, Florence, and published in *Dracula's Guest and Other Weird Stories* (1914). The tale is set in a "lovely spot" between Aberdeen and Peterhead—a spot, then, that roughly maps onto Cruden Bay—and follows the holidaying of Londoner Arthur Markam and his family. Besides the story's sustained interest in the shifting, treacherous quicksand of Crooken Bay, in the fulfilment of a sinister prophecy, and its exceptionally effective deployment of a *doppelgänger*, "Crooken Sands" is also a text scrutinising Anglo-Scottish relations. Markam indulges in apparent seaside frivolities when he decides to dress up as a "Highland chieftain"—an embarrassing (or so his children think) performance of Scottishness, and one, ultimately, he may have been wise to avoid.

M r. Arthur Fernlee Markam, who took what was known as the Red House above the Mains of Crooken, was a London merchant, and, being essentially a cockney, thought it necessary when he went for the summer holidays to Scotland to provide an entire rig-out as a Highland chieftain, as manifested in chromolithographs and on the music-hall stage. He had once seen in the Empire the Great Prance—"The Bounder King"—bring down the house by appearing as "The MacSlogan of that Ilk," and singing the celebrated Scotch song, "There's naethin' like haggis to mak a mon dry!" and he had ever since preserved in his mind a faithful image of the picturesque and warlike appearance which he presented. Indeed, if the true inwardness of Mr. Markam's mind on the subject of his selection of Aberdeenshire as a summer resort were known, it would be found that in the foreground of the holiday locality which his fancy painted stalked the many-hued figure of the MacSlogan of that Ilk.

However, be this as it may, a very kind fortune—certainly so far as external beauty was concerned—led him to the choice of Crooken Bay. It is a lovely spot, between Aberdeen and Peterhead, just under the rock-bound headland whence the long, dangerous reefs known as The Spurs run out into the North Sea. Between this and the "Mains of Crooken"—a village sheltered by the northern cliffs—lies the deep bay, backed with a multitude of bent-grown dunes where the rabbits are to be found in thousands. Thus at either end of the bay is a rocky promontory, and when the dawn or the sunset falls on the rocks of red syenite the effect is very lovely. The bay itself is floored with level sand, and the tide runs far out, leaving a smooth waste of hard sand, on which are dotted here and there the stake-nets and bag-nets of the salmon-fishers. At one end of the bay there is a little group or cluster of rocks whose heads are raised something above high water, except when in rough weather the waves come over them green. At low tide they are exposed down to the sand level; and here is perhaps the only little bit of dangerous sand on this part of the eastern coast. Between the rocks, which are apart about some fifty feet, is a small quicksand, which, like the Goodwins, is dangerous only with the incoming tide. It extends outward till it is lost in the sea, and inward till it fades away in the hard sand of the upper beach. On the slope of the hill which rises beyond the dunes, midway between The Spurs and the Port of Crooken, is the Red House. It rises from the midst of a clump of fir-trees which protect it on three sides, leaving the whole sea-front open. A trim, old-fashioned garden stretches down to the roadway, on crossing which a grassy path, which can be used for light vehicles, threads a way to the shore, winding amongst, the sand-hills.

When the Markam family arrived at the Red House after their thirty-six hours of pitching on the Aberdeen steamer *Ban Righ* from Blackwall, with the subsequent train to Yellon and drive of a dozen miles, they all agreed that they had never seen a more delightful spot. The general satisfaction was more marked as at that very time none of the family were for several reasons inclined to find favourable anything or any place over the Scottish border. Though the family was a large one, the prosperity of the business allowed them all sorts of personal luxuries, amongst which was a wide latitude in the way of dress. The frequency of the Markam girls' new frocks was a source of envy to their bosom friends, and of joy to themselves.

Arthur Fernlee Markam had not taken his family into his confidence regarding his new costume. He was not quite certain that he should be free from ridicule, or at least from sarcasm; and as he was sensitive on the subject he thought it better to be actually in the suitable environment before he allowed the full splendour to burst on them. He had taken some pains to insure the completeness of the Highland costume. For the purpose he had paid many visits to "The Scotch All-Wool Tartan Clothing Mart," which had been lately established in Copthall-court by the Messrs. MacCallum More and Roderick MacDhu. He had anxious consultations with the head of the firm—MacCallum as he called himself, resenting any such additions as "Mr." or "Esquire." The known stock of buckles, buttons, straps, brooches, and ornaments of all kinds were examined in critical detail; and at last an eagle's feather of sufficiently magnificent proportions was discovered, and the equipment was complete. It was only when he saw the finished costume, with the vivid hues of the tartan seemingly modified into comparative sobriety by the multitude of silver fittings, the cairngorm brooches, the philibeg, dirk, and sporran that he was fully and absolutely satisfied with his choice. At first he had thought of the Royal Stuart dress tartan, but abandoned it on the MacCallum pointing out that if he should happen to be in the neighbourhood of Balmoral it might lead to complications. The MacCallum, who, by the way, spoke with a remarkable cockney accent, suggested other plaids in turn; but now that the other question of accuracy had been raised, Mr. Markam foresaw difficulties if he should by chance find himself in the locality of the clan whose colours he had usurped. The MacCallum at last undertook to have, at Markam's expense, a special pattern woven which would not be exactly the same as any existing tartan, though partaking of the characteristics of many. It was based on the Royal Stuart, but contained suggestions as to simplicity of pattern from the Macalister and Ogilvie clans, and as to neutrality of colour from the clans of Buchanan, Macbeth, Chief of Macintosh and Macleod. When the specimen had been shown to Markam he had feared somewhat lest it should strike the eye of his domestic circle as gaudy; but as Roderick MacDhu fell into perfect ecstasies over its beauty he did not make any objection to the completion of the piece. He thought, and wisely, that if a genuine Scotchman like MacDhu liked it, it must be right—especially as the junior partner was a man very much of his own build and appearance. When the MacCallum was receiving his cheque—which, by the way, was a pretty stiff one—he remarked:

"I've taken the liberty of having some more of the stuff woven in case you or any of your friends should want it." Markam was gratified, and told him that he should be only too happy if the beautiful stuff which they had originated between them should become a favourite, as he had no doubt it would in time. He might make and sell as much as he would.

Markam tried the dress on in his office one evening after the clerks had all gone home. He was pleased, though a little frightened, at the result. The MacCallum had done his work thoroughly, and there was nothing omitted that could add to the martial dignity of the wearer.

"I shall not, of course, take the claymore and the pistols with me on ordinary occasions," said Markam to himself as he began to undress. He determined that he would wear the dress for the first time on landing in Scotland; and accordingly on the morning when the *Ban Righ* was hanging off the Girdle Ness lighthouse, waiting for the tide to enter the port of Aberdeen, he emerged from his cabin in all the gaudy splendour of his new costume. The first comment he heard was from one of his own sons, who did not recognise him at first.

"Here's a guy! Great Scott! It's the governor!" And the boy fled forthwith and tried to bury his laughter under a cushion in the saloon. Markam was a good sailor, and had not suffered from the pitching of the boat, so that his naturally rubicund face was even more rosy by the conscious blush which suffused his cheeks when he had found himself at once the cynosure of all eyes. He could have wished that he had not been so bold, for he knew from the cold that there was a big bare spot under one side of his jauntily worn Glengarry cap. However, he faced the group of strangers boldly. He was not, outwardly, upset even when some of their comments reached his ears.

"He's off his bloomin' chump," said a cockney in a suit of exaggerated plaid.

"There's flies on him," said a tall, thin Yankee, pale with seasickness, who was on his way to take up his residence for a time as close as he could get to the gates of Balmoral.

"Happy thought! Let us fill our mulls; now's the chance!" said a young Oxford man on his way home to Inverness. But presently Mr. Markam heard the voice of his eldest daughter.

"Where is he? Where is he?" and she came tearing along the deck with her hat blowing behind her. Her face showed signs of agitation, for her mother had just been telling her of her father's condition; but when she saw him she instantly burst into laughter so violent that it ended in a fit of hysterics. Something of the same kind happened with each of the other children. When they had all had their turn Mr. Markam went to his cabin, and sent his wife's maid to tell each member of the family that he wanted to see them at once. They all made their appearance, suppressing their feelings as well as they could. He said to them very quietly:

"My dears, don't I provide you all with ample allowances?"

"Yes, father!" they all answered gravely, "no one could be more generous!"

"Don't I let you dress as you please?"

"Yes, father!"—this a little sheepishly.

"Then, my dears, don't you think it would be nicer and kinder of you not to try and make me feel uncomfortable, even if I do assume a dress which is ridiculous in your eyes, though quite common enough in the country where we are about to sojourn?" There was no answer except that which appeared in their hanging heads. He was a good father and they all knew it. He was quite satisfied and went on:

"There, now, run away and enjoy yourselves! We sha'n't have another word about it." Then he went on deck again, and stood bravely the fire of ridicule which he recognised around him, though nothing more was said within his hearing.

The astonishment and amusement which his get-up occasioned on the *Ban Righ* were, however, nothing to those which it created in Aberdeen. The boys and loafers, and women with babies, who waited at the landing-shed, followed *en masse* as the Markam party took their way to the railway station; even the porters with their old-fashioned knots and their new-fashioned barrows, who await the traveller at the foot of the gang-plank, followed in wondering delight. Fortunately, the Peterhead train was just about to start, so that the martyrdom was not unnecessarily prolonged. In the carriage the glorious Highland costume was unseen, and as there were but few persons at the station at Yellon, all went well there. When, however, the carriage drew near the Mains of Crooken, and the fisher-folk had run to their doors to see who it was that was passing, the excitement exceeded all bounds. The children with one impulse waved their hats and ran shouting behind the carriage; the men forsook their nets and their baiting and followed; the women clutched their babies and followed also. The horses were tired after their long journey to Yellon and back, and the hill was steep, so that there was ample time for the crowd to gather and even to pass on ahead. Mrs. Markam and the elder girls would have liked to make some protest, or to do something to relieve their feelings of chagrin at the ridicule which they saw on all faces; but there was a look of fixed determination on the face of the seeming Highlander which awed them a little, and they were silent. It might have been that the eagle's feather, even when rising above the bald head—the cairngorm brooch even on the fat shoulder, and the claymore, dirk, and pistols, even when belted round the extensive paunch and protruding from the stocking on the sturdy calf, fulfilled their existence as symbols of martial and terrifying import! When the party arrived at the gate of the Red House there awaited them a crowd of Crooken inhabitants, hatless and respectfully silent; the remainder of the population was painfully toiling up the hill. The silence was broken by only one sound, that of a man with a deep voice.

"Man! but he's forgotten the pipes!"

The servants had arrived some days before, and all things were in readiness. In the glow consequent on a good lunch after a hard journey all the disagreeables of travel and all the chagrin consequent on the adoption of the obnoxious costume were forgotten.

That afternoon Markam, still clad in full array, walked through the Mains of Crooken. He was all alone, for, strange to say, his wife and both daughters had sick headaches, and were, as he was told, lying down to rest after the fatigues of the journey. His eldest son, who claimed to be a young man, had gone out by himself to explore the surroundings of the place, and one of the boys could not be found. The other boy, on being told that his father had sent for him to come for a walk, had managed—by accident, of course—to fall into a water-butt, and had to be dried and rigged out afresh. His clothes not having been as yet unpacked, this was of course impossible without delay.

Mr. Markam was not quite satisfied with his walk. He could not meet any of his neighbours. It was not that there were not enough people about, for every house and cottage seemed to be full; but the people when in the open were either in their doorways some distance behind him, or on the roadway a long distance in front. As he passed he could see the tops of heads and the whites of eyes in the windows or round the corners of doors. The only interview which he had was anything but a pleasant one. This was with an odd sort of old man who was hardly ever heard to speak except to join in the "Amens" in the meeting-house. His sole occupation seemed to be to wait at the window of the post-office from eight o'clock in the morning till the arrival of the mail at one, when he carried the letter-bag to a neighbouring baronial castle. The remainder of his day was spent on a seat in a draughty part of the port, where the offal of the fish, the refuse of the bait, and the house rubbish were thrown, and where the ducks were accustomed to hold high revel. When Saft Tammie beheld him coming he raised his eyes, which were generally fixed on the nothing which lay on the roadway opposite his seat, and, seeming dazzled as if by a burst of sunshine, rubbed them and shaded them with his hand. Then he started up, and raised his hand aloft in a denunciatory manner as he spoke:

"'Vanity of vanities, saith the preacher. All is vanity.' Mon, be warned in time! 'Behold the lilies of the field, they toil not, neither do they spin, yet Solomon in all his glory was not arrayed like one of these.' Mon! mon! Thy vanity is as the quicksand which swallows up all which comes within its circle. Beware vanity! Beware the quicksand, which yawneth for thee, and which will swallow thee up! See thyself! Learn thine own vanity! Meet thyself face to face, and then in that moment thou shalt learn the fatal force of thy vanity. Learn it, know it, and repent ere the quicksand swallow thee!" Then without another word he went back to his seat, and sat there immovable and expressionless as before.

Markam could not but feel a little upset by this tirade. Only that it was spoken by a seeming madman, he would have put it down to some eccentric exhibition of Scottish humour or impudence; but the gravity of the message—for it seemed nothing else—made such a reading impossible. He was, however, determined not to give in to ridicule, and although he had not as yet seen anything in Scotland to remind him even of a kilt, he determined to wear his Highland dress. When he returned home, in less than half an hour, he found that every member of the family was, despite the headaches, out taking a walk. He took the opportunity afforded by their absence to lock himself in his dressing-room, took off the Highland dress, and, putting on a suit of flannels, lit a cigar and had a snooze. He was awakened by the noise of the family coming in, and at once donning his dress made his appearance in the drawing-room for tea. He did not go out again that afternoon; but after dinner he put on his dress again—he had of course dressed for dinner as usual—and went by himself for a walk on the seashore. He had by this time come to the conclusion that he would get by degrees accustomed to the Highland dress before making it his ordinary wear. The moon was up, and he easily followed the path through the sand-hills, and shortly struck the shore. The tide was out, and the beach firm as a rock, so he strolled southward to nearly the end of the bay. Here he was attracted by two isolated rocks some little way out from the edge of the dunes, so he strolled toward them. When he reached the nearest one he climbed it, and sitting there, elevated some fifteen or twenty feet over the waste of sand, enjoyed the lovely, peaceful prospect. The moon was rising behind the headland of Pennyfold, and its light was just touching the top of the furthermost rock of The Spurs, some three quarters of a mile out; the rest of the rocks were in dark shadow. As the moon rose over the headland, the rocks of The Spurs and then the beach by degrees, became flooded with light.

For a good while Mr. Markam sat and looked at the rising moon, and the growing area of light which followed its rise. Then he turned and faced eastward, and sat with his chin in his hand looking seaward, revelling in the peace and beauty and freedom of the scene. The roar of London—the darkness and the strife and weariness of London life—seemed to have passed quite away, and he lived at the moment a freer and higher life. He looked at the glistening water as it stole its way over the flat waste of sand, coming closer and closer insensibly—the tide had turned. Presently he heard a distant shouting along the beach very far off.

"The fishermen calling to each other," he said to himself, and looked around. As he did so he got a horrible shock, for though just then a cloud sailed across the moon he saw, in spite of the sudden darkness around him, his own image. For an instant, on the top of the opposite rock, he could see the bald back of the head and the Glengarry cap with the immense eagle's feather. As he staggered back his foot slipped, and he began to slide down toward the sand between the two rocks. He took no concern as to falling, for the sand was really only a few feet below him, and his mind was occupied with the figure or simulacrum of himself, which had already disappeared. As the easiest way of reaching *terra firma* he prepared to jump the remainder of the distance. All this had taken but a second; but the brain works quickly, and even as he gathered himself for the spring he saw the sand below him lying so marbly level shake and shiver in an odd way. A sudden fear overcame him; his knees failed, and instead of jumping he slid miserably down the rock, scratching his bare legs as he went. His feet touched the sand—went through it like water—and he was down below his knees before he realised that he was in a quicksand.

Wildly he grasped at the rock to keep himself from sinking deeper, and fortunately there was a jutting spur or edge which he was able to grasp instinctively. To this he clung in grim desperation. He tried to shout, but his breath would not come, till after a great effort his voice rang out. Again he shouted, and it seemed as if the sound of his own voice gave him new courage, for he was able to hold on to the rock for a longer time than he thought possible—though he held on only in blind desperation. He was, however, beginning to find his grasp weakening, when, joy of joys! his shout was answered by a rough voice from just above him.

"God be thankit, I'm nae too late!" and a fisherman with great thigh-boots came hurriedly climbing over the rock. In an instant he recognised the gravity of the danger, and with a cheering "Haud fast, mon! I'm comin'!" scrambled down till he found a firm foot-hold. Then, with one strong hand holding the rock above, he leaned down, and, catching Markam's wrist, called out to him, "Haud to me, mon! Haud to me wi' your ither hond!"

Then he lent his great strength, and with a steady, sturdy pull dragged him out of the hungry quicksand and placed him safe upon the rock. Hardly giving him time to draw breath, he pulled and pushed him—never letting him go for an instant—over the rock on to the firm sand beyond it; and finally deposited him, still shaking from the magnitude of his danger, high up on the beach. Then he began to speak:

"Mon! but I was just in time. If I had no laucht at yon foolish lads, and begun to rin at the first, you'd a bin sinkin' doon to the bowels o' the airth be the noo! Wully Beagrie thocht you was a ghaist, and Tom McPhail swore ye was only like a goblin on a puddick-steel! 'Na!' said I. 'Yon's but the daft Englishman—the loony that has escapit frae the waxworks.' I was thinkin' that bein' strange and silly—if not a whole-made feel—ye'd no ken the ways o' the quicksan'. I shouted till warn ye, and then ran to drag ye aff, if need be. But God be thankit, be ye feel or only half-daft wi' yer vanity, that I was no that late!" And he reverently lifted his cap as he spoke.

Mr. Markam was deeply touched and thankful for his escape from a horrible death; but the sting of the charge of vanity thus made once more against him came through his humility. He was about to reply angrily, when suddenly a great awe fell upon him as he remembered the warning words of the half-crazy letter-carrier: "Meet thyself face to face, and repent ere the quicksand shall swallow thee!"

Here, too, he remembered the image of himself that he had seen, and the sudden danger from the deadly quicksand that had followed. He was silent a full minute, and then said:

"My good fellow, I owe you my life!"

The answer came with reverence from the hardy fisherman: "Na! na! Ye owe that to God; but, as for me, I'm only too glad till be the humble instrument o' His mercy."

"But you will let me thank you," said Mr. Markam, taking both the great hands of his deliverer in his, and holding them tight. "My heart is too full as yet, and my nerves are too much shaken to let me say much; but, believe me, I am very, very grateful!" It was quite evident that the poor old fellow was deeply touched, for the tears were running down his cheeks

The fisherman said, with a rough but true courtesy:

"Ay, sir! thank me an ye will—if it 'll do yer poor heart good. An' I'm thinkin' that if it were me I'd like to be thankful, too. But, sir, as for me I need no thanks. I am glad, so I am!"

That Arthur Fernlee Markam was really thankful and grateful was shown practically later on. Within a week's time there sailed into Port Crooken the finest fishing-smack that had ever been seen in the harbour of Peterhead. She was fully found with sails and gear of all kinds, and with nets of the best. Her master and men went away by the coach, after having left with the salmon-fisher's wife the papers which made her over to him.

As Mr. Markam and the salmon-fisher walked together along the shore the former asked his companion not to mention the fact that he had been in such imminent danger, for that it would only distress his dear wife and children. He said that he would warn them all of the quicksand, and for that purpose he, then and there, asked questions about it till he felt that his information on the subject was complete. Before they parted he asked his companion if he had happened to see a second figure, dressed like himself, on the other rock as he had approached to succour him.

"Na! na!" came the answer, "there is nae sic another feel in these pairts. Nor has there been since the time o' Jamie Fleeman—him that was feel to the Laird o' Udney. Why, mon! sic a heathenish dress as ye have on till ye has nae been seen in these pairts within the memory o' mon. An I'm thinkin' that sic a dress never was for sittin' on the cauld rock, as ye done beyont. Mon! but do ye no fear the rheumatism or the lumbagy wi' floppin' doon on to the cauld stanes wi' yer bare flesh! I was thinkin' that it was daft ye waur when I see ye the mornin' doon be the port, but it's feel or eediot ye maun be for the like o' that!"

Mr. Markam did not care to argue the point, and as they were now close to his own home he asked the salmon-fisher to have a glass of whisky—which he did—and they parted for the night. He took good care to warn all his family of the quicksand, telling them that he had himself been in some danger from it.

All that night he never slept. He heard the hours strike one after the other; but try how he would he could not get to sleep. Over and over again he went through the horrible episode of the quicksand, from the time that Saft Tammie had broken his habitual silence to preach to him of the sin of vanity and to warn him. The question kept ever arising in his mind—"Am I then so vain as to be in the ranks of the foolish?" and the answer ever came in the words of the crazy prophet: "'Vanity of vanities! All is vanity.' Meet thyself face to face, and repent ere the quicksand shall swallow thee!" Somehow a feeling of doom began to shape itself in his mind that he would yet perish in that same quicksand, for there he had already met himself face to face.

In the grey of the morning he dozed off, but it was evident that he continued the subject in his dreams, for he was fully awakened by his wife, who said:

"Do sleep quietly! That blessed Highland suit has got on your brain. Don't talk in your sleep, if you can help it!" He was somehow conscious of a glad feeling, as if some terrible weight had been lifted from him, but he did not know any cause for it. He asked his wife what he had said in his sleep, and she answered:

"You said it often enough, goodness knows, for one to remember it—'Not face to face! I saw the eagle plume over the bald head! There is hope yet! Not face to face!' Go to sleep! Do!" And then he did go to sleep, for he seemed to realise that the prophecy of the crazy man had not been fulfilled. He had not met himself face to face—as yet, at all events.

He was awakened early by a maid who came to tell him that there was a fisherman at the door who wanted to see him. He dressed himself as quickly as he could—for he was not yet expert with the Highland dress—and hurried down, not wishing to keep the salmon-fisher waiting. He was surprised, and not altogether pleased, to find that his visitor was none other than Saft Tammie, who at once opened fire on him:

"I maun gang awa't' the post; but I thocht that I would waste an hour on ye, and ca' roond just to see if ye waur still that fou wi' vanity as on the nicht gane by. An' I see that ye've no learned the lesson. Weel! the time is comin', sure eneucht! However, I have all the time i' the marnins to my ain sel', so I'll aye look roond just till see how ye gang yer ain gait to the quicksan', and then to the de'il! I'm aff till ma wark the noo!" And he went straightway, leaving Mr. Markam considerably vexed, for the maids within earshot were vainly trying to conceal their giggles. He had fairly made up his mind to wear on that day ordinary clothes, but the visit of Saft Tammie reversed his decision. He would show them all that he was not a coward, and he would go on as he had begun—come what might. When he came to breakfast in full martial panoply, the children, one and all, held down their heads, and the backs of their necks became very red indeed. As, however, none of them laughed—except Titus, the youngest boy, who was seized with a fit of hysterical choking and was promptly banished from the room—he could not reprove them, but began to break his egg with a sternly determined air. It was unfortunate that as his wife was handing him a cup of tea one of the buttons of his sleeve caught in the lace of her morning wrapper, with the result that the hot tea was spilt over his bare knees. Not unnaturally, he made use of a swear word, whereupon his wife, somewhat nettled, spoke out:

"Well, Arthur, if you will make such an idiot of yourself with that ridiculous costume what else can you expect? You are not accustomed to it—and you never will be!" In answer he began an indignant speech with: "Madam!" but he got no further, for now that the subject was broached, Mrs. Markam intended to have her say out. It was not a pleasant say, and, truth to tell, it was not said in a pleasant manner. A wife's manner seldom is pleasant when she undertakes to tell what she considers "truths" to her husband. The result was that Arthur Fernlee

Markam undertook, then and there, that during his stay in Scotland he would wear no other costume than the one which she abused. Womanlike his wife had the last word—given in this case with tears:

"Very well, Arthur! Of course you will do as you choose. Make me as ridiculous as you can, and spoil the poor girls' chances in life. Young men don't seem to care, as a general rule, for an idiot father-in-law! But I warn you that your vanity will some day get a rude shock—if indeed you are not before then in an asylum, or dead!"

It was manifest after a few days that Mr. Markam would have to take the major part of his outdoor exercise by himself. The girls now and again took a walk with him, chiefly in the early morning or late at night, or on a wet day when there would be no one about; they professed to be willing to go at all times, but somehow something always used to occur to prevent it. The boys could never be found at all on such occasions, and as to Mrs. Markam, she sternly refused to go out with him on any consideration so long as he should continue to make a fool of himself. On the Sunday he dressed himself in his habitual broadcloth, for he rightly felt that church was not a place for angry feelings; but on Monday morning he resumed his Highland garb. By this time he would have given a good deal if he had never thought of the dress, but his British obstinacy was strong, and he would not give in. Saft Tammie called at his house every morning, and, not being able to see him nor to have any message taken to him, used to call back in the afternoon, when the letter-bag had been delivered, and watch for his going out. On such occasions he never failed to warn him against his vanity in the same words which he had used at the first. Before many days were over Mr. Markam had come to look upon him as little short of a scourge.

By the time the week was out the enforced partial solitude, the constant chagrin, and the never-ending brooding which was thus engendered, began to make Mr. Markam quite ill. He was too proud to take any of his family into his confidence, since they had in his view treated him very badly. Then he did not sleep well at night, and when he did sleep he had constantly bad dreams. Merely to assure himself that his pluck was not failing him he made it a practice to visit the quicksand at least once every day; he hardly ever failed to go there the last thing at night. It was perhaps this habit that wrought the quicksand with its terrible experience so perpetually into his dreams. More and more vivid these became, till on waking at times he could hardly realise that he had not been actually in the flesh to visit the fatal spot. He sometimes thought that he might have been walking in his sleep.

One night his dream was so vivid that when he awoke he could not believe that it had been only a dream. He shut his eyes again and again, but each time the vision, if it was a vision, or the reality, if it was a reality, would rise before him. The moon was shining full and yellow over the quicksand as he approached it; he could see the expanse of light shaken and disturbed, and full of black shadows, as the liquid sand quivered and trembled, and wrinkled and eddied, as was its wont between its pauses of marble calm. As he drew close to it another figure came toward it from the opposite side with equal footsteps. He saw that it was his own figure, his very self, and in silent terror, compelled by what force he knew not, he advanced—charmed as the bird is by the snake, mesmerised or hypnotised—to meet this other self. As he felt the yielding sand closing over him he awoke in the agony of death, trembling with fear, and, strange to say, with the silly man's prophecy seeming to sound in his ears: "'Vanity of vanities! All is vanity!' See thyself and repent ere the quicksand swallow thee!"

So convinced was he that this was no dream that he arose, early as it was, and, dressing himself without disturbing his wife, took his way to the shore. His heart fell when he came across a series of footsteps on the sands, which he at once recognised as his own. There was the same wide heel, the same square toe; he had no doubt now that he had actually been there, and half horrified, and half in a state of dreamy stupor, he followed the footsteps, and found them lost in the edge of the yielding quicksand. This gave him a terrible shock, for there were no return steps marked on the sand, and he felt that there was some dread mystery which he could not penetrate, and the penetration of which would, he feared, undo him.

In this state of affairs he took two wrong courses. Firstly, he kept his trouble to himself, and, as none of his family had any clue to it, every innocent word or expression which they used supplied fuel to the consuming fire of his imagination. Secondly, he began to read books professing to bear upon the mysteries of dreaming and of mental phenomena generally, with the result that every wild imagining of every crank or half-crazy philosopher became a living germ of unrest in the fertilising soil of his disordered brain. Thus negatively and positively all things began to work to a common end. Not the least of his disturbing causes was Saft Tammie, who had now become at certain times of the day a fixture at his gate. After a while, being interested in the previous state of this individual, he made inquiries regarding his past with the following result.

Saft Tammie was popularly believed to be the son of a laird in one of the counties round the Firth of Forth. He had been partially educated for the ministry, but for some cause which no one ever knew threw up his prospects suddenly, and, going to Peterhead in its days of whaling prosperity, had there taken service on a whaler. Here off and on he had remained for some years, getting gradually more and more silent in his habits, till finally his shipmates protested against so taciturn a mate, and he had found service among the fishing-smacks of the northern fleet. He had worked for many years at the fishing with always the reputation of being "a wee bit daft," till at length he had gradually settled down at Crooken, where the laird, doubtless knowing something of his family history, had given him a job which practically made him a pensioner. The minister who gave the information finished thus:

"It is a very strange thing, but the man seems to have some odd kind of gift. Whether it be that 'second sight' which we Scotch people are so prone to believe in, or some other occult form of knowledge, I know not, but nothing of a disastrous tendency ever occurs in this place but the men with whom he lives are able to quote after the event some saying of his which certainly appears to have foretold it. He gets uneasy or excited—wakes up in fact—when death is in the air!"

This did not in any way tend to lessen Mr. Markam's concern, but on the contrary seemed to impress the prophecy more deeply on his mind. Of all the books which he had read on his new subject of study none interested him so much as a German one, "Die Doppelgänger," by Dr. Heinrich von Aschenberg, formerly of Bonn. Here he learned for the first time of cases where men had led a double existence—each nature being quite apart from the other—the body being always a reality with one spirit, and a simulacrum with the other. Needless to say that Mr. Markam realised this theory as exactly suiting his own case. The glimpse which he had of his own back the night of his escape from the quicksand—his own footmarks disappearing into the quicksand with no return steps visible—the prophecy of Saft Tammie about his meeting himself and perishing in the quicksand—all lent aid to the conviction that he was in his own person an instance of the doppelgänger. Being then conscious of a double life he took steps to prove its existence to his own satisfaction. To this end on one night before going to bed he wrote his name in chalk on the soles of his shoes. That night he dreamed of the quicksand, and of his visiting it—dreamed so vividly that on waking in the grey of the dawn he could not believe that he had not been there. Arising, without disturbing his wife, he sought his shoes.

The chalk signatures were undisturbed! He dressed himself and stole out softly. This time the tide was in, so he crossed the dunes and struck the shore on the further side of the quicksand. There, oh, horror of horrors! he saw his own footprints dying into the abyss!

He went home a desperately sad man. It seemed incredible that he, an elderly commercial man, who had passed a long and uneventful life in the pursuit of business in the midst of roaring, practical London, should thus find himself enmeshed in mystery and horror, and that he should discover that he had two existences. He could not speak of his trouble even to his own wife, for well he knew that she would at once require the fullest particulars of that other life—the one which she did not know; and that she would at the start not only imagine but charge him with all manner of infidelities on the head of it. And so his brooding grew deeper and deeper still. One evening—the tide then going out and the moon being at the full—he was sitting waiting for dinner when the maid announced that Saft Tammie was making a disturbance outside because he would not be let in to see him. He was very indignant, but did not like the maid to think that he had any fear on the subject, and so told her to bring him in. Tammie entered, walking more briskly than ever, with his head up and a look of vigorous decision in the eyes that were so generally cast down. As soon as he entered he said:

"I have come to see ye once again—once again; and there ye sit, still just like a cockatoo on a pairch. Weel, mon, I forgie ye! Mind ye that, I forgie ye!" And without a word more he turned and walked out of the house, leaving the master in speechless indignation.

After dinner he determined to pay another visit to the quicksand—he would not allow even to himself that he was afraid to go. And so, about nine o'clock, in full array, he marched to the beach, and passing over the sands sat on the skirt of the nearer rock. The full moon was behind him, and its light lit up the bay so that its fringe of foam, the dark outline of the headland, and the stakes of the salmon-nets, were all emphasised. In the brilliant yellow glow the lights in the windows of Port Crooken, and in those of the distant castle of the laird, trembled like stars through the sky. For a long time he sat and drank in the beauty of the scene, and his soul seemed to feel a peace that it had not known for many days. All the pettiness and annoyance and silly fears of the past weeks seemed blotted out, and a new and holy calm took the vacant place. In this sweet and solemn mood he reviewed his late action calmly, and felt ashamed of himself for his vanity and for the obstinacy which had followed it. And then and there he made up his mind that the present would be the last time he would wear the costume which had so estranged him from those whom he loved, and which had caused him so many hours and days of chagrin, vexation, and pain.

But almost as soon as he arrived at this conclusion another voice seemed to speak within him, and mockingly to ask him if he should ever get the chance to wear the suit again—that it was too late—he had chosen his course and must now abide the issue.

"It is not too late," came the quick answer of his better self; and, full of the thought, he rose up to go home and divest himself, right away, of the now hated costume. He paused for one look at the beautiful scene. The light lay pale and mellow, softening every outline of rock and tree and housetop, and deepening the shadows into velvety black, and lighting, as with a pale flame, the incoming tide, that now crept fringelike across the flat waste of sand. Then he left the rock and stepped out for the shore.

But as he did so a frightful spasm of horror shook him, and, for an instant, the blood rushing to his head shut out all the light of the full moon. Once more he saw that fatal image of himself moving beyond the quicksand from the opposite rock to the shore. The shock was all the greater for the contrast with the spell of peace which he had just enjoyed; and, almost paralysed in every sense, he stood and watched the fatal vision and the wrinkly, crawling quicksand that seemed to writhe and yearn for something that lay between. There could be no mistake this time, for though the moon behind threw the face into shadow he could see there the same shaven cheeks as his own, and the small stubbly moustache of a few weeks' growth. The light shone on the brilliant tartan, and on the eagle's plume. Even the bald space at one side of the Glengarry cap glistened, as did the cairngorm brooch on the shoulder and the tops of the silver buttons. As he looked he felt his feet slightly sinking, for he was still near the edge of the belt of quicksand, and he stepped back. As he did so the other figure stepped forward, so that the space between them was preserved. So the two stood facing each other, as though in some weird fascination; and in the rushing of the blood through his brain Markam seemed to hear the words of the prophecy: "See thyself face to face, and repent ere the quicks and swallow thee." He did stand face to face with himself, he had repented; and now he was sinking in the quicksand—the warning and prophecy were coming true!

Above him the seagulls screamed, circling round the fringe of the incoming tide, and the sound being entirely mortal recalled him to himself. On the instant he stepped back a few quick steps, for as yet only his feet were merged in the soft sand. As he did so the other figure stepped forward, and coming within the deadly grip of the quicksand began to sink. It seemed to Markam that he was looking at himself going down to his doom, and on the instant the anguish of his soul found vent in a terrible cry. There was at the same instant a terrible cry from the other figure, and as Markam threw up his hands the figure did the same. With horror-struck eyes he saw him sink deeper into the quicksand; and then impelled by what power he knew not, he advanced again toward the sand to meet his fate. But as his more forward foot began to sink he heard again the cries of the seagulls, which seemed to restore his benumbed faculties. With a mighty effort he drew his foot out of the sand which seemed to clutch it, leaving his shoe behind, and then in sheer terror he turned and ran from the place, never stopping till his breath and strength failed him, and he sank half swooning on the grassy path through the sand-hills.

Arthur Markam made up his mind not to tell his family of his terrible adventure—until at least such time as he should be complete master of himself. Now that the fatal double—his other self—had been engulfed in the quicksand he felt something like his old peace of mind.

That night he slept soundly and did not dream at all; and in the morning was quite his old self. It really seemed as though his newer and lower self had disappeared for ever; and strangely enough Saft Tammie was absent from his post that morning and never appeared there again, but sat in his old place watching nothing, as of old, with lack-lustre eye. In accordance with his resolution Markam did not wear his Highland suit again, but one evening tied it up in a bundle,—claymore, dirk, and philibeg and all,—and bringing it secretly with him threw it into the quicksand. With a feeling of intense pleasure he saw it sucked below the sand, which closed above it into marble smoothness. Then he went home and announced cheerily to his family assembled for evening prayers:

"Well! my dears, you will be glad to hear that I have abandoned my idea of wearing the Highland dress. I see now what a vain old fool I was, and how ridiculous I made myself! You shall never see it again!"

"Where is it, father?" asked one of the girls, wishing to say something so that such a self-sacrificing announcement as her father's should not be passed in absolute silence. His answer was so sweetly given that the girl rose from her seat and came and kissed him. It was:

"In the quicksand, my dear! and I hope that my lower self is buried there along with it—for ever."

The remainder of the summer was passed at Crooken with delight by all the family, and on his return to town Mr. Markam had almost forgotten the whole of the incident of the quicksand, and all touching on it, when one day he got a letter from the MacCallum More which caused him much thought, though he said nothing of it to his family, and left it, for certain reasons, unanswered. It ran as follows:

THE MACCALLUM MORE & RODERICK MACDHU.
THE SCOTCH ALL-WOOL TARTAN CLOTHING MART,
COPTHALL COURT, E. C.,
30TH SEPTEMBER, 1892.

DEAR SIR: I trust you will pardon the liberty which I take in writing to you, but I am desirous of making an inquiry, and I am informed that you have been sojourning during the summer in Aberdeenshire, Scotland (N. B.). My partner, Mr. Roderick MacDhu,—as he appears, for business reasons, on our bill-heads and in our advertisements, his real name being Emmanuel Moses Marks, of London,—went early last month to Scotland (N. B.) for a tour, but as I have only once heard from him, shortly after his departure, I am anxious lest any misfortune may have befallen him. As I have been unable to obtain any news of him on making all inquiries in my power, I venture to appeal to you. His letter was written in deep dejection of spirit, and mentioned that he feared a judgment had come upon him for wishing to appear as a Scotchman on Scottish soil, as he had one moonlight night, shortly after his arrival, seen his 'wraith.' He evidently alluded to the fact that before his departure he had procured for himself a Highland costume similar to that which we had the honour to supply to you, with which, as perhaps you will remember, he was much struck. He may, however, never have worn it, as he was, to my own knowledge, diffident about putting it on, and even went so far as to tell me that he would at first only venture to wear it late at night or very early in the morning, and then only in remote places, until such time as he should get accustomed to it. Unfortunately he did not advise me of his route, so that I am in complete ignorance of his whereabouts; and I venture to ask if you may have seen or heard of a Highland costume similar to your own having been seen anywhere in the neighbourhood in which I am told you have recently purchased the estate which you temporarily occupied. I shall not expect an answer to this letter unless you can give me some information regarding my friend and partner, so pray do not trouble yourself to reply unless there be cause. I am encouraged to think that he may have been in your neighbourhood as, though his letter is not dated, the envelope is marked with the postmark of Yellon, which I find is in Aberdeenshire, and not far from the Mains of Crooken.

I HAVE THE HONOUR TO BE, DEAR SIR,

YOURS VERY RESPECTFULLY,

JOSHUA SHEENY COHEN BENJAMIN.

(THE MACCALLUM MORE.)

THE SEA RAIDERS

H. G. Wells

In "The Sea Raiders", famed science fiction author H. G. Wells (1866–1946) explores one of his favourite ideas about humanity's dethronement by evolutionary processes from its complacent position of superiority over nature, familiar from his best-known scientific romances such as *The Time Machine* (1895) and *The Island of Doctor Moreau* (1896). In this case, a hitherto unknown species of giant squid, *Haploteuthis ferox*, menaces fishermen and holidaymakers along the south coast of England for a few weeks one summer, before disappearing back into the ocean.

Haploteuthis ferox is an alarmingly intelligent animal with a taste for human flesh and the ability to move swiftly on land as well as in water. First published in the *Weekly Sun Literary Supplement* in 1896, "The Sea Raiders" was later collected in *The Plattner Story and Others* (1897). Like "The Plattner Story", "The Sea Raiders" is told in a characteristic Wellsian matter-of-fact style, accumulating verifiable details and witness accounts to frame events with a scaffold of authenticity that accentuates, rather than downplays, the horror of these creatures' fatal attacks. Yet in one of the story's most striking moments, the monsters become something beautiful when glimpsed sleeping and suspended in thirty feet of water, "creatures of moonshine" that glow with bioluminescence in the blackness of the night-time sea.

Until the extraordinary affair at Sidmouth, the peculiar species *Haploteuthis ferox* was known to science only generically, on the strength of a half-digested tentacle obtained near the Azores, and a decaying body pecked by birds and nibbled by fish, found early in 1896 by Mr. Jennings, near Land's End.

In no department of zoological science, indeed, are we quite so much in the dark as with regard to the deep-sea cephalopods. A mere accident, for instance, it was that led to the Prince of Monaco's discovery of nearly a dozen new forms in the summer of 1895, a discovery in which the before-mentioned tentacle was included. It chanced that a cachalot was killed off Terceira by some sperm whalers, and in its last struggles charged almost to the Prince's yacht, missed it, rolled under, and died within twenty yards of his rudder. And in its agony it threw up a number of large objects, which the Prince, dimly perceiving they were strange and important, was, by a happy expedient, able to secure before they sank. He set his screws in motion, and kept them circling in the vortices thus created until a boat could be lowered. And these specimens were whole cephalopods and fragments of cephalopods, some of gigantic proportions, and almost all of them unknown to science!

It would seem, indeed, that these large and agile creatures, living in the middle depths of the sea, must, to a large extent, for ever remain unknown to us, since under water they are too nimble for nets, and it is only by such rare unlooked-for accidents that specimens can be obtained. In the case of *Haploteuthis ferox*, for instance, we are still altogether ignorant of its habitat, as ignorant as we are of the breeding-ground of the herring or the sea-ways of the salmon. And zoologists are altogether at a loss to account for its sudden appearance on our coast. Possibly it was the stress of a hunger migration that drove it hither out of the deep. But it will be, perhaps, better to avoid necessarily inconclusive discussion, and to proceed at once with our narrative.

The first human being to set eyes upon a living *Haploteuthis*—the first human being to survive, that is, for there can be little doubt now that the wave of bathing fatalities and boating accidents that travelled along the coast of Cornwall and Devon in early May was due to this cause—was a retired tea-dealer of the name of Fison, who was stopping at a Sidmouth boarding-house. It was in the afternoon, and he was walking along the cliff path between Sidmouth and Ladram Bay. The cliffs in this direction are very high, but down the red face of them in one place a kind of ladder staircase has been made. He was near this when his attention was attracted by what at first he thought to be a cluster of birds struggling over a fragment of food that caught the sunlight, and glistened pinkish-white. The tide was right out, and this object was not only far below him, but remote across a broad waste of rock reefs covered with dark seaweed and interspersed with silvery shining tidal pools. And he was, moreover, dazzled by the brightness of the further water.

In a minute, regarding this again, he perceived that his judgment was in fault, for over this struggle circled a number of birds, jackdaws and gulls for the most part, the latter gleaming blindingly when the sunlight smote their wings, and they seemed minute in comparison with it. And his curiosity was, perhaps, aroused all the more strongly because of his first insufficient explanations.

As he had nothing better to do than amuse himself, he decided to make this object, whatever it was, the goal of his afternoon walk, instead of Ladram Bay, conceiving it might perhaps be a great fish of some sort, stranded by some chance, and flapping about in its distress. And so he hurried down the long steep ladder, stopping at intervals of thirty feet or so to take breath and scan the mysterious movement.

At the foot of the cliff he was, of course, nearer his object than he had been; but, on the other hand, it now came up against the incandescent sky, beneath the sun, so as to seem dark and indistinct. Whatever was pinkish of it was now hidden by a skerry of weedy boulders. But he perceived that it was made up of seven rounded bodies, distinct or connected, and that the birds kept up a constant croaking and screaming, but seemed afraid to approach it too closely.

Mr. Fison, torn by curiosity, began picking his way across the wave-worn rocks, and, finding the wet seaweed that covered them thickly rendered them extremely slippery, he stopped, removed his shoes and socks, and coiled his trousers above his knees. His object was, of course, merely to avoid stumbling into the rocky pools about him, and perhaps he was rather glad, as all men are, of an excuse to resume, even for a moment, the sensations of his boyhood. At anyrate, it is to this, no doubt, that he owes his life.

He approached his mark with all the assurance which the absolute security of this country against all forms of animal life gives its inhabitants. The round bodies moved to and fro, but it was only when he surmounted the skerry of boulders I have mentioned that he realised the horrible nature of the discovery. It came upon him with some suddenness.

The rounded bodies fell apart as he came into sight over the ridge, and displayed the pinkish object to be the partially devoured body of a human being, but whether of a man or woman he was unable to say. And the rounded bodies were new and ghastly-looking creatures, in shape somewhat resembling an octopus, and with huge and very long and flexible tentacles, coiled copiously on the ground. The skin had a glistening texture, unpleasant to see, like shiny leather. The downward bend of the tentacle-surrounded mouth, the curious excrescence at the bend, the tentacles, and the large intelligent eyes, gave the creatures a grotesque suggestion of a face. They were the size of a fair-sized swine about the body, and the tentacles seemed to him to be many feet in length. There were, he thinks, seven or eight at least of the creatures. Twenty yards beyond them, amid the surf of the now returning tide, two others were emerging from the sea.

Their bodies lay flatly on the rocks, and their eyes regarded him with evil interest; but it does not appear that Mr. Fison was afraid, or that he realised that he was in any danger. Possibly his confidence is to be ascribed to the limpness of their attitudes. But he was horrified, of course, and intensely excited and indignant at such revolting creatures preying upon human flesh. He thought they had chanced upon a drowned body. He shouted to them, with the idea of driving them off, and, finding they did not budge, cast about him, picked up a big rounded lump of rock, and flung it at one.

And then, slowly uncoiling their tentacles, they all began moving towards him—creeping at first deliberately, and making a soft purring sound to each other.

In a moment Mr. Fison realised that he was in danger. He shouted again, threw both his boots, and started off, with a leap, forthwith. Twenty yards off he stopped and faced about, judging them slow, and behold! the tentacles of their leader were already pouring over the rocky ridge on which he had just been standing!

At that he shouted again, but this time not threatening, but a cry of dismay, and began jumping, striding, slipping, wading across the uneven expanse between him and the beach. The tall red cliffs seemed suddenly at a vast distance, and he saw, as though they were creatures in another world, two minute workmen engaged in the repair of the ladder-way, and little suspecting the race for life that was beginning below them. At one time he could hear the creatures splashing in the pools not a dozen feet behind him, and once he slipped and almost fell.

They chased him to the very foot of the cliffs, and desisted only when he had been joined by the workmen at the foot of the ladder-way up the cliff. All three of the men pelted them with stones for a time, and then hurried to the cliff top and along the path towards Sidmouth, to secure assistance and a boat, and to rescue the desecrated body from the clutches of these abominable creatures.

II

And, as if he had not already been in sufficient peril that day, Mr. Fison went with the boat to point out the exact spot of his adventure.

As the tide was down, it required a considerable detour to reach the spot, and when at last they came off the ladder-way, the mangled body had disappeared. The water was now running in, submerging first one slab of slimy rock and then another, and the four men in the boat—the workmen, that is, the boatman, and Mr. Fison—now turned their attention from the bearings off shore to the water beneath the keel.

At first they could see little below them, save a dark jungle of laminaria, with an occasional darting fish. Their minds were set on adventure, and they expressed their disappointment freely. But presently they saw one of the monsters swimming through the water seaward, with a curious rolling motion that suggested to Mr. Fison the spinning roll of a captive balloon. Almost immediately after, the waving streamers of laminaria were extraordinarily perturbed, parted for a moment, and three of these beasts became darkly visible, struggling for what was probably some fragment of the drowned man. In a moment the copious olive-green ribbons had poured again over this writhing group.

At that all four men, greatly excited, began beating the water with oars and shouting, and immediately they saw a tumultuous movement among the weeds. They desisted to see more clearly, and as soon as the water was smooth, they saw, as it seemed to them, the whole sea bottom among the weeds set with eyes.

"Ugly swine!" cried one of the men. "Why, there's dozens!"

And forthwith the things began to rise through the water about them. Mr. Fison has since described to the writer this startling eruption out of the waving laminaria meadows. To him it seemed to occupy a considerable time, but it is probable that really it was an affair of a few seconds only. For a time nothing but eyes, and then he speaks of tentacles streaming out and parting the weed fronds this way and that. Then these things, growing larger, until at last the bottom was hidden by their intercoiling forms, and the tips of tentacles rose darkly here and there into the air above the swell of the waters.

One came up boldly to the side of the boat, and, clinging to this with three of its sucker-set tentacles, threw four others over the gunwale, as if with an intention either of oversetting the boat or of clambering into it. Mr. Fison at once caught up the boathook, and, jabbing furiously at the soft tentacles, forced it to desist. He was struck in the back and almost pitched overboard by the boatman, who was using his oar to resist a similar attack on the other side of the boat. But the tentacles on either side at once relaxed their hold at this, slid out of sight, and splashed into the water.

"We'd better get out of this," said Mr. Fison, who was trembling violently. He went to the tiller, while the boatman and one of the workmen seated themselves and began rowing. The other workman stood up in the fore part of the boat, with the boathook, ready to strike any more tentacles that might appear. Nothing else seems to have been said. Mr. Fison had expressed the common feeling beyond amendment. In a hushed, scared mood, with faces white and drawn, they set about escaping from the position into which they had so recklessly blundered.

But the oars had scarcely dropped into the water before dark, tapering, serpentine ropes had bound them, and were about the rudder; and creeping up the sides of the boat with a looping motion came the suckers again. The men gripped their oars and pulled, but it was like trying to move a boat in a floating raft of weeds. "Help here!" cried the boatman, and Mr. Fison and the second workman rushed to help lug at the oar.

Then the man with the boathook—his name was Ewan, or Ewen— sprang up with a curse, and began striking downward over the side, as far as he could reach, at the bank of tentacles that now clustered along the boat's bottom. And, at the same time, the two rowers stood up to get a better purchase for the recovery of their oars. The boatman handed his to Mr. Fison, who lugged desperately, and, meanwhile, the boatman opened a big clasp-knife, and, leaning over the side of the boat, began hacking at the spiring arms upon the oar shaft.

Mr. Fison, staggering with the quivering rocking of the boat, his teeth set, his breath coming short, and the veins starting on his hands as he pulled at his oar, suddenly cast his eyes seaward. And there, not fifty yards off, across the long rollers of the incoming tide, was a large boat standing in towards them, with three women and a little child in it. A boatman was rowing, and a little man in a pink-ribboned straw hat and whites stood in the stern, hailing them. For a moment, of course, Mr. Fison thought of help, and then he thought of the child. He abandoned his oar forthwith, threw up his arms in a frantic gesture, and screamed to the party in the boat to keep away "for God's sake!" It says much for the modesty and courage of Mr. Fison that he does not seem to be aware that there was any quality of heroism in his action at this juncture. The oar he had abandoned was at once drawn under, and presently reappeared floating about twenty yards away.

At the same moment Mr. Fison felt the boat under him lurch violently, and a hoarse scream, a prolonged cry of terror from Hill, the boatman, caused him to forget the party of excursionists altogether. He turned, and saw Hill crouching by the forward rowlock, his face convulsed with terror, and his right arm over the side and drawn tightly down. He gave now a succession of short, sharp cries, "Oh! oh! oh!—oh!" Mr. Fison believes that he must have been hacking at the tentacles below the waterline, and have been grasped by them, but, of course, it is quite impossible to say now certainly what had happened. The boat was heeling over, so that the gunwale was within ten inches of the water, and both Ewan and the other labourer were striking down into the water, with oar and boathook, on either side of Hill's arm. Mr. Fison instinctively placed himself to counterpoise them.

Then Hill, who was a burly, powerful man, made a strenuous effort, and rose almost to a standing position. He lifted his arm, indeed, clean out of the water. Hanging to it was a complicated tangle of brown ropes; and the eyes of one of the brutes that had hold of him, glaring straight and resolute, showed momentarily above the surface. The boat heeled more and more, and the green-brown water came pouring in a cascade over the side. Then Hill slipped and fell with his ribs across the side, and his arm and the mass of tentacles about it splashed back into the water. He rolled over; his boot kicked Mr. Fison's knee as that gentleman rushed forward to seize him, and in another moment fresh tentacles had whipped about his waist and neck, and after a brief, convulsive struggle, in which the boat was nearly capsized, Hill was lugged overboard. The boat righted with a violent jerk that all but sent Mr. Fison over the other side, and hid the struggle in the water from his eyes.

He stood staggering to recover his balance for a moment, and as he did so, he became aware that the struggle and the inflowing tide had carried them close upon the weedy rocks again. Not four yards off a table of rock still rose in rhythmic movements above the in-wash of the tide. In a moment Mr. Fison seized the oar from Ewan, gave one vigorous stroke, then, dropping it, ran to the bows and leapt. He felt his feet slide over the rock, and, by a frantic effort, leapt again towards a further mass. He stumbled over this, came to his knees, and rose again.

"Look out!" cried someone, and a large drab body struck him. He was knocked flat into a tidal pool by one of the workmen, and as he went down he heard smothered, choking cries, that he believed at the time came from Hill. Then he found himself marvelling at the shrillness and variety of Hill's voice. Someone jumped over him, and a curving rush of foamy water poured over him, and passed. He scrambled to his feet dripping, and, without looking seaward, ran as fast as his terror would let him shoreward. Before him, over the flat space of scattered rocks, stumbled the two workmen—one a dozen yards in front of the other.

He looked over his shoulder at last, and, seeing that he was not pursued, faced about. He was astonished. From the moment of the rising of the cephalopods out of the water, he had been acting too swiftly to fully comprehend his actions. Now it seemed to him as if he had suddenly jumped out of an evil dream.

For there were the sky, cloudless and blazing with the afternoon sun, the sea weltering under its pitiless brightness, the soft creamy foam of the breaking water, and the low, long, dark ridges of rock. The righted boat floated, rising and falling gently on the swell about a dozen yards from shore. Hill and the monsters, all the stress and tumult of that fierce fight for life, had vanished as though they had never been.

Mr. Fison's heart was beating violently; he was throbbing to the finger-tips, and his breath came deep.

There was something missing. For some seconds he could not think clearly enough what this might be. Sun, sky, sea, rocks—what was it? Then he remembered the boatload of excursionists. It had vanished. He wondered whether he had imagined it. He turned, and saw the two workmen standing side by side under the projecting masses of the tall pink cliffs. He hesitated whether he should make one last attempt to save the man Hill. His physical excitement seemed to desert him suddenly, and leave him aimless and helpless. He turned shoreward, stumbling and wading towards his two companions.

He looked back again, and there were now two boats floating, and the one farthest out at sea pitched clumsily, bottom upward.

III

So it was *Haploteuthis ferox* made its appearance upon the Devonshire coast. So far, this has been its most serious aggression. Mr. Fison's account, taken together with the wave of boating and bathing casualties to which I have already alluded, and the absence of fish from the

Cornish coasts that year, points clearly to a shoal of these voracious deep-sea monsters prowling slowly along the sub-tidal coastline. Hunger migration has, I know, been suggested as the force that drove them hither; but, for my own part, I prefer to believe the alternative theory of Hemsley. Hemsley holds that a pack or shoal of these creatures may have become enamoured of human flesh by the accident of a foundered ship sinking among them, and have wandered in search of it out of their accustomed zone; first waylaying and following ships, and so coming to our shores in the wake of the Atlantic traffic. But to discuss Hemsley's cogent and admirably-stated arguments would be out of place here.

It would seem that the appetites of the shoal were satisfied by the catch of eleven people—for so far as can be ascertained, there were ten people in the second boat, and certainly these creatures gave no further signs of their presence off Sidmouth that day. The coast between Seaton and Budleigh Salterton was patrolled all that evening and night by four Preventive Service boats, the men in which were armed with harpoons and cutlasses, and as the evening advanced, a number of more or less similarly equipped expeditions, organised by private individuals, joined them. Mr. Fison took no part in any of these expeditions.

About midnight excited hails were heard from a boat about a couple of miles out at sea to the southeast of Sidmouth, and a lantern was seen waving in a strange manner to and fro and up and down. The nearer boats at once hurried towards the alarm. The venturesome occupants of the boat, a seaman, a curate, and two schoolboys, had actually seen the monsters passing under their boat. The creatures, it seems, like most deep-sea organisms, were phosphorescent, and they had been floating, five fathoms deep or so, like creatures of moonshine through the blackness of the water, their tentacles retracted and as if asleep, rolling over and over, and moving slowly in a wedge-like formation towards the south-east.

These people told their story in gesticulated fragments, as first one boat drew alongside and then another. At last there was a little fleet of eight or nine boats collected together, and from them a tumult, like the chatter of a marketplace, rose into the stillness of the night. There was little or no disposition to pursue the shoal, the people had neither weapons nor experience for such a dubious chase, and presently—even with a certain relief, it may be—the boats turned shoreward.

And now to tell what is perhaps the most astonishing fact in this whole astonishing raid. We have not the slightest knowledge of the subsequent movements of the shoal, although the whole south-west coast was now alert for it. But it may, perhaps, be significant that a cachalot was stranded off Sark on June 3. Two weeks and three days after this Sidmouth affair, a living *Haploteuthis* came ashore on Calais sands. It was alive, because several witnesses saw its tentacles moving in a convulsive way. But it is probable that it was dying. A gentleman named Pouchet obtained a rifle and shot it.

That was the last appearance of a living *Haploteuthis*. No others were seen on the French coast. On the 15th of June a dead body, almost complete, was washed ashore near Torquay, and a few days later a boat from the Marine Biological station, engaged in dredging off Plymouth, picked up a rotting specimen, slashed deeply with a cutlass wound. How the former specimen had come by its death it is impossible to say. And on the last day of June, Mr. Egbert Caine, an artist, bathing near Newlyn, threw up his arms, shrieked, and was drawn under. A friend bathing with him made no attempt to save him, but swam at once for the shore. This is the last fact to tell of this extraordinary raid from the deeper sea. Whether it is really the last of these horrible creatures it is, as yet, premature to say. But it is believed, and certainly it is to be hoped, that they have returned now, and returned for good, to the sunless depths of the middle seas, out of which they have so strangely and so mysteriously arisen.

THE SEA FIT

Algernon Blackwood

Algernon Blackwood (1869–1951) rightly numbers among the most celebrated writers of weird fiction and folk horror. He is a writer very much in his element in strange and marginal spaces, in those uncanny regions haunted by pagan or quasi-mythical creatures and the half-forgotten deities of the natural world. "The Sea Fit" was originally published on 25 June 1910 in *Country Life* magazine. It was printed in the magazine's recurring "Tales of Country Life" feature—this was a venue Blackwood used numerous times, though one hopes the tales are not awfully representative of rural living...

"The Sea Fit" is one of Blackwood's less famous stories, but it develops some familiar themes, most notably the idea that the old gods still wield much power over the material world inhabited by mortals. The story offers an evocative portrait of an Ancient Mariner thoroughly soaked by the lore of the sea after a life lived on the waves. We meet him entertaining friends in his small beach hut on a sandy spit of land by Poole Harbour—possibly Sandbanks. The tale gives us two different ways to understand its title: the sea fit refers both to the sea frets which grow in intensity across the tale and to the passion (or tempest) into which the protagonist, Erricson, is thrown by the "loneliness of the sand-spit" and the "melancholy singing of the sea". "The Sea Fit" is an account of a cosmic encounter on the seashore, but also of the enduring, even hypnotic, allure of sea stories themselves: Blackwood's weird tale is one with the "extraordinary tale[s]" Erricson is telling when we first meet him.

The sea that night sang rather than chanted; all along the far-running shore a rising tide dropped thick foam, and the waves, white-crested, came steadily in with the swing of a deliberate purpose. Overhead, in a cloudless sky, that ancient Enchantress, the full moon, watched their dance across the sheeted sands, guiding them carefully while she drew them up. For through that moonlight, through that roar of surf, there penetrated a singular note of earnestness and meaning—almost as though these common processes of Nature were instinct with the flush of an unusual activity that sought audaciously to cross the borderland into some subtle degree of conscious life. A gauze of light vapour clung upon the surface of the sea, far out—a transparent carpet through which the rollers drove shorewards in a moving pattern.

In the low-roofed bungalow among the sand-dunes the three men sat. Foregathered for Easter, they spent the day fishing and sailing, and at night told yarns of the days when life was younger. It was fortunate that there were three—and later four—because in the mouths of several witnesses an extraordinary thing shall be established—when they agree. And although whisky stood upon the rough table made of planks nailed to barrels, it is childish to pretend that a few drinks invalidate evidence, for alcohol, up to a certain point, intensifies the consciousness, focusses the intellectual powers, sharpens observation; and two healthy men, certainly three, must have imbibed an absurd amount before they all see, or omit to see, the same things.

The other bungalows still awaited their summer occupants. Only the lonely tufted sand-dunes watched the sea, shaking their hair of coarse white grass to the winds. The men had the whole spit to themselves—with the wind, the spray, the flying gusts of sand, and that great Easter full moon. There was Major Reese of the Gunners and his half-brother, Dr. Malcolm Reese, and Captain Erricson, their host, all men whom the kaleidoscope of life had jostled together a decade ago in many adventures, then flung for years apart about the globe. There was also Erricson's body-servant, "Sinbad," sailor of big seas, and a man who had shared on many a ship all the lust of strange adventure that distinguished his great blonde-haired owner—an ideal servant and dog-faithful, divining his master's moods almost before they were born. On the present occasion, besides crew of the fishing-smack, he was cook, valet, and steward of the bungalow smoking-room as well.

"Big Erricson," Norwegian by extraction, student by adoption, wanderer by blood, a Viking reincarnated if ever there was one, belonged to that type of primitive man in whom burns an inborn love and passion for the sea that amounts to positive worship—devouring tide, a lust and fever in the soul. "All genuine votaries of the old sea-gods have it," he used to say, by way of explaining his carelessness of worldly ambitions. "We're never at our best away from salt water—never quite right. I've got it bang in the heart myself. I'd do a bit before the mast sooner than make a million on shore. Simply can't help it, you see, and never could! It's our gods calling us to worship." And he had never tried to "help it," which explains why he owned nothing in the world on land except this tumble-down, one-storey bungalow—more like a ship's cabin than anything else, to which he sometimes asked his bravest and most faithful friends—and a store of curious reading gathered in long, becalmed days at the ends of the world. Heart and mind, that is, carried a queer cargo. "I'm sorry if you poor devils are uncomfortable in her. You must ask Sinbad for anything you want and don't see, remember." As though Sinbad could have supplied comforts that were miles away, or converted a draughty wreck into a snug, taut, brand-new vessel.

Neither of the Reeses had cause for grumbling on the score of comfort, however, for they knew the keen joys of roughing it, and both weather and sport besides had been glorious. It was on another score this particular evening that they found cause for uneasiness, if not for actual grumbling. Erricson had one of his queer sea fits on— the Doctor was responsible for the term—and was in the thick of it, plunging like a straining boat at anchor, talking in a way that made them both feel vaguely uncomfortable and distressed. Neither of them knew exactly perhaps why he should have felt this growing *malaise*, and each was secretly vexed with the other for confirming his own unholy instinct that something uncommon was astir. The loneliness of the sand-spit and that melancholy singing of the sea before their very door may have had something to do with it, seeing that both were landsmen; for Imagination is ever Lord *of* the Lonely Places, and adventurous men remain children to the last. But, whatever it was that affected both men in different fashion, Malcolm Reese, the doctor, had not thought it necessary to mention to his brother that Sinbad had tugged his sleeve on entering and whispered in his ear significantly: "Full moon, sir, please, and he's better without too much! These high spring tides get him all caught off his feet sometimes—clean sea-crazy"; and the man had contrived to let the doctor see the hilt of a small pistol he carried in his hip-pocket.

For Erricson had got upon his old subject: that the gods were not dead, but merely withdrawn, and that even a single true worshipper was enough to draw them down again into touch with the world, into the sphere of humanity, even into active and visible manifestation. He spoke of queer things he had seen in queerer places. He was serious, vehement, voluble; and the others had let it pour out unchecked, hoping thereby for its speedier exhaustion. They puffed their pipes in comparative silence, nodding from time to time, shrugging their shoulders, the soldier mystified and bewildered, the doctor alert and keenly watchful.

"And I like the old idea," he had been saying, speaking of these departed pagan deities, "that sacrifice and ritual feed their great beings, and that death is only the final sacrifice by which the worshipper becomes absorbed into them. The devout worshipper"—and there was a singular drive and power behind the words—"should go to his death singing, as to a wedding—the wedding of his soul with the particular deity he has loved and served all his life." He swept his tow-coloured beard with one hand, turning his shaggy head towards the window, where the moonlight lay upon the procession of shaking waves. "It's playing the whole game, I always think, man-fashion... I remember once, some years ago, down there off the coast by Yucatan—"

And then, before they could interfere, he told an extraordinary tale of something he had seen years ago, but told it with such a horrid earnestness of conviction—for it was dreadful, though fine, this adventure—that his listeners shifted in their wicker chairs, struck matches unnecessarily, pulled at their long glasses, and exchanged glances that attempted a smile yet did not quite achieve it. For the tale had to do with sacrifice of human life and a rather haunting pagan ceremonial of the sea, and at its close the room had changed in some indefinable manner—was not exactly as it had been before perhaps—as though the savage earnestness of the language had introduced some new element that made it less cosy, less cheerful, even less warm. A secret lust in the man's heart, born of the sea, and of his intense admiration of the pagan gods called a light into his eye not altogether pleasant.

"They were great Powers, at any rate, those ancient fellows," Erricson went on, refilling his huge pipe bowl; "too great to disappear altogether, though today they may walk the earth in another manner. I swear they're still going it—especially the—" (he hesitated for a mere second) "the old water Powers—the Sea Gods. Terrific beggars, every one of 'em."

"Still move the tides and raise the winds, eh?" from the Doctor.

Erricson spoke again after a moment's silence, with impressive dignity. "And I like, too, the way they manage to keep their names before us," he went on, with a curious eagerness that did not escape the Doctor's observation, while it clearly puzzled the soldier. "There's old Hu, the Druid god of justice, still alive in 'Hue and Cry'; there's Typhon hammering his way against us in the typhoon; there's the mighty Hurakar, serpent god of the winds, you know, shouting to us in hurricane and *ouragan*; and there's—"

"Venus still at it as hard as ever," interrupted the Major, facetiously, though his brother did not laugh because of their host's almost sacred earnestness of manner and uncanny grimness of face. Exactly how he managed to introduce that element of gravity—of conviction—into such talk neither of his listeners quite understood, for in discussing the affair later they were unable to pitch upon any definite detail that betrayed it. Yet there it was, alive and haunting, even distressingly so. All day he had been silent and morose, but since dusk, with the turn of the tide, in fact, these queer sentences, half mystical, half unintelligible, had begun to pour from him, till now that cabin-like room among the sand-dunes fairly vibrated with the man's emotion. And at last Major Reese, with blundering good intention, tried to shift the key from this portentous subject of sacrifice to something that might eventually lead towards comedy and laughter, and so relieve this growing pressure of melancholy and incredible things. The Viking fellow had just spoken of the possibility of the old gods manifesting themselves visibly, audibly, physically, and so the Major caught him up and made light mention of spiritualism and the so-called "materialisation séances," where physical bodies were alleged to be built up out of the emanations of the medium and the sitters. This crude aspect of the Supernatural was the only possible link the soldier's mind could manage. He caught his brother's eye too late, it seems, for Malcolm Reese realised by this time that something untoward was afoot, and no longer needed the memory of Sinbad's warning to keep him sharply on the look-out. It was not the first time he had seen Erricson "caught" by the sea; but he had never known him quite so bad, nor seen his face so flushed and white alternately, nor his eyes so oddly shining. So that Major Reese's well-intentioned allusion only brought wind to fire.

The man of the sea, once Viking, roared with a rush of boisterous laughter at the comic suggestion, then dropped his voice to a sudden hard whisper, awfully earnest, awfully intense. Any one must have started at the abrupt change and the life-and-death manner of the big man. His listeners undeniably both did.

"Bunkum!" he shouted, "bunkum, and be damned to it all! There's only one real materialisation of these immense Outer Beings possible, and that's when the great embodied emotions, which are their sphere of action"—his words became wildly incoherent, painfully struggling to get out—"derived, you see, from their honest worshippers the world over—constituting their Bodies, in fact—come down into matter and get condensed, crystallised into form—to claim that final sacrifice I spoke about just now, and to which any man might feel himself proud and honoured to be summoned... No dying in bed or fading out from old age, but to plunge full-blooded and alive into the great Body of the god who has deigned to descend and fetch you—"

The actual speech may have been even more rambling and incoherent than that. It came out in a torrent at white heat. Dr. Reese
kicked his brother beneath the table, just in time. The soldier looked
thoroughly uncomfortable and amazed, utterly at a loss to know how
he had produced the storm. It rather frightened him.

"I know it because I've seen it," went on the sea man, his mind
and speech slightly more under control. "Seen the ceremonies that
brought these whopping old Nature gods down into form—seen
'em carry off a worshipper into themselves—seen that worshipper,
too, go off singing and happy to his death, proud and honoured to
be chosen."

"Have you really—by George!" the Major exclaimed. "You tell us
a queer thing, Erricson"; and it was then for the fifth time that Sinbad
cautiously opened the door, peeped in and silently withdrew after
giving a swiftly comprehensive glance round the room.

The night outside was windless and serene, only the growing
thunder of the tide near the full woke muffled echoes among the
sand-dunes.

"Rites and ceremonies," continued the other, his voice booming with a singular enthusiasm, but ignoring the interruption, "are
simply means of losing one's self by temporary ecstasy in the God
of one's choice—the God one has worshipped all one's life—of
being partially absorbed into his being. And sacrifice completes the
process—"

"At death, you said?" asked Malcolm Reese, watching him keenly.

"Or voluntary," was the reply that came flash-like. "The devotee
becomes wedded to his Deity—goes bang into him, you see, by fire
or water or air—as by a drop from a height—according to the nature
of the particular God; at-one-ment, of course. A man's death that!
Fine, you know!"

The man's inner soul was on fire now. He was talking at a fearful pace, his eyes alight, his voice turned somehow into a kind of singsong that chimed well, singularly well, with the booming of waves outside, and from time to time he turned to the window to stare at the sea and the moon-blanched sands. And then a look of triumph would come into his face—that giant face framed by slow-moving wreaths of pipe smoke.

Sinbad entered for the sixth time without any obvious purpose, busied himself unnecessarily with the glasses and went out again, lingeringly. In the room he kept his eye hard upon his master. This time he contrived to push a chair and a heap of netting between him and the window. No one but Dr. Reese observed the manoeuvre. And he took the hint.

"The port-holes fit badly, Erricson," he laughed, but with a touch of authority. "There's a five-knot breeze coming through the cracks worse than an old wreck!" And he moved up to secure the fastening better.

"The room *is* confoundedly cold," Major Reese put in; "has been for the last half-hour, too." The soldier looked what he felt—cold—distressed—creepy. "But there's no wind really, you know," he added.

Captain Erricson turned his great bearded visage from one to the other before he answered; there was a gleam of sudden suspicion in his blue eyes. "The beggar's got that back door open again. If he's sent for any one, as he did once before, I swear I'll drown him in fresh water for his impudence—or perhaps—can it be already that he expects—?" He left the sentence incomplete and rang the bell, laughing with a boisterousness that was clearly feigned. "Sinbad, what's this cold in the place? You've got the back door open. Not expecting any one, are you—?"

"Everything's shut tight, Captain. There's a bit of a breeze coming up from the east. And the tide's drawing in at a raging pace—"

"We can all hear *that*. But are you expecting any one? I asked," repeated his master, suspiciously, yet still laughing. One might have said he was trying to give the idea that the man had some land flirtation on hand. They looked one another square in the eye for a moment, these two. It was the straight stare of equals who understood each other well.

"Some one—might be—on the way, as it were, Captain. Couldn't say for certain."

The voice almost trembled. By a sharp twist of the eye, Sinbad managed to shoot a lightning and significant look at the Doctor.

"But this cold—this freezing, damp cold in the place? Are you sure no one's come—by the back ways?" insisted the master. He whispered it. "Across the dunes, for instance?" His voice conveyed awe and delight, both kept hard under.

"It's all over the house, Captain, already," replied the man, and moved across to put more sea-logs on the blazing fire. Even the soldier noticed then that their language was tight with allusion of another kind. To relieve the growing tension and uneasiness in his own mind he took up the word "house" and made fun of it.

"As though it were a mansion," he observed, with a forced chuckle, "instead of a mere sea-shell!" Then, looking about him, he added: "But, all the same, you know, there *is* a kind of fog getting into the room—from the sea, I suppose; coming up with the tide, or something, eh?" The air had certainly in the last twenty minutes turned thickish; it was not all tobacco smoke, and there was a moisture that began to precipitate on the objects in tiny, fine globules. The cold, too, fairly bit.

"I'll take a look round," said Sinbad, significantly, and went out. Only the Doctor perhaps noticed that the man shook, and was white down to the gills. He said nothing, but moved his chair nearer to the window and to his host. It was really a little bit beyond comprehension how the wild words of this old sea-dog in the full sway of his "sea fit" had altered the very air of the room as well as the personal equations of its occupants, for an extraordinary atmosphere of enthusiasm that was almost splendour pulsed about him, yet vilely close to something that suggested terror! Through the armour of every-day common sense that normally clothed the minds of these other two, had crept the faint wedges of a mood that made them vaguely wonder whether the incredible could perhaps sometimes—by way of bewildering exceptions—actually come to pass. The moods of their deepest life, that is to say, were already affected. An inner, and thoroughly unwelcome, change was in progress. And such psychic disturbances once started are hard to arrest. In this case it was well on the way before either the Army or Medicine had been willing to recognise the fact. There was something coming—coming from the sand-dunes or the sea. And it was invited, welcomed at any rate, by Erricson. His deep, volcanic enthusiasm and belief provided the channel. In lesser degree they, too, were caught in it. Moreover, it was terrific, irresistible.

And it was at this point—as the comparing of notes afterwards established—that Father Norden came in, Norden, the big man's nephew, having bicycled over from some point beyond Corfe Castle and raced along the hard Studland sand in the moonlight, and then hullood till a boat had ferried him across the narrow channel of Poole Harbour. Sinbad simply brought him in without any preliminary question or announcement. He could not resist the splendid night and the spring air, explained Norden. He felt sure his uncle could "find a hammock" for him somewhere aft, as he put it. He did not add that Sinbad had telegraphed for him just before sundown from the coastguard hut. Dr. Reese already knew him, but he was introduced to the

Major. Norden was a member of the Society of Jesus, an ardent, not clever, and unselfish soul.

Erricson greeted him with obviously mixed feelings, and with an extraordinary sentence: "It doesn't really matter," he exclaimed, after a few commonplaces of talk, "for all religions are the same if you go deep enough. All teach sacrifice, and, without exception, all seek final union by absorption into their Deity." And then, under his breath, turning sideways to peer out of the window, he added a swift rush of half-smothered words that only Dr. Reese caught: "The Army, the Church, the Medical Profession, and Labour—if they would only all come! What a fine result, what a grand offering! Alone—I seem so unworthy—insignificant...!"

But meanwhile young Norden was speaking before any one could stop him, although the Major did make one or two blundering attempts. For once the Jesuit's tact was at fault. He evidently hoped to introduce a new mood—to shift the current already established by the single force of his own personality. And he was not quite man enough to carry it off.

It was an error of judgment on his part. For the forces he found established in the room were too heavy to lift and alter, their impetus being already acquired. He did his best, anyhow. He began moving with the current—it was not the first sea fit he had combated in this extraordinary personality—then found, too late, that he was carried along with it himself like the rest of them.

"Odd—but couldn't find the bungalow at first," he laughed, somewhat hardly. "It's got a bit of sea-fog all to itself that hides it. I thought perhaps my pagan uncle—"

The Doctor interrupted him hastily, with great energy. "The fog *does* lie caught in these sand hollows—like steam in a cup, you know," he put in. But the other, intent on his own procedure, missed the cue.

"—thought it was smoke at first, and that you were up to some heathen ceremony or other," laughing in Erricson's face; "sacrificing to the full moon or the sea, or the spirits of the desolate places that haunt sand-dunes, eh?"

No one spoke for a second, but Erricson's face turned quite radiant.

"My uncle's such a pagan, you know," continued the priest, "that as I flew along those deserted sands from Studland I almost expected to hear old Triton blow his wreathèd horn... or see fair Thetis's tinsel-slippered feet..."

Erricson, suppressing violent gestures, highly excited, face happy as a boy's, was combing his great yellow beard with both hands, and the other two men had begun to speak at once, intent on stopping the flow of unwise allusion. Norden, swallowing a mouthful of cold soda-water, had put the glass down, spluttering over its bubbles, when the sound was first heard at the window. And in the back room the manservant ran, calling something aloud that sounded like "It's coming, God save us, it's coming in...!" Though the Major swears some name was mentioned that he afterwards forgot—Glaucus—Proteus—Pontus—or some such word. The sound itself, however, was plain enough—a kind of imperious tapping on the window-panes as of a multitude of objects. Blown sand it might have been or heavy spray or, as Norden suggested later, a great water-soaked branch of giant seaweed. Every one started up, but Erricson was first upon his feet, and had the window wide open in a twinkling. His voice roared forth over those moonlit sand-dunes and out towards the line of heavy surf ten yards below.

"All along the shore of the Ægean," he bellowed, with a kind of hoarse triumph that shook the heart, "that ancient cry once rang. But it was a lie, a thumping and audacious lie. And He is not the only one. Another still lives—and, by Poseidon, He comes! He knows His own and His own know Him—and His own shall go to meet Him...!"

That reference to the Ægean "cry"! It was so wonderful. Every one, of course, except the soldier, seized the allusion. It was a comprehensive, yet subtle, way of suggesting the idea. And meanwhile all spoke at once, shouted rather, for the Invasion was somehow—monstrous.

"Damn it—that's a bit too much. Something's caught my throat!" The Major, like a man drowning, fought with the furniture in his amazement and dismay. Fighting was his first instinct, of course. "Hurts so infernally—takes the breath," he cried, by way of explaining the extraordinarily violent impetus that moved him, yet half ashamed of himself for seeing nothing he could strike. But Malcolm Reese struggled to get between his host and the open window, saying in tense voice something like "Don't let him get out! Don't let him get out!" While the shouts of warning from Sinbad in the little cramped back offices added to the general confusion. Only Father Norden stood quiet—watching with a kind of admiring wonder the expression of magnificence that had flamed into the visage of Erricson.

"Hark, you fools! Hark!" boomed the Viking figure, standing erect and splendid.

And through that open window, along the far-drawn line of shore from Canford Cliffs to the chalk bluffs of Studland Bay, there certainly ran a sound that was no common roar of surf. It was articulate—a message from the sea—an announcement—a thunderous warning of approach. No mere surf breaking on sand could have compassed so deep and multitudinous a voice of dreadful roaring—far out over the entering tide, yet at the same time close in along the entire sweep of shore, shaking all the ocean, both depth and surface, with its deep vibrations. Into the bungalow chamber came—the SEA!

Out of the night, from the moonlit spaces where it had been steadily accumulating, into that little cabined room so full of humanity and tobacco smoke, came invisibly—the Power of the Sea. Invisible, yes, but mighty, pressed forward by the huge draw of the moon, soft-coated with brine and moisture—the great Sea. And with it, into the minds of those three other men, leaped instantaneously, not to be denied, overwhelming suggestions of water-power, the tear and strain of thousand-mile currents, the irresistible pull and rush of tides, the suction of giant whirlpools—more, the massed and awful impetus of whole driven oceans. The air turned salt and briny, and a welter of seaweed clamped their very skins.

"Glaucus! I come to Thee, great God of the deep Waterways... Father and Master!" Erricson cried aloud in a voice that most marvellously conveyed supreme joy.

The little bungalow trembled as from a blow at the foundations, and the same second the big man was through the window and running down the moonlit sands towards the foam.

"God in Heaven! Did you all see *that*?" shouted Major Reese, for the manner in which the great body slipped through the tiny window-frame was incredible. And then, first tottering with a sudden weakness, he recovered himself and rushed round by the door, followed by his brother. Sinbad, invisible, but not inaudible, was calling aloud from the passage at the back. Father Norden, slimmer than the others—well controlled, too—was through the little window before either of them reached the fringe of beach beyond the sand-dunes. They joined forces halfway down to the water's edge. The figure of Erricson, towering in the moonlight, flew before them, coasting rapidly along the wave-line.

No one of them said a word; they tore along side by side, Norden a trifle in advance. In front of them, head turned seawards, bounded Erricson in great flying leaps, singing as he ran, impossible to overtake.

Then, what they witnessed all three witnessed; the weird grandeur of it in the moonshine was too splendid to allow the smaller emotions of personal alarm, it seems. At any rate, the divergence of opinion afterwards was unaccountably insignificant. For, on a sudden, that heavy roaring sound far out at sea came close in with a swift plunge of speed, followed simultaneously—accompanied, rather—by a dark line that was no mere wave moving: enormously, up and across, between the sea and sky it swept close in to shore. The moonlight caught it for a second as it passed, in a cliff of her bright silver.

And Erricson slowed down, bowed his great head and shoulders, spread his arms out and...

And what? For no one of those amazed witnesses could swear exactly what then came to pass. Upon this impossibility of telling it in language they all three agreed. Only those eyeless dunes of sand that watched, only the white and silent moon overhead, only that long, curved beach of empty and deserted shore retain the complete record, to be revealed some day perhaps when a later Science shall have learned to develop the photographs that Nature takes incessantly upon her secret plates. For Erricson's rough suit of tweed went out in ribbons across the air; his figure somehow turned dark like strips of tide-sucked seaweed; something enveloped and overcame him, half shrouding him from view. He stood for one instant upright, his hair wild in the moonshine, towering, with arms again outstretched; then bent forward, turned, drew out most curiously sideways, uttering the singing sound of tumbling waters. The next instant, curving over like a falling wave, he swept along the glistening surface of the sands—and was gone. In fluid form, wave-like, his being slipped away into the Being of the Sea. A violent tumult convulsed the surface of the tide near in, but at once, and with amazing speed, passed careering away into the deeper water—far out. To his singular death, as to a wedding, Erricson had gone, singing, and well content.

"May God, who holds the sea and all its powers in the hollow of His mighty hand, take them *both* into Himself!" Norden was on his knees, praying fervently.

The body was never recovered... and the most curious thing of all was that the interior of the cabin, where they found Sinbad shaking with terror when they at length returned, was splashed and sprayed, almost soaked, with salt water. Up into the bigger dunes beside the bungalow, and far beyond the reach of normal tides, lay, too, a great streak and furrow as of a large invading wave, caking the dry sand. A hundred tufts of the coarse grass tussocks had been torn away.

The high tide that night, drawn by the Easter full moon, of course, was known to have been exceptional, for it fairly flooded Poole Harbour, flushing all the coves and bays towards the mouth of the Frome. And the natives up at Arne Bay and Wych always declare that the noise of the sea was heard far inland even up to the nine Barrows of the Purbeck Hills—triumphantly singing.

HAVEN HOTEL

1910

WHERE THE TIDES
EBB AND FLOW

Lord Dunsany

Lord Dunsany (1878–1957), or Edward John Moreton Drax Plunkett, 18th Baron of Dunsany, to give him his full name, was an Anglo-Irish writer, known for his contributions to early fantasy writing and weird tales. His major works include *The King of Elfland's Daughter* (1924) and numerous short stories such as those collected in *Time and the Gods* (1906). "Where the Tides Ebb and Flow" was published as part of the collection *A Dreamer's Tales* (1917) and belongs to a strand of coastal fiction set in (or on) London's River Thames.

The story is a deliciously oozy dream vision of the tidal mudflats of the Thames—and beyond. Dunsany adopts a narrative perspective that has us, along with the unfortunate soul who narrates this dream, gazing up and out of that shore. It is a classically liminal imagining of this region: as the first line of the story tells us, the narrator dreams he has done something terrible that denies him burial "either in soil or sea", and so his body must rest in the mud-banks. Except, of course, with the comings and goings of the tide and those strange beings who populate this realm, there is no rest. Instead, the undead and undying narrator is forced to bear witness to a world that changes around him. A stormy sea offers brief respite here, but this is a tale that excels in its attention to the sludgy, viscous matter of the foreshore.

I dreamt that I had done a horrible thing, so that burial was to be denied me either in soil or sea, neither could there be any hell for me.

I waited for some hours, knowing this. Then my friends came for me, and slew me secretly and with ancient rite, and lit great tapers, and carried me away.

It was all in London that the thing was done, and they went furtively at dead of night along grey streets and among mean houses until they came to the river. And the river and the tide of the sea were grappling with one another between the mud-banks, and both of them were black and full of lights. A sudden wonder came into the eyes of each, as my friends came near to them with their glaring tapers. All these things I saw as they carried me dead and stiffening, for my soul was still among my bones, because there was no hell for it, and because Christian burial was denied me.

They took me down a stairway that was green with slimy things, and so came slowly to the terrible mud. There, in the territory of forsaken things, they dug a shallow grave. When they had finished they laid me in the grave, and suddenly they cast their tapers to the river. And when the water had quenched the flaring lights the tapers looked pale and small as they bobbed upon the tide, and at once the glamour of the calamity was gone, and I noticed then the approach of the huge dawn; and my friends cast their cloaks over their faces, and the solemn procession was turned into many fugitives that furtively stole away.

Then the mud came back wearily and covered all but my face. There I lay alone with quite forgotten things, with drifting things that the tides will take no farther, with useless things and lost things, and with the horrible unnatural bricks that are neither stone nor soil. I was rid of feeling, because I had been killed, but perception and thought were in my unhappy soul. The dawn widened, and I saw the desolate houses that crowded the marge of the river, and their dead windows peered into my dead eyes, windows with bales behind them instead of human souls. I grew so weary looking at these forlorn things that I wanted to cry out, but could not, because I was dead. Then I knew, as I had never known before, that for all the years that herd of desolate houses had wanted to cry out too, but, being dead, were dumb. And I knew then that it had yet been well with the forgotten drifting things if they had wept, but they were eyeless and without life. And I, too, tried to weep, but there were no tears in my dead eyes. And I knew then that the river might have cared for us, might have caressed us, might have sung to us, but he swept broadly onwards, thinking of nothing but the princely ships.

At last the tide did what the river would not, and came and covered me over, and my soul had rest in the green water, and rejoiced and believed that it had the Burial of the Sea. But with the ebb the water fell again, and left me alone again with the callous mud among the forgotten things that drift no more, and with the sight of all those desolate houses, and with the knowledge among all of us that each was dead.

In the mournful wall behind me, hung with green weeds, forsaken of the sea, dark tunnels appeared, and secret narrow passages that were clamped and barred. From these at last the stealthy rats came down to nibble me away, and my soul rejoiced thereat and believed that he would be free perforce from the accursed bones to which burial was refused. Very soon the rats ran away a little space and whispered among themselves. They never came any more.

When I found that I was accursed even among the rats I tried to weep again.

Then the tide came swinging back and covered the dreadful mud, and hid the desolate houses, and soothed the forgotten things, and my soul had ease for a while in the sepulture of the sea. And then the tide forsook me again.

To and fro it came about me for many years. Then the County Council found me, and gave me decent burial. It was the first grave that I had ever slept in. That very night my friends came for me. They dug me up and put me back again in the shallow hole in the mud.

Again and again through the years my bones found burial, but always behind the funeral lurked one of those terrible men who, as soon as night fell, came and dug them up and carried them back again to the hole in the mud.

And then one day the last of those men died who once had done to me this terrible thing. I heard his soul go over the river at sunset.

And again I hoped.

A few weeks afterwards I was found once more, and once more taken out of that restless place and given deep burial in sacred ground, where my soul hoped that it should rest.

Almost at once men came with cloaks and tapers to give me back to the mud, for the thing had become a tradition and a rite. And all the forsaken things mocked me in their dumb hearts when they saw me carried back, for they were jealous of me because I had left the mud. It must be remembered that I could not weep.

And the years went by seawards where the black barges go, and the great derelict centuries became lost at sea, and still I lay there without any cause to hope, and daring not to hope without a cause, because of the terrible envy and the anger of the things that could drift no more.

Once a great storm rode up, even as far as London, out of the sea from the South; and he came curving into the river with the fierce East wind. And he was mightier than the dreary tides, and went with great leaps over the listless mud. And all the sad forgotten things rejoiced, and mingled with things that were haughtier than they, and rode once more amongst the lordly shipping that was driven up and down. And out of their hideous home he took my bones, never again, I hoped, to be vexed with the ebb and flow. And with the fall of the tide he went riding down the river and turned to the southwards, and so went to his home. And my bones he scattered among many isles and along the shores of happy alien mainlands. And for a moment, while they were far asunder, my soul was almost free.

Then there arose, at the will of the moon, the assiduous flow of the tide, and it undid at once the work of the ebb, and gathered my bones from the marge of sunny isles, and gleaned them all along the mainland's shores, and went rocking northwards till it came to the mouth of the Thames, and there turned westwards its relentless face, and so went up the river and came to the hole in the mud, and into it dropped my bones; and partly the mud covered them and partly it left them white, for the mud cares not for its forsaken things.

Then the ebb came, and I saw the dead eyes of the houses and the jealousy of the other forgotten things that the storm had not carried thence.

And some more centuries passed over the ebb and flow and over the loneliness of things forgotten. And I lay there all the while in the careless grip of the mud, never wholly covered, yet never able to go free, and I longed for the great caress of the warm Earth or the comfortable lap of the Sea.

Sometimes men found my bones and buried them, but the tradition never died, and my friends' successors always brought them back.

At last the barges went no more, and there were fewer lights; shaped timbers no longer floated down the fair-way, and there came instead old wind-uprooted trees in all their natural simplicity.

At last I was aware that somewhere near me a blade of grass was growing, and the moss began to appear all over the dead houses. One day some thistledown went drifting over the river.

For some years I watched these signs attentively, until I became certain that London was passing away. Then I hoped once more, and all along both banks of the river there was anger among the lost things that anything should dare to hope upon the forsaken mud. Gradually the horrible houses crumbled, until the poor dead things that never had had life got decent burial among the weeds and moss. At last the may appeared and the convolvulus. Finally, the wild rose stood up over mounds that had been wharves and warehouses. Then I knew that the cause of Nature had triumphed, and London had passed away.

The last man in London came to the wall by the river, in an ancient cloak that was one of those that once my friends had worn, and peered over the edge to see that I still was there. Then he went, and I never saw men again: they had passed away with London.

A few days after the last man had gone the birds came into London, all the birds that sing. When they first saw me they all looked sideways at me, then they went away a little and spoke among themselves.

"He only sinned against Man," they said; "it is not our quarrel."

"Let us be kind to him," they said.

Then they hopped nearer me and began to sing. It was the time of the rising of the dawn, and from both banks of the river, and from the sky, and from the thickets that were once the streets, hundreds of birds were singing. As the light increased the birds sang more and more; they grew thicker and thicker in the air above my head, till there were thousands of them singing there, and then millions, and at last I could see nothing but a host of flickering wings with the sunlight on them, and little gaps of sky. Then when there was nothing to be heard in London but the myriad notes of that exultant song, my soul rose up from the bones in the hole in the mud and began to climb up the song heavenwards. And it seemed that a laneway opened amongst the wings of the birds, and it went up and up, and one of the smaller gates of Paradise stood ajar at the end of it. And then I knew by a sign that the mud should receive me no more, for suddenly I found that I could weep.

At this moment I opened my eyes in bed in a house in London, and outside some sparrows were twittering in a tree in the light of the radiant morning; and there were tears still wet upon my face, for one's restraint is feeble while one sleeps. But I arose and opened the window wide, and, stretching my hands out over the little garden, I blessed the birds whose song had woken me up from the troubled and terrible centuries of my dream.

FOUR FOLK TALES

Sophia *Morrison*

Sophia Morrison (1859–1917) was an important advocate of Manx culture and was recognised in her day as a foremost authority on folklore
particular to the Isle of Man. The short pieces of folklore included
here come from her most famous work, *Manx Fairy Tales* (1911); she
was also the editor of the Manx journal *Mannin* from 1913–17, and published numerous other works on the history and culture of the island,
including a cookbook (co-written with her sister Louisa), a book of
Manx proverbs, and book of quotations of the Manx poet T. E. Brown.

In keeping with the abiding concerns we encounter in strange tales
of the coast, Morrison's tales make a claim on a distinctive regional
history. As she notes in her preface to the volume, the "fairies" of her
tales are "never called Fairies by the Manx, but Themselves, or the
Little People", and they "are not the tiny creatures who flutter about
in many English Fairy tales". As a text like "The Making of Mann" further suggests, coastal narratives help us better understand archipelagic
relations of the British Isles: here, the Isle of Man's creation narrative
is rooted in conflict between Scotland and Ireland. The Isle of Man's
own wider gothic culture includes most notably several romances by
Hall Caine—the "Hommy-Beg" (or "Little Tommy") to whom *Dracula*
was dedicated. In stories like *She's All the World to Me* (1885) and *The
Deemster* (1887), shorelines, harbours, and coastal cliff-faces occupy
conspicuous roles in the narrative, as sites of wreckings, drownings,
and the washings ashore of corpses.

The Making of Mann

Thousands of years ago, at the time of the Battles of the Giants in Ireland, Finn Mac Cooil was fighting with a great, red-haired Scotch giant who had come over to challenge him. He beat him and chased him eastwards towards the sea. But the Scotch giant was a faster runner and began to get ahead of him, so Finn, who was afraid that he would jump into the sea and escape, stooped down and clutched a great handful of the soil of Ireland to throw at him. He cast it, but he missed his enemy, and the great lump of earth fell into the midst of the Irish Sea. It is the Isle of Mann, and the great hole which Finn made, where he tore it up, is Lough Neagh.

There were men, too, in Ireland in those days as well as giants, and to some of them it seemed to happen in a different way. Men do not always understand the doings of giants, because men live, it may be said, in the footprints of the giants. It seems that at this time the Irish tribes were gathered in two great forces getting ready to meet the plunderers who had left Scotland and were at work on their own coast. Their blood got too hot and they went into each other in downright earnest, to show how they would do with the rascals when they came. To their confusion, for they lost hold over themselves, they got into boggy ground and were in great danger. The leaders, seeing that it was going to mean a big loss of life, got all their men together on a big patch of dry ground that happened to be in the bog-land, when all of a sudden a darkness came overhead and the ground began to shake and tremble with the weight of the people and the stir there was at them, and then it disappeared, people and all. Some said that it took plunge and sank into the bog with the people on it. Others said that it was lifted up, and the people on it dropped off into the swamp. No doubt the darkness that was caused by the hand of Finn made it hard to see just how it happened. However that may be, a while after this they said the sea was surging dreadful, and the men in the boats had to hold to the sides, or it's out they'd have been thrown. And behold ye, a few days after this there was land seen in the middle of the sea, where no man ever saw the like before.

You may know that this story is true because the Irish have always looked on the Isle of Mann as a parcel of their own land. They say that when Saint Patrick put the blessing of God on the soil of Ireland and all creatures that might live upon it, the power of that blessing was felt at the same time in the Island.

> Saint Patrick was a mighty man,
> He was a Saint so clever,
> He gave the snakes and toads a twisht!
> And banished them for ever.

And there is proof of the truth of the saying to this day, for while such nasty things do live in England they cannot breathe freely on the blessed soil.

The island was much larger then than it is now, but the magician who for a time ruled over it, as a revenge on one of his enemies, raised a furious wind in the air and in the bosom of the earth. This wind tore several pieces off the land and cast them into the sea. They floated about and were changed into the dangerous rocks which are now so much feared by ships. The smaller pieces became the shifting sands which wave round the coast, and are sometimes seen and sometimes disappear. Later the island was known as Ellan Sheaynt, the Isle of Peace, or the Holy Island. It was a place where there was always sunshine, and the singing of birds, the scent of sweet flowers, and apple-trees blossoming the whole year round. There was always enough there to eat and drink, and the horses of that place were fine and the women beautiful.

Little Footprints

C lose to the Niarbyl, the great tail of rock that stretches into the sea at Dalby, is a little house on the strand. It is sheltered behind by the high rock which rises above its thatched roof. Before it lies Bay Mooar, the great bay, held by a chain of mountains purple with ling. Standing before its door and looking to the west, you may see the sun set behind the distant Mourne Mountains. At dawn you may see him rise over Cronk-yn-Irree-Laa, the Hill of the Rising Day. Here lived Juan, the fisherman.

He knew, as well as any person, that the Little People were all around. When he was a boy he had many a time looked out of the door on moonlight nights to try if he could put sight on them dancing on the lonely shore. He had not seen them—they make themselves invisible when they know that mortal eyes are on them. But he had seen the tiny riding lights of their herring fleet in the bay, and had helped his father to draw in the nets full of good fish, which were sure to be caught the night after. Many a time he had wakened from his sleep in the dark, and, in the pauses of the wind and the lull of the great breakers, he had heard the sound of hammering. He knew it was the Little People hammering at their herring barrels in Ooig-ny-Seyir, the Coopers' Cave, under the hills, and that as the chips flew out on to the waves they became ships.

He had heard the story of the fisherman, a friend of his father's, who was fishing one night at Lag-ny-Keilley, when a dense grey mist rolled in. He thought he had best make for home while the footpath

237

above the rocks was visible. When he was getting his things together he heard what sounded like a lot of children coming out of school. He lifted his head, and, behold, there was a fleet of fairy boats each side of the rock, their riding lights shining like little stars on a frosty night. The crews seemed busy preparing to come on shore, and he heard one little fellow shout:

"Hraaghyn boght as earish broigh, skeddan dy liooar ec yn mooinjer seihll shoh, cha nel veg ain!"

Poor times and dirty weather, herring enough at the people of this world, nothing at us!

"Then," said the fisherman, "they dropped off and went agate o' the flitters."

When Juan was a big boy he himself saw a thing which he never forgot. One day he left a boat over at the farther side of Bay Mooar, and at night he had to go over to fetch it. It was a moonlight night and the bay was as smooth as glass as he rowed across. There was no sound but the lapping of the little waves on the shore, and now and again the cry of a gannet. Juan found his boat on the strand where he had left her and was setting to work to launch her, when he thought he saw a glimmering light, which was not the light of the moon, in one of the caves near him. He stood where he was, and listened, and he heard the sound of faint music. Then he went as silently as he was able to the cave, and looked in. No light was there but the dim light of the moon. The shadows in the corners of the cave were as black as pitch.

Juan was trembling all over, and at first he was blinking his eyes and could see nothing. But after some minutes he saw a great stone in the midst of the cave and the floor of fine white sand. And on the sand around that stone there were little footprints—marks of tiny clogs they were, no bigger than his thumb!

The Witch of Slieu Whallian

It was Midsummer Day, and the Peel Herring Fleet, with sails half set, was ready for sea. The men had their barley sown, and their potatoes down, and now their boats were rigged and nets stowed on board and they were ready for the harvest of the sea. It was a fine day, the sky was clear and the wind was in the right airt, being from the north. But, as they say, "If custom will not get custom, custom will weep." A basinful of water was brought from the Holy Well and given to the Wise Woman that sold fair winds, as she stood on the harbour-side with the women and children to watch the boats off. They told her to look and tell of the luck of the Herring Fleet. She bent over the water and, as she looked, her face grew pale with fear, and she gasped: "Hurroose, hurroose! An' do ye know what I'm seeing?"

"Let us hear," said they.

> I'm seeing the wild waves lashed to foam away by great
>   Bradda Head,
> I'm seeing the surge round the Chicken's Rock an' the
>   breaker's lip is red;
> I'm seeing where corpses toss in the Sound, with nets an'
>   gear an' spars,
> An' never a one of the Fishing Fleet is riding under the
>   stars.

There was a dead hush, and the men gathered close together, muttering, till Gorry, the Admiral of the Fishing Fleet, stepped forward, caught the basin out of her hands and flung it out to sea, growling:

"Sure as I'm alive, sure as I'm alive, woman, I've more than half a mind to heave you in after it. If I had my way, the like of you an' your crew would be run into the sea. Boys, are we goin' to lose a shot for that bleb? Come on, let's go an' chonce it with the help of God."

"Aye, no herring, no wedding. Let's go an' chonce it," said young Cashen.

So hoisting sails they left the port and when the land was fairly opened out, so that they could see the Calf, they headed for the south and stood out for the Shoulder. Soon a fine breeze put them in the fishing-ground, and every man was looking out for signs of herring—perkins, gannets, fish playing on the surface, oily water, and such like. When the sun was set and the evening was too dark to see the Admiral's Flag, the skipper of each lugger held his arm out at full length, and when he could no longer see the black in his thumb-nail he ordered the men to shoot their nets. And as they lay to their trains it all fell out as the witch had said. Soon the sea put on another face, the wind from westward blew a sudden gale and swelled up the waves with foam. The boats were driven hither and thither, and the anchors dragged quickly behind them. Then the men hoisted sail before the wind and struggled to get back to land, and the lightning was all the light they had. It was so black dark that they could see no hill, and above the uproar of the sea they could hear the surges pounding on the rocky coast. The waves were rising like mountains, breaking over the boats and harrying them from stem to stern. They were dashed to pieces on the rocks of the Calf, and only two men escaped with their lives.

But there was one boat that had got safe back to port before the storm, and that was the boat of the Seven Boys. She was a Dalby boat and belonged to seven young men who were all unmarried. They were always good to the Dooinney Marrey, the Merman, and when they were hauling their nets they would throw him a dishful of herring, and in return they had always good luck with their fishing. This night, after the Fleet had shot their nets sometime, the night being still fine and calm, the Seven Boys heard the voice of the Merman hailing them and saying:

"It is calm and fine now; there will be storm enough soon!"

When the Skipper heard this he said: "Every herring must hang by its own gills," and he and his crew at once put their nets on board and gained the harbour. And it was given for law ever after that no crew was to be made up of single men only; there was to be at least one married man on board and no man was bound by his hiring to fish in this same south sea, which was called "The Sea of Blood" from that day.

As for the witch, they said she had raised the storm by her spells and they took her to the top of the great mountain Slieu Whallian, put her into a spiked barrel and rolled her from the top to the bottom, where the barrel sank into the bog. For many and many a long year there was a bare track down the steep mountain-side, where grass would never grow, nor ling, nor gorse. They called it "The Witch's Way," and they say that her screams are heard in the air every year on the day she was put to death.

The City Under the Sea

Now where Langness runs its long nose into the sea, and on a place now always covered by the waves, there was once a fine city with many towers and gilded domes. Great ships went sailing from its port to all parts of the world, and round it were well-grassed lands with cattle and sheep. Even now sailors sometimes see it through the clear, deep waters, and hear dimly the bleating of sheep, the barking of dogs, and the muffled chiming of bells—"Nane, jees, three, kiare, queig." But no man can walk its streets.

For once upon a time, in the days when there were giants in the Isle of Mann, Finn Mac Cool had his home near this city. He lived at the Sound to keep his eye on Erinn, and to watch the sea. But he was very seldom in Mann, and wherever he was he was always doing some mischief, so that his enemies were many. One day he was in such a hurry to reach his home that he jumped from Erinn and landed in the island on the rocks above the Sound. He came down with such force that he left his footmarks in the hard stone, and the place has been called ever since, Slieu ynnyd ny Cassyn, or the Mountain of the place of the Feet. His first act when he reached home was to get in a red rage with the people of the city close by; his next act was to turn them all into blocks of granite. In his passion he struck the ground so hard with his club that he made a great dent in it—the waves rushed into the deep hollow and the roaring sea drowned the din of the city. Its towers and domes were covered by the green water; its streets and market-place, its harbour and its crowded quays, disappeared from sight. And there it lies to this day.

But there is a strange story told of a man that went down to it more than two hundred years ago. A ship was searching for sunken treasure in those parts and this man was let down to the bottom of the sea in a kind of ancient diving bell. He was to pull the rope when he wished to be let down further. He pulled and pulled till the men on the ship knew that he was as deep down in the sea as the moon is high up in the sky; then there was no more rope and they had to draw him up again. When he was on deck he told them that if he could have gone further he would have made the most wonderful discoveries. They begged him to tell them what he had seen, and when he had drunk a cup of wine he told his story.

First he had passed through the waters in which the fishes live; then he came into the clear and peaceful region where storms never come, and saw the bottom of the World-under-Sea shining with coral and bright pebbles. When the diving bell rested on the ground he looked through its little windows and saw great streets decorated with pillars of crystal glittering like diamonds, and beautiful buildings made of mother-of-pearl, with shells of every colour set in it. He longed to go into one of these fine houses, but he could not leave his diving bell, or he would have been drowned. He managed to move it close to the entrance of a great hall, with a floor of pearls and rubies and all sorts of precious stones, and with a table and chair of amber. The walls were of jasper, and strings of lovely jewels were hanging on them. The man wished to carry some away with him, but he could not reach them—the rope was at an end. As he rose up again towards the air he met many handsome Mermen and beautiful Mermaids, but they were afraid of him, and swam away as fast as they could.

That was the end of the man's story. After that he grew so sad with longing to go back to the World-under-Sea and stay there for ever, that he cared for nothing on earth, and soon died of grief.

OUT OF THE EARTH

Arthur Machen

"Out of the Earth" is a chilling, understated story that hints of elusive mysteries. Arthur Machen (1863–1947) is best known for "The Bowmen" (1914) and his urban Gothic novels *The Great God Pan* (1895) and *The Three Impostors* (1894). The latter are set in London but nevertheless, like "Out of the Earth", both depend upon the pagan histories and mysteries of rural Wales, where Machen grew up. Machen credits his birthplace, Caerleon, in Gwent, with the mystical qualities that infuse so much of his fiction. Like Sophia Morrison, Machen drew upon stories of "fairies" and developed his own mythos of a sinister "Little People" belonging to a hidden, alternative existence that occasionally impinges, often fatally, on the world of humans. "Out of the Earth" is one such tale, recounting the corruption of a lonely Welsh coastal town by peculiar "children" only visible to other children.

The story is told as an accumulation of rumours that reach a narrator who poses as Machen himself and begins by referencing "The Bowmen". Machen's famous story of spirits fighting with British soldiers in the First World War contributed to the legend of the Angel of Mons and became, as he remarks in "Out of the Earth", a "mythological monster". The parallels between the two stories invite reflection on the sense-making power of rumour and belief. "Out of the Earth", however, is a story of spiritual forces inimical to human life, and may, like the hostile animals of "The Terror" (1917), suggest the negative reaction of the non-human world to the activities of a warmongering modernity.

There was some sort of confused complaint during last August of the ill-behaviour of the children at certain Welsh watering-places. Such reports and vague rumours are most difficult to trace to their heads and fountains; none has better reason to know that than myself. I need not go over the old ground here, but I am afraid that many people are wishing by this time that they had never heard my name; again, a considerable number of estimable persons are concerning themselves gloomily enough, from my point of view, with my everlasting welfare. They write me letters, some in kindly remonstrance, begging me not to deprive poor sick-hearted souls of what little comfort they possess amidst their sorrows. Others send me tracts and pink leaflets with allusions to "the daughter of a well-known canon"; others again are violently and anonymously abusive. And then in open print, in fair book-form, Mr. Begbie has dealt with me righteously but harshly, as I cannot but think.

Yet, it was all so entirely innocent, nay casual, on my part. A poor linnet of prose, I did but perform my indifferent piping in the "Evening News" because I wanted to do so, because I felt that the story of "The Bowmen" ought to be told. An inventor of fantasies is a poor creature, heaven knows, when all the world is at war; but I thought that no harm would be done, at any rate, if I bore witness, after the fashion of the fantastic craft, to my belief in the heroic glory of the English host who went back from Mons fighting and triumphing.

And then, somehow or other, it was as if I had touched a button and set in action a terrific, complicated mechanism of rumours that pretended to be sworn truth, of gossips that posed as evidence, of wild tarradiddles that good men most firmly believed. The supposed testimony of that "daughter of a well-known canon" took parish magazines by storm, and equally enjoyed the faith of dissenting divines. The "daughter" denied all knowledge of the matter, but people still quoted her supposed sure word; and the issues were confused with tales, probably true, of painful hallucinations and deliriums of our retreating soldiers, men fatigued and shattered to the very verge of death. It all became worse than the Russian myths, and as in the fable of the Russians, it seemed impossible to follow the streams of delusion to their fountain-head—or heads. Who was it who said that "Miss M. knew two officers who, etc., etc."? I suppose we shall never know his lying, deluding name.

And so, I dare say, it will be with this strange affair of the troublesome children of the Welsh seaside town, or rather of a group of small towns and villages lying within a certain "section" or zone, which I am not going to indicate more precisely than I can help, since I love that country, and my recent experiences with "The Bowmen" have taught me that no tale is too idle to be believed. And, of course, to begin with, nobody knew how this odd and malicious piece of gossip originated. So far as I know, it was more akin to the Russian myth than to the tale of "The Angels of Mons." That is, rumour preceded print; the thing was talked of here and there and passed from letter to letter long before the papers were aware of its existence. And—here it resembles rather the Mons affair—London and Manchester, Leeds and Birmingham were muttering vague unpleasant things while the little villages concerned basked innocently in the sunshine of an unusual prosperity.

In this last circumstance, as some believe, is to be sought the root of the whole matter. It is well known that certain East-Coast towns suffered from the dread of air-raids, and that a good many of their usual visitors went westward for the first time. So there is a theory that the East Coast was mean enough to circulate reports against the West Coast out of pure malice and envy. It may be so; I do not pretend to know. But here is a personal experience, such as it is, which illustrates the way in which the rumour was circulated. I was lunching one day at my Fleet Street tavern—this was early in July—and a friend of mine, a solicitor, of Serjeants' Inn, came in and sat at the same table. We began to talk of holidays and my friend Eddis asked me where I was going. "To the same old place," I said. "Manavon. You know we always go there." "Are you really?" said the lawyer; "I thought that coast had gone off a lot. My wife has a friend who's heard that it's not at all that it was."

I was astonished to hear this, not seeing how a little village like Manavon could have "gone off." I had known it for ten years as having accommodation for about twenty visitors, and I could not believe that rows of lodging houses had sprung up since the August of 1914. Still I put the question to Eddis: "Trippers?" I asked, knowing firstly that trippers hate the solitudes of the country and the sea; secondly, that there are no industrial towns within cheap and easy distance, and thirdly, that the railways were issuing no excursion tickets during the war.

"No, not exactly trippers," the lawyer replied. "But my wife's friend knows a clergyman who says that the beach at Tremaen is not at all pleasant now, and Tremaen's only a few miles from Manavon, isn't it?"

"In what way not pleasant?" I carried on my examination. "Pierrots and shows, and that sort of thing?" I felt that it could not be so, for the solemn rocks of Tremaen would have turned the liveliest Pierrot to stone. He would have frozen into a crag on the beach, and the seagulls would carry away his song and make it a lament by lonely booming caverns that look on Avalon. Eddis said he had heard nothing about showmen; but he understood that since the war the children of the whole district had got quite out of hand.

"Bad language, you know," he said, "and all that sort of thing, worse than London slum children. One doesn't want one's wife and children to hear foul talk at any time, much less on their holiday. And they say that Castell Coch is quite impossible; no decent woman would be seen there!"

I said: "Really, that's a great pity," and changed the subject. But I could not make it out at all. I knew Castell Coch well—a little bay bastioned by the dunes of red sandstone cliffs, rich with greenery. A stream of cold water runs down there to the sea; there is the ruined Norman Castle, the ancient church and the scattered village; it is altogether a place of peace and quiet and great beauty. The people there, children and grown-ups alike, were not merely decent but courteous folk: if one thanked a child for opening a gate, there would come the inevitable response: "And welcome kindly, sir." I could not make it out at all. I didn't believe the lawyer's tales; for the life of me I could not see what he could be driving at. And, for the avoidance of all unnecessary mystery, I may as well say that my wife and child and myself went down to Manavon last August and had a most delightful holiday. At the time we were certainly conscious of no annoyance or unpleasantness of any kind. Afterwards, I confess, I heard a story that puzzled and still puzzles me, and this story, if it be received, might give its own interpretation to one or two circumstances which seemed in themselves quite insignificant.

But all through July I came upon traces of evil rumours affecting this most gracious corner of the earth. Some of these rumours were repetitions of Eddis's gossip; others amplified his vague story and made it more definite. Of course, no first-hand evidence was available. There never is any first-hand evidence in these cases. But A knew B who had heard from C that her second-cousin's little girl had been set upon and beaten by a pack of young Welsh savages. Then people quoted "a doctor in large practice in a well-known town in the Midlands," to the effect that Tremaen was a sink of juvenile depravity. They said that a responsible medical man's evidence was final and convincing; but they didn't bother to find out who the doctor was, or whether there was any doctor at all—or any doctor relevant to the issue. Then the thing began to get into the papers in a sort of oblique, by-the-way sort of manner. People cited the case of these imaginary bad children in support of their educational views. One side said that "these unfortunate little ones" would have been quite well-behaved if they had had no education at all; the opposition declared that continuation schools would speedily reform them and make them into admirable citizens. Then the poor Arfonshire children seemed to become involved in quarrels about Welsh Disestablishment and in the question of the miners; and all the while they were going about behaving politely and admirably as they always do behave. I knew all the time that it was all nonsense, but I couldn't understand in the least what it meant, or who was pulling the wires of rumour, or their purpose in so pulling. I began to wonder whether the pressure and anxiety and suspense of a terrible war had unhinged the public mind, so that it was ready to believe any fable, to debate the reasons for happenings which had never happened. At last, quite incredible things began to be whispered: visitors' children had not only been beaten, they had been tortured; a little boy had been found impaled on a stake in a lonely field near Manavon; another child had been lured to destruction over the cliffs at Castell Coch. A London paper sent a good man down quietly to Arfon to investigate. He was away for a week, and at the end of that period returned to his office and, in his own phrase, "threw the whole story down." There was not a word of truth, he said, in any of these rumours; no vestige of a foundation for the mildest forms of all this gossip. He had never seen such a beautiful country; he had never met pleasanter men, women or children; there was not a single case of anyone having been annoyed or troubled in any sort or fashion.

Yet all the while the story grew, and grew more monstrous and incredible. I was too much occupied in watching the progress of my own mythological monster to pay much attention. The Town Clerk of Tremaen, to which the legend had at length penetrated, wrote a brief letter to the Press indignantly denying that there was the slightest foundation for "the unsavoury rumours" which, he understood, were being circulated; and about this time we went down to Manavon and, as I say, enjoyed ourselves extremely. The weather was perfect: blues of paradise in the skies, the seas all a shimmering wonder, olive greens and emeralds, rich purples, glassy sapphires changing by the rocks; far away a haze of magic lights and colours at the meeting of sea and sky. Work and anxiety had harried me; I found nothing better than to rest on the thymy banks by the shore, finding an infinite balm and refreshment in the great sea before me, in the tiny flowers beside me. Or we would rest all the summer afternoon on a "shelf" high on the grey cliffs and watch the tide creaming and surging about the rocks, and listen to it booming in the hollows and caverns below. Afterwards, as I say, there were one or two things that struck cold. But at the time those were nothing. You see a man in an odd white hat pass by and think little or nothing about it. Afterwards, when you hear that a man wearing just such a hat had committed murder in the next street five minutes before, then you find in that hat a certain interest and significance. "Funny children," was the phrase my little boy used; and I began to think they were "funny" indeed.

If there be a key at all to this queer business, I think it is to be found in a talk I had not long ago with a friend of mine named Morgan. He is a Welshman and a dreamer, and some people say he is like a child who has grown up and yet has not grown up like other children of men. Though I did not know it, while I was at Manavon, he was spending his holiday time at Castell Coch. He was a lonely man and he liked lonely places, and when we met in the autumn he told me how, day after day, he would carry his bread and cheese and beer in a basket to a remote headland on that coast known as the Old Camp. Here, far above the waters, are solemn age-old walls, turf-grown; circumvallations rounded and smooth with the passing of many thousand years. At one end of this most ancient place there is a tumulus, a tower of observation, perhaps, and underneath it slinks the green deceiving ditch that seems to wind into the heart of the camp, but in reality rushes down to sheer rock and a precipice over the waters.

Here came Morgan daily, as he said, to dream of Avalon, to purge himself from the fuming corruption of the streets.

And so, as he told me, it was with singular horror that one afternoon as he dozed and dreamed and opened his eyes now and again to watch the miracle and magic of the sea, as he listened to the myriad murmurs of the waves, his meditation was broken by a sudden burst of horrible raucous cries—and the cries of children, too, but children of the lowest type. Morgan says that the very tones made him shudder—"They were to the ear what slime is to the touch," and then the words: every foulness, every filthy abomination of speech; blasphemies that struck like blows at that sky, that sank down into the pure shining depths, defiling them! He was amazed. He peered over the green wall of the fort, and there in the ditch he saw a swarm of noisome children, horrible little stunted creatures with old men's faces, with bloated faces, with little sunken eyes, with leering eyes. It was worse than uncovering a brood of snakes or a nest of worms.

No; he would not describe what they were about. "Read about Belgium," said Morgan, "and think they couldn't have been more than five or six years old." There was no infamy, he said, that they did not perpetrate; they spared no horror of cruelty. "I saw blood running in streams, as they shrieked with laughter, but I could not find the mark of it on the grass afterwards."

Morgan said he watched them and could not utter a word; it was as if a hand held his mouth tight. But at last he found his voice and shrieked at them, and they burst into a yell of obscene laughter and shrieked back at him, and scattered out of sight. He could not trace them; he supposes that they hid in the deep bracken behind the Old Camp.

"Sometimes I can't understand my landlord at Castell Coch," Morgan went on. "He's the village postmaster and has a little farm of his own—a decent, pleasant, ordinary sort of chap. But now and again he will talk oddly. I was telling him about these beastly children and wondering who they could be when he broke into Welsh, something like 'the battle that is for age unto ages; and the people take delight in it'."

So far Morgan, and it was evident that he did not understand at all. But this strange tale of his brought back an odd circumstance or two that I recollected: a matter of our little boy straying away more than once, and getting lost among the sand dunes and coming back screaming, evidently frightened horribly, and babbling about "funny children." We took no notice; did not trouble, I think, to look whether there were any children wandering about the dunes or not. We were accustomed to his small imaginations.

But after hearing Morgan's story I was interested, and I wrote an account of the matter to my friend, old Doctor Duthoit, of Hereford. And he:

"They were only visible, only audible to children and the child-like. Hence the explanation of what puzzled you at first; the rumours, how did they arise? They arose from nursery gossip, from scraps and odds and ends of half-articulate children's talk of horrors that they didn't understand, of words that shamed their nurses and their mothers.

"These little people of the earth rise up and rejoice in these times of ours. For they are glad, as the Welshman said, when they know that men follow their walks."

A TALE OF AN EMPTY HOUSE

E. F. Benson

There was clearly something in the water in the Benson household. Edward Frederic Benson (1867–1940) comes from a family of ghost story writers and ghost hunters. Benson's father, Edward White Benson, was an Archbishop of Canterbury and formalised the Service of Nine Lessons and Carols—now most famously associated with King's College, Cambridge, and connected thereby to another important ghost story tradition. Edward Benson senior also co-founded the Cambridge Association for Spiritual Inquiry, a precursor of sorts to the more celebrated Society for Psychical Research, and provided Henry James with a ghost story that would help shape *The Turn of the Screw* (1898). E. F. Benson's brothers, A. C. and R. H. Benson, both also produced supernatural tales among their varied literary output.

"A Tale of an Empty House" (1925) takes us to the Norfolk coast—to Blakeney Point. Its evocation of a coastal region of uncertain size—the coming and going of the tide dramatically changing the topography of the tale—enables us to think about some of the features peculiar to East Anglia's rich tradition of weird writing. M. R. James was an acquaintance of Benson's, and it is perhaps he who is most readily associated with this region, though James' tales more frequently take the southern Suffolk shoreline as their setting. Benson takes us to the northern coast, where the distinctive flat topography of the Norfolk marshes and Fens offers a chance to re-conceptualise the relationship between land and sea: what might it mean, Benson's tale asks, to live on land so regularly and dramatically reclaimed by the tides? Other writers of weird fiction who make much of this region include E. G. Swain (in *The Stoneground Ghost Tales* [1912]) and R. H. Malden (in *Nine Ghosts* [1942])—both of whom were also friends with James.

It had been a disastrous afternoon: rain had streamed incessantly from a low grey sky, and the road was of the vilest description. There were sections consisting of sharp flints, newly laid down and not yet rolled into amenity, and the stretches in between were worn into deep ruts and bouncing holes, so that it was impossible anywhere to travel at even a moderate speed. Twice we had punctured, and now, as the stormy dusk began to fall, something went wrong with the engine, and after crawling on for a hundred yards or so we stopped. My driver, after a short investigation, told me that there was a half-hour's tinkering to be done, and after that we might, with luck, trundle along in a leisurely manner, and hope eventually to arrive at Crowthorpe, which was the proposed destination.

We had come, when this stoppage occurred, to a crossroad. Through the driving rain I could see on the right a great church, and in front a huddle of houses. A consultation of the map seemed to indicate that this was the village of Riddington, The guide-book added the information that Riddington possessed an hotel, and the signpost at the corner endorsed them both. To the right along the main road, into which we had just struck, was Crowthorpe, fifteen miles away, and straight in front of us, half a mile distant, was the hotel.

The decision was not difficult. There was no reason why I should get to Crowthorpe tonight instead of tomorrow, for the friend whom I was to meet there would not arrive until next afternoon and it was surely better to limp half a mile with a spasmodic engine than to attempt fifteen on this inclement evening.

"We'll spend the night here," I said to my chauffeur. "The road dips downhill, and it's only half a mile to the hotel. I dare say we shall get there without using the engine at all. Let's try, anyhow."

We hooted and crossed the main road, and began to slide very slowly down a narrow street. It was impossible to see much, but on either side there were little houses with lights gleaming through blinds, or with blinds still undrawn, revealing cosy interiors. Then the incline grew steeper, and close in front of us I saw masts against a sheet of water that appeared to stretch unbroken into the rain-shrouded gloom of the gathering night.

Riddington, then, must be on the open sea, though how it came about that boats should be tied up to an open quay-wall was a puzzle, but perhaps there was some jetty, invisible in the darkness, which protected them. I heard the chauffeur switch on his engine as we made a sharp turn to the left, and we passed below a long row of lighted windows, shining out on to a rather narrow road, on the right edge of which the water lapped. Again he turned sharply to the left, described a half-circle on crunching gravel, and drew up at the door of the hotel. There was a room for me, there was a garage, there was a room for him, and dinner had not long begun.

Among the little excitements and surprises of travel there is none more delightful than that of waking in a new place at which one has arrived after nightfall on the previous evening. The mind has received a few hints and dusky impressions, and probably during sleep it has juggled with these, constructing them into some sort of coherent whole, and next morning its anticipations are put to the proof. Usually the eye has seen more than it has consciously registered, and the brain has fitted together as in the manner of a jigsaw puzzle a very fair presentment of its immediate surroundings. When I woke next morning a brilliantly sunny sky looked in at my windows; there was no sound of wind or of breaking waves, and before getting up and verifying my impressions of the night before I lay and washed in my imagined picture. In front of my windows there would be a narrow roadway bordered by a quay-wall: there would be a breakwater, forming a harbour for the boats that lay at anchor there, and away, away to the horizon would stretch an expanse of still and glittering sea. I ran over these points in my mind; they seemed an inevitable inference from the glimpses of the night before and then, assured of my correctness, I got out of bed and went to the window.

I have never experienced so complete a surprise. There was no harbour, there was no breakwater, and there was no sea. A very narrow channel, three-quarters choked with sand-banks on which now rested the boats whose masts I had seen the previous evening, ran parallel to the road, and then turned at right-angles and went off into the distance. Otherwise no water of any sort was visible; right and left and in front stretched a limitless expanse of shining grasses with tufts of shrubby growth, and great patches of purple sea-lavender. Beyond were tawny sand-banks, and further yet a line of shingle and scrub and sand-dunes. But the sea which I had expected to fill the whole circle of the visible world till it met the sky on the horizon had totally disappeared.

After the first surprise at this colossal conjuring trick was over, I dressed quickly, in order to ascertain from local authorities how it was done. Unless some hallucination had poisoned my perceptive faculties, there must be an explanation of this total disappearance, alternately, of sea and land, and the key, when supplied, was simple enough. That line of shingle and scrub and sand-dunes on the horizon was a peninsula running for four or five miles parallel with the land, forming the true beach, and it enclosed this vast basin of sand-banks and mud-banks and level lavender-covered marsh, which was submerged at high tide, and made an estuary. At low tide it was altogether empty but for the stream that struggled out through various channels to the mouth of it two miles away to the left, and there was easy passage across it for a man who carried his shoes and stockings, to the far sand-dunes and beaches which terminated at Riddington Point, while at high tide you could sail out from the quay just in front of the hotel and be landed there.

The tide would be out of the estuary for five or six hours yet; I could spend the morning on the beach, or, taking my lunch, walk out to the Point, and be back before the returning waters rendered the channel impassable. There was good bathing on the beach, and there was a colony of terns who nested there.

Already, as I ate my breakfast at a table in the window overlooking the marsh, the spell and attraction of it had begun to work. It was so immense and so empty; it had the allure of the desert about it, with none of the desert's intolerable monotony, for companies of chiding gulls hovered over it, and I could hear the pipe of redshank and the babble of curlews. I was due to meet Jack Granger in Crowthorpe that evening, but if I went I knew that I should persuade him to come back to Riddington, and from my knowledge of him I was aware that he would feel the spell of the place not less potent than I. So, having ascertained that there was a room for him here, I wrote him a note saying that I had found the most amazing place in the world, and told my chauffeur to take the car into Crowthorpe to meet the train that afternoon and bring him here. And with a perfectly clear conscience I set off with a towel and a packet of lunch in my pocket to explore vaguely and goallessly that beckoning immensity of lavender-covered, bird-haunted expanse.

My way, as pointed out to me, led first along a sea-bank which defended the drained pastureland on the right of it from the high tides, and at the corner of that I struck into the basin of the estuary. A contour-line of jetsam, withered grass, strands of seaweed, and the bleached shells of little crabs showed where the last tide had reached its height, and inside it the marsh-growth was still wet. Then came a stretch of mud and pebbles, and presently I was wading through the stream that flowed down to the sea. Beyond that were banks of ribbed sand swept by the incoming tides, and soon I regained the wide green marshes on the further side, beyond which was the bar of shingle that fringed the sea.

I paused as I reshod myself. There was not a sign of any living human being within sight, but never have I found myself in so exhilarating a solitude. Right and left were spread the lawns of sea-lavender, starred with pink tufts of thrift and thickets of suaeda bushes. Here and there were pools left in depressions of the ground by the retreated tide, and here were patches of smooth black mud, out of which grew, like little spikes of milky-green asparagus, a crop of glasswort, and all these happy vegetables flourished in sunshine, or rain, or the salt of the flooding tides with impartial amphibiousness. Overhead was the immense arc of the sky, across which flew now a flight of duck, hurrying with necks outstretched, and now a lonely black-backed gull, flapping his ponderous way seawards. Curlews were bubbling, and redshank and ringed plover fluting, and now as I trudged up the shingle-bank, at the bottom of which the marsh came to an end, the sea, blue and waveless, lay stretched and sleeping, bordered by a strip of sand, on which far off a mirage hovered. But from end to end of it, as far as eye could see, there was no sign of human presence.

I bathed and basked on the hot beach, walked along for half a mile, and then struck back across the shingle into the marsh. And then with a pang of disappointment I saw the first evidence of the intrusion of man into this paradise of solitude, for on a stony spit of ground that ran like some great rib into the amphibious meadows, there stood a small square house built of brick, with a tall flagstaff set up in front of it. It had not caught my eye before, and it seemed an unwarrantable invasion of the emptiness. But perhaps it was not so gross an infringement of it as it appeared, for it wore an indefinable look of desertion, as if man had attempted to domesticate himself here and had failed. As I approached it this impression increased, for the chimney was smokeless, and the closed windows were dim with the film of salt air and the threshold of the closed door was patched with lichen and strewn with debris of withered grasses. I walked twice round it, decided that it was certainly uninhabited, and finally, leaning against the sunbaked wall, ate my lunch.

The glitter and heat of the day were at their height. Warmed and exercised, and invigorated by my bathe, I felt strung to the supreme pitch of physical well-being, and my mind, quite vacant except for these felicitous impressions, followed the example of my body, and basked in an unclouded content. And, I suppose by a sense of the Lucretian luxury of contrast, it began to picture to itself, in order to accentuate these blissful conditions, what this sunlit solitude would be like when some November night began to close in underneath a low, grey sky and a driving storm of sleet. Its solitariness would be turned into an abominable desolation: if from some unconjecturable cause one was forced to spend the night here, how the mind would long for any companionship, how sinister would become the calling of the birds, how weird the whistle of the wind round the cavern of this abandoned habitation. Or would it be just the other way about, and would one only be longing to be assured that the seeming solitude was real, and that no invisible but encroaching presence, soon to be made manifest, was creeping nearer under cover of the dusk, and be shuddering to think that the wail of the wind was not only the wind, but the cry of some discarnate being, and that it was not the curlews who made that melancholy piping? By degrees the edge of thought grew blunt, and melted into inconsequent imaginings, and I fell asleep.

I woke with a start from the trouble of a dream that faded with waking, but felt sure that some noise close at hand had aroused me. And then it came again: it was the footfall of someone moving about inside the deserted house, against the wall of which my back was propped. Up and down it went, then paused and began again; it was like that of a man who waited with impatience for some expected arrival. I noticed also that the footfall had an irregular beat, as if the walker went with a limp. Then in a minute or two the sound ceased altogether.

An odd uneasiness came over me, for I had been so certain that the house was uninhabited. Then turning my head I noticed that in the wall just above me was a window, and the notion, wholly irrational and unfounded, entered my mind that the man inside who tramped was watching me from it. When once that idea got hold of me, it became impossible to sit there in peace any more, and I got up and shovelled into my knapsack my towel and the remains of my meal. I walked a little further down the spit of land which ran out into the marsh, and turning looked at the house again, and again to my eyes it seemed absolutely deserted. But, after all, it was no concern of mine and I proceeded on my walk, determining to inquire casually on my return to the hotel who it was that lived in so hermetical a place, and for the present dismissed the matter from my mind.

It was some three hours later that I found myself opposite the house again, after a long, wandering walk. I saw that, by making an only slightly longer detour, I could pass close to the house again, and I knew that the sound of those footsteps within it had raised in me a curiosity that I wanted to satisfy. And then, even as I paused, I saw that a man was standing by the door: how he came there I had no idea, for the moment before he had not been there, and he must have come out of the house. He was looking down the path that led through the marsh, shielding his eyes against the sun, and presently he took a step or two forward, and he dragged his left leg as he walked, limping heavily. It was his step, then, which I had heard within, and any mystery about the matter was of my own making. I therefore took the shorter path, and got back to the hotel to find that Jack Granger had just arrived.

We went out again in the gleam of the sunset, and watched the tide sweeping in and pouring up the dykes, until again the great conjuring trick was accomplished, and the stretch of marsh with its fields of sea-lavender was a sheet of shining water. Far away across it stood the house by which I had lunched, and just as we turned Jack pointed to it.

"That's a queer place for a house," he said. "I suppose no one lives there."

"Yes, a lame man," said I; "I saw him today. I'm going to ask the hotel porter who he is."

The result of this inquiry was unexpected.

"No; the house has been uninhabited several years," he said. "It used to be a watch-house from which the coastguards signalled if there was a ship in distress, and the lifeboat went out from here. But now the lifeboat and the coastguards are at the end of the Point."

"Then who is the lame man I saw walking about there, and heard inside the house?" I asked.

He looked at me, I thought, queerly.

"I don't know who that could be," he said. "There's no lame man about here to my knowledge."

The effect on Jack of the marshes and their gorgeous emptiness, of the sun and the sea, was precisely what I had anticipated. He vowed that any day spent anywhere than on these beaches and fields of sea-lavender was a day wasted, and proposed that the tour, of which the main object had originally been the golf links of Norfolk, should for the present be cancelled. In particular, it was the birds of this long solitary headland that enchanted him.

"After all, we can play golf anywhere," he said.

"There's an oyster-catcher scolding, do you hear?—and how silly to whack a little white ball—ringed plover, but what's that calling as well?—when you can spend the day like this! Oh, don't let us go and bathe yet: I want to wander along that edge of the marsh—ha, there's a company of turnstones; they make a noise like the drawing of a cork—there they are, those little chaps with chestnut-coloured patches! Let's go along the near edge of the marsh, and come out by the house where your lame man lives."

We took, therefore, the path with the longer detour, which I had abandoned last night. I had said nothing to him of what the hotel porter had told me—that the house was unlived in—and all he knew was that I had seen a lame man, apparently in occupation there. My reason for not doing so (to make the confession at once) was that I already half believed that the steps I had heard inside, and the lame man I had seen watching outside, did not imply in the porter's sense of the word that the house was occupied, and I wanted to see whether Jack as well as myself would be conscious of any such tokens of a presence there. And then the oddest thing happened.

All the way up to the house his attention was alert on the birds, and in especial on a piping note which was unfamiliar to him. In vain he tried to catch sight of the bird that uttered it, and in vain I tried to hear it. "It doesn't sound like any bird I know," he said; "in fact, it doesn't sound like a bird at all, but like some human being whistling. There it is again! Is it possible you don't hear it?"

We were now quite close to the house.

"There must be someone there who is whistling," he said; "it must be your lame man... Lord, yes, it comes from inside the house. So that's explained, and I hoped it was some new bird. But why can't you hear it?"

"Some people can't hear a bat's squeak," said I.

Jack, satisfied with the explanation, took no more interest in the matter, and we struck across the shingle, bathed and lunched, and tramped on to the tumble of sand-dunes in which the Point ended. For a couple of hours we strolled and lazed there in the liquid and sunny air, and reluctantly returned in order to cross the ford before the tide came in. As we retraced our way, I saw coming up from the west a huge continent of cloud; and just as we reached the spit of land on which the house stood, a jagged sword of lightning flickered down to the low-lying hills across the estuary, and a few big raindrops plopped on the shingle.

"We're in for a drenching," he said. "Ha! Let's ask for shelter at your lame man's house. Better run for it!" Already the big drops were falling thickly, and we scuttled across the hundred yards that lay between us and the house, and came to the door just as the sluices of heaven were pulled wide. He rapped on it, but there came no answer; he tried the handle of it, but the door did not yield, and then, by a sudden inspiration, he felt along the top of the lintel and found a key. It fitted into the wards and next moment we stood within.

We found ourselves in a slip of a passage, at the end of which went up the staircase to the floor above. On each side of it was a room, one a kitchen, the other a living-room, but in neither was there any stick of furniture. Discoloured paper was peeling off the walls, the windows were thick with spidery weavings, the air heavy with unventilated damp.

"Your lame man dispenses with the necessities as well as the luxuries of life," said Jack. "A spartan fellow."

We were standing in the kitchen: outside the hiss of the rain had grown to a roar, and the bleared window was suddenly lit up with a flare of lightning. A crack of thunder answered it, and in the silence that followed there came from just outside, audible now to me, the sound of a piping whistle. Immediately afterwards I heard the door by which we had just entered violently banged, and I remembered that I had left it open.

His eyes met mine.

"But there's no breath of wind," I said. "What made it bang like that?"

"And that was no bird that whistled," said he.

There was the shuffle in the passage outside of a limping step: I could hear the drag of a man's lame foot along the boards.

"He has come in," said Jack.

Yes, he had come in, and who had come in? At that moment not fright, but fear, which is a very different matter, closed in on me. Fright, as I understand it, is an emotion, startling, but not unnerving; you may under the finger of fright spring aside, you may scream, you may shout, you have the command of your muscles. But as that limping step moved down the passage I felt fear, the hand of the nightmare that, as it clutches, paralyses and inhibits not action only, but thought. I waited frozen and speechless for what should happen next.

Exactly opposite the open door of the kitchen in which we stood the step stopped. And then, soundlessly and invisibly, the presence that had made itself manifest to the outward ear entered. Suddenly I heard Jack's breath rattle in his throat.

"Oh, my God!" he cried in a voice hoarse and strangled, and he threw his left arm across his face as if defending himself, and his right arm, shooting out seemed to hit at something which I could not see, and his fingers crooked themselves as if clutching at that which had evaded his blow. His body was bent back as if resisting some invisible pressure, then lunged forward again, and I heard the noise of a resisting joint, and saw on his throat the shadow (or so it seemed) of a clutching hand. At that some power of movement came back to me, and I remember hurling myself at the empty space between him and me, and felt under my grip the shape of a shoulder and heard on the boards of the floor the slip and scoop of a foot. Something invisible, now a shoulder, now an arm, struggled in my grasp, and I heard a panting respiration that was not Jack's, nor mine, and now and then in my face I felt a hot breath that stank of corruption and decay. And all the time this physical contention was symbolical only: what he and I wrestled with was not a thing of flesh and blood, but some awful spiritual presence. And then...

There was nothing. The ghostly invasion ceased as suddenly as it had begun, and there was Jack's face gleaming with sweat close to mine, as we stood with dropped arms opposite each other in an empty room, with the rain beating on the roof and the gutters chuckling. No word passed between us, but next moment we were out in the pelting rain, running for the ford. The deluge was sweet to my soul, it seemed to wash away that horror of great darkness and that odour of corruption in which we had been plunged.

Now, I have no certain explanation to give of the experience which has here been shortly recounted, and the reader may or may not connect with it a story that I heard a week or two later on my return to London.

A friend of mine and I had been dining at my house one evening, and we had discussed a murder trial then going on of which the papers were full.

"It isn't only the atrocity that attracts," he said, "I think it is the place where the murder occurs that is the cause of the interest in it. A murder at Brighton, or Margate, or Ramsgate, any place which the public associates with pleasure trips, attracts them because they know the place and can visualise the scene. But when there is a murder at some small, unknown spot, which they have never heard of, there is no appeal to their imagination. Last spring, for instance, there was the murder at that small village on the coast of Norfolk. I've forgotten the name of the place, though I was in Norwich at the time of the trial and was present in court. It was one of the most awful stories I ever heard, as ghastly and sensational as this last affair, but it didn't attract the smallest attention. Odd that I can't remember the name of the place when all the rest is so vivid to me!"

"Tell me about it," I said; "I never heard of it."

"Well, there was this little village, and just outside it was a farm, owned by a man called John Beardsley. He lived there with his only daughter, an unmarried woman of about thirty, a good-looking, sensible creature apparently, the last in the world you would have thought to do anything unexpected. There worked at the farm as a day-labourer a young fellow called Alfred Maldon, who in the trial of which I am speaking was the prisoner. He had one of the most dreadful faces I ever saw, a catlike receding forehead, a broad, short nose, and a great red sensual mouth, always on the grin. He seemed positively to enjoy being the central figure around whom all the interest of those ghoulish women who thronged the court was concentrated, and when he shambled into the witness-box—"

"Shambled?" I asked.

"Yes; he was lame; his left foot dragged along the floor as he walked. As he shambled into the witness-box he nodded and smiled to the judge, and clapped his counsel on the shoulder, and leered at the gallery... He worked on the farm, as I was saying, doing jobs that were within his capacity, among which was certain house-work, carrying coals and what-not, for John Beardsley, though very well-off, kept no servant, and this daughter Alice—that was her name—ran the house. And what must she do but fall in love, it was no less than that, with this monstrous and misshapen fellow. One afternoon her father came home unexpectedly and caught them together in the parlour, kissing and cuddling. He turned the man out of the house, neck and crop, gave him his week's wages, and dismissed him, threatening him with a fine thrashing if he ever caught him hanging about the place. He forbade his daughter ever to speak to him again, and in order to keep watch over her, got in a woman from the village who would be there all day while he was out on the farm.

"Young Maldon, deprived of his job, tried to get work in the village, but none would employ him, for he was a black-tempered fellow ready to pick a quarrel with anyone, and an unpleasant opponent, for, with all his lameness, he was of immense muscular strength. For some weeks he idled about in the village, getting a chance job occasionally, and no doubt, as you will see, Alice Beardsley managed to meet him. The village—its name still escapes me—lay on the edge of a big tidal estuary, full at high water, but on the ebb of a broad stretch of marsh and sand and mud-banks, beyond which ran a long belt of shingle that formed the seaward side of the estuary. On it stood a disused coastguard house, a couple of miles away from the village, and in as lonely a place as you would find anywhere in England. At low tide there was a shallow ford across to it, and in the sand-banks round about it some beds of cockle. Maldon, unable to get regular work, took to cockle-digging, and during the summer, when the tide was low, Alice (it was no new thing with her) used to go over the ford to the beach beyond and bathe. She would go across the sand-banks where the cockle-diggers, Maldon among them, were at work, and if he whistled as she passed that was the signal between them that he would slip away presently and join her at the disused coastguard house, and there throughout the summer they used to meet.

"As the weeks went on her father saw the change that was coming in her, and suspecting the cause, often left his work and, hidden behind some sea-bank, used to watch her. One day he saw her cross the ford, and soon after she had passed he saw Maldon, recognisable from a long way off by his dragging leg, follow her. He went up the path to the coastguard house, and entered. At that John Beardsley crossed the ford, and hiding in the bushes near the house, saw Alice coming back from her bathe. The house was off the direct path to the ford, but she went round that way, and the door was opened to her, and closed behind her. He found them together, and mad with rage attacked the man. They fought and Maldon got him down and then and there in front of his daughter strangled him.

"The girl went off her head, and is in the asylum at Norwich now. She sits all day by the window whistling. The man was hanged."

"Was Riddington the name of the village?" I asked.

"Yes. Riddington, of course," he said. "I can't think how I forgot it."

ON THE ISLE OF BLUE MEN

Robert W. Sneddon

Lovecraftian horrors abound in "On the Isle of Blue Men", a weird tale of the Outer Hebrides by Robert W. Sneddon (1880–1944), first published in the April 1927 edition of *Ghost Stories*. Sneddon was born in Scotland but moved to the US in 1910, where he became a prolific writer of horror fiction.

"On the Isle of Blue Men" is set in and around the Flannan Isles Lighthouse—the real-life counterpart of which was manned until its automation in 1971. The story follows a young couple on a yachting excursion who seek refuge in the lighthouse during a storm; one of the lighthouse keepers is distinctly uncomfortable with the couple's presence, especially the red-haired Alice who, it seems, may very well prompt the fulfilment of a terrible prophecy. The tentacled blue men of the story would appear to be Sneddon's take on the blue men of the Minch, creatures of folklore who haunt the waters around the Isle of Lewis and have the power to conjure storms and send sailors to watery graves. Sneddon's story also provides an opportunity to acknowledge the importance of lighthouses to the coastal weird tradition—from Ann Radcliffe to Jeff VanderMeer. These beacons of preservation are also suggestive sites of terror, isolation, and madness.

The re-publication history of this tale is also worth raising. The only noteworthy reprinting of the tale since its original publication is in the 1993 *Lighthouse Horrors* anthology. The editors of this volume note, however, that they have amended—or "restored"—"what we believe to have been the author's original ending". Other changes are silently made, too, including the removal of the opening frame narrative and subsequent references to it. We are pleased to be able to present the tale in its original form for the first time since, we believe, its initial appearance in *Ghost Stories*.

From the Curious Manuscript of "The Solitary"

"Incredible, impossible, this relation of extraordinary happenings—the ravings of a madman, the distortions of a disordered brain." Such were my thoughts on the first reading of the document which had come to my hands through the agency of the wireless operator.

Even the manner in which he had come into possession of the document was extraordinary. He had been wrecked on the shores of Portugal—but that's a story in itself which I shall delay telling 'til I have given you the story of the Isle of Blue Men.

This must be fiction, I said to myself; but drawn on by curiosity, by the tempting lure of discovery that there might be truth in these statements set down with such an impressive semblance of verity, I began to investigate. And gradually, from many sources, came verification of certain facts so astounding and convincing that I could not help being all but persuaded that the story of the man known to the Portuguese fisherman as "The Solitary," was true. And, now, sharing this story with the readers of *Ghost Stories* Magazine, it is in hope that perhaps among them may be someone who can shed further light on the mysterious and inexplicable tragedy which compelled a brilliant man to forsake Society and bury himself in a living death, alone with haunting and terrible memories.

Inasmuch as I suspect with reason that certain names have been changed, I am led to believe that the name of the writer, too, is not that with which he was baptised. That name now, is lost in a merciful oblivion However—

With this preamble I shall let The Solitary tell his story.

Sometimes I sit for hours weighing myself in the balance of reason. Have I dreamed all this? Am I what I am, a castaway? Have I always been the creature, scarce human, whom the fishermen regard with pity and compassion, thinking me mad? Or have I really been John Scott of New York, the painter of pictures which hang in the Metropolitan Museum of New York, the Corcoran Art Gallery of Washington, the Philadelphia Art Gallery, the Luxemburg of Paris? Surely knowing these names indicates my knowledge of art, yet were canvas and palette set before me I would hesitate to touch them. I shall never paint again.

I shrink from the task I have set myself. Can I bear to relive those days of horror? And yet there is some power stronger than my puny will that prompts me to write, to assure myself I am still capable of sane and ordered thought. I have begged pen, ink, and paper from the schoolmaster. He gave them to me as though to a child, and I felt his little eyes follow me with a strange surmise.

And when I have written, what then? What shall I have proved? I do not know—

Summer had crept into fall. We had seen the heather turn purple on the hills of this remote island of the Hebrides which lies off the North of Scotland, and winter still found us lingering. The few tourists had long since gone. In the little, low stone cottage with its thatched roof held down by heavy stones, the peat fire burned night and day. Only two lovers in the divinest of sympathy could have existed as we did, so remote from human intercourse, our only visitors a shepherd or a fisherman. Sometimes they had no English and we knew no Gaelic, but we nodded and grinned amiably at each other as we bartered for a piece of mutton or a basket of herring. A few of them spoke English with a soft, caressing accent, in which they lingered over each "s" or converted hard sounds into soft.

I seem to hear old Hamish, our man-of-all-work, saying:

"I am thinking it was time you were going away, you and your leddy. Soon it will be blowing great gales of wind, whatever."

But Alice was content to wait, to see me cover canvas after canvas with those majestic, rocky, snow-capped peaks, sometimes sharp against a brilliant blue sky, sometimes wrapped in a misty veil. And I shivered many a day on the rocks by the sea, striving to capture the secret of the surge and swell of the tossing waters.

God in heaven! I read this which I have written, and I am sure I am sane. These things really happened.

We had a taut little yacht, of seagoing qualities that I had tested many a time. Alice was as good a skipper as I, and we were fearless.

Would to God we had known the terrors of the deeps, clung like cowards to the shore. Would to God I had never conceived the wild fancy which assailed me, to tempt the voyage to the Isles of the Seven Hunters when others less adventurous and foolhardy were snug in cities thinking of Christmas, of gifts and lighted stores and goodwill and peace toward men.

Twenty-five miles from the inlet in which our yacht rode at anchor, lies an outpost of civilisation. Seven little islands, hardly more than rocks they are, and beyond them is the Atlantic Ocean, the farthest surges of which beat upon the coast of my own country. On the largest of the islands stands a lighthouse which flashes its warning rays forty miles out to sea, and guides daring vessels passing around the North of Scotland to Scandinavian ports.

Now I had heard stories of this island. On it was a ruined church, the Gaelic name of which was translated to me as she "Temple of Blessing." It had been founded by a sixteenth century monk, still held in reverence. Until the past year when the lighthouse had reached completion, the only visitors to the island were the fishermen who went to gather seafowl eggs and to kill birds for their feathers. Strange old customs were observed there. The men went in pairs, and did everything in unison. One could not take as much as a drink of water alone unless his comrade did likewise. On landing they took off their upper garments, laid them on a stone and went toward the chapel, praying at intervals. No man must kill a bird with a stone, or after evening prayer.

The name of the island must not be mentioned. It was always spoken of as "The Country."

Little did I know what a country of horrors unspeakable I was to find it, though I might have guessed something from the reluctance of those about me to give me any information.

The day was clear when we left the shores of Loch Roig and put out into the unknown, Alice and I, with a good store of provisions and some presents that we knew would please the lighthouse keepers. It was cold, but we were well muffled up; we laughed gaily as a couple of school-children when the wind caught our sails.

As we approached the egg-shaped rock with its grey cliffs rising sheer, and caught the glint of turf patches gleaming with frost crystals and the tall white tower of the lighthouse, its base 200 feet or so above sea level, Alice clapped her hands. It was a spectacle of stern and menacing beauty from which, had we but known, we would have fled as from a plague ship.

Already we could see two men hastening down a zigzag stair cut in the rock, and making for the landing place visible to us. As we came in we could see the amazement on their faces, and there was amazement in the voices that hailed us. They threw us a rope, and we drew into the stone landing. I moored the boat so that it would not knock to pieces on the rocks, and then we scrambled ashore. They stood staring at us, two men sea-tanned, with wrinkled eyes under the woollen tams they wore, rather solemn looking, and saying not a word as I explained.

Could we spend the night? Any shakedown of a bed they could give us would be all right. We had provisions of our own—and would they accept the bundle of magazines and tins of tobacco we had brought?

I could see they were troubled, and especially about Alice.

"It was a rash-like thing, sir," said one of them, at length. "There is no accommodation for visitors. But it is plain you cannot be going back the day, for there is a storm on the way."

"Then we stay," I said cheerfully.

They helped us to carry our bundles to the lighthouse, and the third man came out, Jamieson, they called him, a short stout man with eyes which seemed to look beyond us. When he saw us, he got to his feet quickly, and seemed under the control of some strange fear. Why our presence should inspire Jamieson with fear I did not then know.

"Angus," said one of our guides who had told us his name was Ross, "the gentleman and leddy are stopping with us over night. There will be nothing in the regulations against that, now?"

Jamieson appeared strangely troubled and looked behind him one or twice, with an abrupt turn of his head,

"The woman!" he said at last in a husky voice. "*They* will not be wanting her here. The curse will fall! The curse— Is it not a fact that no woman has set foot on the country since—since the time—" And he added something in Gaelic.

"Man," said Ross roughly, "will you ever be letting alone these old wive's tales? It's bad enough when you are glooming over the fire of a night, but here in broad daylight, what is there to fear? Put an end to it, Angus Jamieson."

I could see Alice was upset by this show of ungraciousness.

"Perhaps we'd better try and get back," she suggested.

"No! No! That would be madness indeed," protested the third, McLeod. "Would you be driving the leddy out into the night? Stay you here and welcome, ma'am."

We had come up a narrow winding iron stair, past the oil tanks and storage room, into a circular living room.

"We sleep above," McLeod continued; "so maybe you can be making shift here with some rugs and the like."

We told him anything would do, and so the matter was settled.

I went up with Ross into the lamp room, saw him light the wicks and set the clockwork going, and then we came down to a meal to which we were happy to contribute some dainties. Afterward we settled round the fire. Jamieson, to my surprise, busied himself knitting a coarse wool sock.

"Angus is not much for reading," said McLeod, "but there is not a woman can make a better pair of socks, whatever. It is a good thing you stayed, for hark to it now."

Indeed, the wind was blattering upon the smooth pillar raising its head in defiance, and I had a vision of the yacht grating its planking to shreds; but there was nothing to be done that night.

Suddenly Alice raised her head. I, too, heard what had attracted her attention—a steady body of sound, like some ancient religious composition, like an unknown Wagnerian opera played by some vast orchestra and taken up by other orchestras.

"Oh, how wonderful!" she said softly.

Ross laughed slyly. "The birds, ma'am," he said; "the puffins and the gulls, the divers and the cormorants. There's no counting the beasties."

The night choir of the seabirds swelled solemnly, majestically, then died away, to recur again with such awe-inspiring notes that I felt my flesh creep. Then all at once, as though stilled by a master leader's baton, the wild sea music ceased. A thin flutter of ashes ascended from the peat fire. Something made me look at Jamieson, who sat staring into blank space beyond him, his knitting needles motionless as though he heard sounds not audible to our ears.

All at once there reached us dimly through the thick walls a screeching so hellish that my blood ran cold.

"In God's name!" cried Ross, rising to his feet and looking about the room. "A year I've been stationed here, yet never heard I the like."

"Nor I," added McLeod.

"What would it be?" said Jamieson in a quick, tense tone as he set his needles in motion once more. "What but the *sluagh*?"

I caught at the word. "What's that?"

"It will be some of the old tales, sir. Be paying no heed to Angus," said Ross slowly. "He's meaning the host of the dead that are about us."

"Ay!" said Jamieson in a strange, remote tone, "the grey, watery forms of ghosts. Maybe worse."

"Tush!" said Ross roughly. "Will you be frightening the leddy, Angus?"

Jamieson looked at us, and I fancied there was real concern in his look, and this caused vague uneasiness in my mind,

"God forbid, leddy. But I will be telling you, John Ross, and you, Donald McLeod, see to it this night that the door be locked and all shut tight and close. Something is speaking within me, and I am seeing beyond. The call is coming. Aye! The dark one is at hand, the dread one that we will be calling The Kindly—"

"Peace, man," said Ross. "You and your death fancies, and we as snug here as any man could be asking! What could be the hurt of us?" He looked at his watch. "Time it is you were keeping your watch, Angus."

Jamieson rose to his feet and disappeared up the spiral stairway without another word.

"They will be saying," explained Ross, lowering his voice, "that Angus has the gift of the second-sight."

"Do you believe in that?" asked Alice, with a shudder. "Do you think he really can see into the future?"

"Ma'am," said Ross, with an odd expression, "I could be telling you things that are better left unsaid. Angus Jamieson is a strange lad, and whatever be his power, it is true that he sees more than the rest of us. But rest your mind. There's safety here for yourself and your gentleman this night. And now, by your leave, we'll be going upstairs and having our sleep."

We heard their heavy tread die away on the iron steps. Drawing our blankets over to the fire, we lay down.

Suddenly Alice clung to me, whispering: "I'm frightened. I never felt like this in all my life. That queer Angus—and what was that screech?"

"Some seal, probably, or the sea in a hollow cave," I said, but as I spoke I knew I lied.

All night long as I lay there my flesh tingled, and it seemed to me that the tower of the lighthouse was beset with stealthy prowling horrors to which I could give neither shape nor name, and Alice moaned in her sleep and more than once put out an appealing hand to mine.

The morning came cold, brisk, and wild. While McLeod busied himself over the cookstove, I climbed to the lantern and looked abroad. One look was enough to tell me we could not leave the island that day. We were surrounded by a circle of tempestuous seas, rising and falling in monstrous surges.

We were sitting at breakfast when Jamieson came down to join us. Scarcely had he nodded to us than I saw a terrified light flash into his eyes, and he half rose from his seat with a hoarse exclamation:

"The red-haired woman!"

Alice looked at him with surprise in her blue eyes. Her hand went up to her hair.

"Yes, it is red," she said, smiling faintly.

"I did not notice it last night," muttered Jamieson, with his eyes still upon her, his face convulsed with an emotion which was communicated to us all. "God have mercy upon us!"

"What is the matter with red hair, my friend?" I asked abruptly. "Don't you admire it?"

Jamieson swayed in his seat.

"What is the matter?" I asked, turning to McLeod.

"I don't know, sir," he said slowly. "I never saw him act this way before. Angus, my man, will you be feeling sick this day?"

I never saw such a desperate look on any man's face as that which Jamieson turned to us.

"It is not sickness!" he cried suddenly. "It is death that is all about. Oh, it was an ill day that brought a red-haired woman to The Country.

Did I not hear them crying aloud last night, licking their mouths for their victims?"

"You are *fey*, Angus Jamieson," said Ross harshly. "Cease your wild talk."

"No, there is no madness in my brain," said Jamieson with solemn sincerity. "Oh, sir"—he turned to me—"will you not be leaving us now—this very minute—you and the leddy, before They come upon us and destroy us?"

"How can we put to sea? Look for yourself, man," I shouted, losing my temper. "It's utterly impossible. I'm sorry we're so unwelcome."

Ross laid his hand on my arm.

"Wheesht, sir. There is no need to be saying that. McLeod and me will not hear of your going."

But I was determined to get to the root and bottom of the business.

"What's all this talk about destroying—what will come upon us—who are licking their mouths for victims?"

Jamieson looked as though stunned by my vehemence. Then he put his hands to his eyes as though to shut out some terrifying sight. A strange babble of sound came from his lips.

"What is he saying, Ross?" I cried. "What is *Na fir gorma?*"

Ross drew a long breath, then rolled his eyes toward heaven.

"The blue men, sir... But never heed him. I'll see to him."

He caught Jamieson roughly by the shoulder and propelled him toward the ladder. I heard him speak soothingly in Gaelic, and then we were left alone.

McLeod sat looking at us in silence; then as the stillness weighed upon us, he cleared his throat.

"It's the lonely life here," he said as if in apology. "It would be a wonder indeed if it did not go to the head sometimes, sir and ma'am. Angus will be all right after a bit of sleep. Angus is perfectly harmless, leddy. You need not be afraid. You see, he is full of old stories... and it is well known no woman has ever set foot on this island."

"Why not?" asked Alice. "And why doesn't he like my red hair?"

"Well," answered McLeod with evident uneasiness, "there's an old saying about this part—'The red-haired witch and the blue men come together.'"

"A witch!" cried Alice, opening her pretty eyes wide. "I like that. So he thinks I'm a witch!"

"Oh, 'deed no, ma'am," said McLeod hastily; "but there's a prejudice against the red hair among some of them that live hereabouts. Poor creatures! I come from Oban myself, where we're civilised—yes, indeed."

"But the blue men? What are they?" I asked. "What does he mean?"

"I don't know," said McLeod simply. "Some other old tale, no doubt."

Alice appeared comforted, but I noticed that when Ross came down again, he was stern and uncommunicative.

"You'll excuse him, leddy," he said; "and now, Donald, we'll be cleaning the lenses and trimming the wicks."

"We'll go out and get the air," I suggested.

"Very good," Ross answered with an air of relief. "A good blow will do good, but do not be going close to the water. It has a trick of heaving itself up and not a warning. A cruel, treacherous thing, the sea."

As we passed through the low iron door to the cemented square in front of it, I slipped on something.

"Why, how odd!" said Alice. "A piece of seaweed. Fancy it being up here."

"Carried up by the wind, I suppose," and I kicked it carelessly aside. "What a strange smell, though."

"Hasn't it?"

"It's a sea smell, and yet... Did you ever smell a tank of seals? Like that. That's odd."

Alice laughed. "Everything's queer here. Don't you think we ought to see how *The Sprite* is?"

"Nice thing if she's knocked to pieces and we're marooned here till the Northern Lighthouse Board tender comes to relieve the men."

"I suppose they take turns."

"Yes, there're four of them, Ross tells me. Three on duty, one on shore. The tender isn't due for ten days or so."

"Oh, be careful," Alice begged as we hugged the rock in our descent of the zigzag steps. "There's more of that weed here. Oh look, *The Sprite*'s all safe, but what is that on the landing?"

"A seal, probably. You wait here. I'll go down and see."

I came gingerly down, and as I reached the bottom step the seal slithered into the water with a loud *plop*. I stood there, staring, rubbing my eyes wet with the salt spray.

And then I found myself shuddering. With incredulous eyes I peered into the water. I caught a glint of a blue-black, shadowy, twisting thing—and then it was gone, melted into the waters, as though it possessed a protective coloration which blended with that of the sea.

I heard Alice shout, and in unreasoning alarm scrambled back to her.

"You scared it," she said.

"Yes," I answered curtly, clenching my jaws tight. My pulse was drumming so loudly I thought she must have heard it. I would never confess to her what I had seen or fancied I had seen—not a harmless seal, but a froglike monster such as I had never heard of, nor seen pictured in any work on natural history.

"Come along!" I said roughly. "It's perishing cold here. Let's get out of the wind."

She did not seem to wonder at my abruptness, but followed me obediently. Strive as I would, however, I could not help turning my head to look behind, but all I could see was the spray flung high into the air.

We sat huddled together in a cranny. Never had I felt Alice so close to my heart as in that hour. A strange, fatal apprehension was upon me, a mad desire to get aboard *The Sprite* and flee the island, yet cold common sense, that bondage which civilisation has cast upon us, told me that to do this would be folly unspeakable. We could not hope to reach shore in that sea.

How many times since have I not shouted my curses on this obstinacy, casting those curses in the teeth of the sea as it flung itself on this desolate shore? But we are all children who learn our lesson too late. I have turned my back upon reason, upon logic, upon all that condemned my darling to a death which has made me what I am today, I who have set down these things with untold heart burnings, with a cankerous remorse and grief that nothing may assuage.

After a time we returned to the lighthouse. Alice went up to the living room, leaving me with Ross busy at work on the oil tanks.

I sat down on a box. "Ross," I said, "I imagine there's lots of strange fish in these waters."

"I dare say," he answered carelessly. "There are some will be saying they have seen the sea-serpent, and 'deed, the way the water comes plunging up sometimes, it looks like maybe he'd be kicking down at the bottom."

"I don't suppose you ever came across anything like a monstrous frog."

He stopped work to look at me.

"No, indeed. I never heard of frogs in the sea, sir. They're made for the fresh water, surely."

"So I always thought." I hesitated. "There was something like a frog—looked as big as a man—on the east landing, but it dived in before I got a look at it properly."

He shook his head at that.

"A seal, I'll be thinking. They twist that quick, you'll hardly get a look at them. But a frog—That's a good one."

He laughed easily, and somehow my memory became disconcerted. Of course the thing must have been a seal. My eyes were nipping with cold and salt, and it was natural I had not seen straight.

"Well, we'll keep the discovery to ourselves," I said, with a mockery of a laugh.

"Yes, indeed. If Angus were to get wind of this, we'd be having another mouthful of nonsense. 'Deed, company has a bad effect on him."

The sea-fog rose so high that afternoon that there was no thought of us venturing forth, so we spent the time in our several ways. Alice sewed, while Ross, McLeod, and I played endless games with a grimy deck of cards. Jamieson, apparently normal again, sat with his knitting. The beacon was lighted early, and faintly from above came the monotonous *tick-tock* of the clockwork which revolved it.

All at once McLeod raised his head. "Did you bolt that downstairs door, John?" he asked Ross.

"That I did. Why?"

McLeod stirred uneasily in his seat. "It sounded like it was giving a bit of a squeak. I'll put the oil can to the hinges in the morning."

He appeared reassured, but I noticed his eyes turn now and then to the trapdoor in the flooring. At length he rose and went down. When he returned, he was sniffing.

"There's a queer kind of smell on the air this night," he said.

"I noticed it this morning—we both did, my wife and I," I said as I shuffled the cards for another deal.

He sat down, but made no effort to pick up his cards.

"There's times," he said slowly, "when I am thinking I would like a wee farm a long way from the sea. Yes! A long way."

"Are you married, Mr. McLeod?" Alice asked.

"Yes, ma'am. But what kind of a life is it for a married couple? Here I am, six weeks on duty, then two ashore. You're fortunate, sir, to have your leddy with you all the time."

"I am, indeed, McLeod," I agreed.

I turned to smile at Alice, but to my amazement she had risen to her feet and was staring at the little window in the thick wall, her hand to her side as though it hurt.

"Why—" I started to say, and at that moment Ross uttered a startled: "God spare us all, what's yon?"

Pressed against the thick glass was a white something, a blob of flesh in which two dead, unwinking, fishy eyes rose above an enormous gaping mouth set with jagged teeth.

McLeod took a step forward, and on that instant the thing vanished. I caught Alice to me. I saw Ross run to a wall rack and take down a double-barrelled shotgun.

We heard him run hastily downstairs, heard the clang of the iron door as he flung it open. Mingled with the whiff of sea air which blew up to us, was a strangely musty, rank odour. I listened for the shot which never came. McLeod had tumbled after Ross. In a few moments the pair came upstairs, somewhat shame-faced.

"Not a thing," said Ross, "but the fog's that thick you cannot see your hand in front of your face."

"I'm thinking," added McLeod, with a look at Alice, "this fog makes strange shapes on the windows. It's not the first time I've got a fright out of nothing, a gull blown against the glass, like. Put down your sock, Angus. Get your melodeon and give us a song. He's the bonny singer, is Angus."

Jamieson rose and brought out an accordeon from a cupboard. I think at that moment his voice, untrained, yet with a pleasing tenderness, sounded better than that of any opera star. Somehow the music seemed to discharge the electric state of our nerves, so that when, after half an hour bed was proposed, I agreed willingly.

Twice through the night I was aroused by the hideous screeching I had heard the night of our arrival, but if any one else heard it, it excited no stir. All was quiet above me. Only Alice moaned in her sleep.

Next morning the fog still clung about us, a great stillness. For the fury of the wind we had exchanged that more exacting jailer. There was no hope of us leaving the island.

Though I said nothing to Alice, I was afraid. A vague terror was instilling its insidious venom into my heart. Perhaps I was mistaken, but I believe the other men felt it, also. Coming into the beacon chamber, I found Angus on his knees in prayer. And Ross, in the tank room, was cleaning his gun, squinting through its barrels and whistling a dismal air through puckered lips. I sat watching him in silence, and finally he spoke.

"I'll take a stroll down by the landing, and have a look at your boatie. I'll take the gun. Maybe I'll get a shot at something."

"Good idea!" I agreed. "I'll go with you."

When we got outside, I came to the point. "What do you make of that thing last night, Ross?"

He sighed. "I cannot be saying, sir, unless it was some kind of bird, though I never saw its like. Did you ever see an octopus? Well, to me it had the looks of the eyes and mouth of one of them, though how it got up to the window I cannot be imagining, no indeed. Two hundred feet... Stick close to me, sir, and look to your footing."

We moved slowly through the clinging fog. Indeed, it needed all my attention to keep from falling. I had an unaccountable fancy that on either side of us moved creatures, step for step, just beyond our vision. But we came to the descending steps without mishap.

"We can't do anything down there," I said. "Never mind the boat."

He would go down, however, and I saw him fade from my sight. I heard his shout rise up to me, dulled by the fog, and then a heavy silence blanketed all sound. I listened with beating heart, and then began to fumble my way down.

I had gone only a few feet of the distance when something ascending hastily ran into me.

"Ouch!" I ejaculated.

"That you, sir? Thank God!"

Ross was gasping. He sat down heavily and groaned.

"What's the matter? Boat gone?"

"No, no! She's there all right." He turned on me fiercely, and I felt his hand grip my arm. "Man, you wouldn't be saying I was mad?"

"Heavens, no! Why?"

"Not a word to your leddy—I got down to the landing, and I bent down by the water to give a tug to the mooring rope to see if all was secure, and as sure as God is my maker, sir, the sea was full of faces staring up at me, mouthing and gaping, hungering for my flesh—just like yon we saw last night! The water was alive with bodies—aye, like human bodies, but all bloated like. And the colour of the water was so blue and black you could scarce tell where they began and where they ended."

"I saw something of the same kind yesterday as I told you—that frog..." I stopped suddenly. Far behind us a faint cry rose on the air, more like the thin scream of a trapped rabbit than anything.

"What's that?" I asked sharply.

We both listened intently, but no other sound followed.

"I'm only a plain man without much book knowledge," said Ross simply. "I've followed the sea all my life and been in foreign ports, but this is beyond me, sir."

He pointed a shaking finger downward.

"Yon are devils, sir, devils!"

"Nonsense," I said roughly. "I can't explain it, but when you come to think of it, Ross, here's a part of the world that might as well be at the North Pole for all we know of it. It's quite natural there may be some creatures—sea-creatures flung up by some submarine upheaval—primitive things like those flying lizards and other monsters. You'd never believe there had been such things except in the imagination, unless you had seen the remains of them, as I have, in museums and the like. I don't know but what we may consider ourselves very fortunate in being able to get a look at them."

"I could well be spared the sight," he said drily, as he nursed his gun between his knees. "Maybe you're right, and they're naught but some kind of fishy creature. But for the sake of all concerned I wish we were rid of them. We'd best be getting back. I don't like the looks of it, at all, at all whatever."

"You don't expect them to attack us, surely?" I said. "They never could flounder up to the lighthouse."

"Where came that one we caught a glimpse of last night?"

"That's right," I said. "My God, that's right!"

This realisation came upon me suddenly and with such force that I began to tremble.

"My wife!" I said brokenly.

"Ay!" Ross replied. "Give her the word not to go beyond the door. We may be wrong, and they may be harmless, but it is best not to take a chance. Man, I'm glad I have a good supply of shells for my gun."

"Yes. Let's be getting back. I hate to think of her there."

"McLeod and Jamieson are there."

"Yes, that's true."

But I was distraught with anxiety till we managed to reach the lighthouse, scrambling our way through the fog. I was relieved to hear Alice answer my hail. McLeod came to the trap.

"Did you no meet Angus?" he called down.

Ross started.

"No! Where is he?"

McLeod came down, his rugged face filled with surprise.

"He was sitting here, when all at once he rose up as if his mind was set on something, and he spoke to your leddy, sir, in a queer kind of a way. 'God be kind to you, ma'am, and keep you from harm of them,' and then he turns to me: 'I'll be going after them, Donald. My mind is ill at ease about the gentleman and John Ross.' And what was on his mind, I cannot be saying, but as he went out the door he turned to me: 'I am a single man, Donald, and my time is come. Maybe they that are seeking blood will be satisfied with me'—and with that he was gone."

"The poor lad!" said Ross in a strained voice. "That was strange talk. Poor lad! He never should have taken to this work."

But I saw further. "Ross, Ross, don't you see?" I said wretchedly. "He knew more than we did—his second sight—He thought he might save us by giving himself as a sacrifice to—to—"

All I could do more was point toward the sea.

Ross thrust his face forward to mine, and our glances met. "The blue men Angus was talking about"—he said abruptly, tensely. "If I was thinking he had done that—Bide you here, Donald, with the leddy. And you, sir, take that crowbar and come with me."

I followed, leaving McLeod agape at the door.

"That cry!" I stammered. "That cry!"

I clenched my hand on the cold bar of iron I carried.

"God help him," muttered Ross as we hurried forward. He raised his voice in a shout of "Angus!" "Angus, are you there?" but no response was heard.

Suddenly I stumbled.

"Ross!" I said sharply, and we stooped to look.

For a long moment neither of us touched the thing which lay at our feet. Then Ross gave a choked sob.

"The poor lad!" he said again and again. "Poor Angus!"

I am sure no thought of our own terrible danger was in our minds.

"His arm!" I said in a whisper. "Torn from his shoulder!"

"Aye!" muttered Ross as he bent lower.

All at once he raised himself to his full height. His heavy chest swelled. He threw the gun to his shoulder, and a furious bellow came from his lips:

"Come out o' the fog, you skulking things. Angus, where are you? Say the word, and I'll let hell loose. Angus! For the sake of Heaven give us a shout. Angus, my poor lad, speak!"

But both challenge and plea went without answer.

"They must have caught him near-by," said Ross, more calmly.

"Devil's work. Oh, my heart is sore for that poor lad. He had neither kith nor kin, wife nor mother, to mourn him. Rest his soul in peace if he be dead, and I'm praying he may be soon if there is life left in him, wherever he be lying."

"If this fog would only lift for a minute!"

"Fog or no fog, I'm going to get them that maimed him," said Ross between clenched teeth. "Bide you here, sir."

Before I could say a word, he was lost in the fog. I stood there, every nerve atingle, filled with a strange awe and reverence. Angus undoubtedly had laid down his life for us, and yet I felt with strange intuition his sacrifice had been in vain, and the end was not yet.

Suddenly I saw something move upon the ground. I took a step forward, and then my heart stood still. My nostrils were full of the musky stench. Something had caught my ankle in a strong, tenacious grip. I did not stop to look down, but with my bar struck repeatedly on some flabby substance, and the clutch upon the ankle gave way. I was conscious of a bulk scrambling past me, blundering with a rush that knocked me on the flat of my back. Then I was up and shouting "Ross!—Ross!"

"Sir!" came an answering hail. Never was voice so welcome. Ross was at my side in a few seconds, breathless.

"One of them caught me by the ankle," I told him excitedly.

"So!" he said and bent to the ground. "The arm's gone," he cried, his voice rising to an inhuman screech. "Back to the lighthouse, sir, back this minute. We can do nothing for the dead. It's the living, now, the living."

He caught me by the arm, and, guided by him, we came to the lighthouse. He pulled open the door, thrust me in, then slammed the iron barrier in place.

McLeod came down. "Did you find Angus?" he inquired anxiously.

"No," said Ross; "but no doubt he'll be back soon, Donald. It's gey and thick out."

He thrust his mouth to my ear.

"I'll tell him when I get the chance but not a word to your leddy. D'ye hear me? Swallow your food down. Put a good face on it. We need all our strength against yon, whatever they be."

"Is there any hope of help—if we need it?"

"God spare us," he said solemnly, "none. The tender's not due for another seven days."

"If you were to fail to light the beacon, wouldn't they think something was wrong?"

"Never!" he said fiercely. "I'd sooner die than fail in my duty. No mention of that, sir."

"I beg your pardon, Ross," I said, gripping his hand.

"Oh, I understand, sir," he said brokenly. "Your wife—but I have a wife too on shore. We can only do our best. Ech, sir, I should be writing up the slate, but I haven't the heart to do it the day."

"The slate?" I queried.

"Ay! The log. We keep a log like on board ship, but it can wait. What can I say about Angus—what, that they would believe?"

When we gathered about the table for lunch, I knew by McLeod's face that he sensed the truth, though he tried to preserve something of his usual easy manner.

"Isn't Mr. Jamieson coming?" asked Alice innocently.

"We're looking for him any minute, ma'am," said Ross, avoiding her glance. "He'll be down by the crane splicing a rope, no doubt."

"What made him act so strangely?" she continued.

"Och, just his way of talking," suggested McLeod. "Yes, that will be it. He is very religious, ma'am."

Ross took the first chance he had to tell me he had run up a distress signal, but he feared there was little likelihood of its being seen in the fog. And so we settled for the day, besieged, set about by an unseen army of devils, whose power we had no way of reckoning. What would the end be? God! If I had known then, I'd have taken Ross' gun and shot the life out of Alice—Alice, my darling!

Darkness fell early. By the time the lamps were lit, Alice had begun to worry about Angus and to question us all, until Ross could stand it no longer.

"Ma'am," he said simply, "I'm thinking we'll never be seeing Angus Jamieson again. He met with an accident going down the steps, and fell into the water. He was carried away at once surely, for your good man and me could find no trace of him. Aye, you may let the tears fall, ma'am. Yon was a good lad, none better."

Under pretence of getting my help to do some slight repair to the mechanism of the beacon, Ross took me up the iron steps. In that narrow chamber with McLeod, we considered what was to be done.

"I'm thinking," said Ross, "if you and your leddy were to get away early in the morn, you could make the land and get a message to the board."

"What!" I said. "Leave you two here? That's out of the question. You'd better come with us if we're going. You can come back."

But he shook his head.

"It cannot be done, sir." He hesitated. "You'll forgive me—there's just a thought in my mind. Maybe there was sense in what Angus said. We've been here close on a year now, and never saw nor heard of yon hellish things till—till your leddy came. There never was a woman set foot on the island here. It might be—it was the woman—that they had got the wind of—and's drawing them out from their lurking places."

I looked at him in silence, at his honest, rugged face, the blue eyes which sought mine so earnestly.

"I mean no offence, God knows that," he added hastily.

"So you think if my wife and I went," I said, "there would be an end to this business?"

"Just that, sir."

"Very well, Ross," I said at last. "We'll make a dash for it tomorrow morning, at dawn. But I swear I'll be back with help just as soon as I can gather it together. A few charges of dynamite dropped in would make short work of these things."

"Donald and myself will see you off. I wonder how the weather is. It looks like clearing."

We went out onto the gallery, and as we did so I clung to the rail in a spasm of loathing.

About the base of the lighthouse crawled groups of the creatures so closely massed that their shapes were indeterminate. They moved with a strange undulation, and for the moment I had the impression I looked down on waves. There was a flickering movement on their surface, and after a little I was able to see that their upper limbs terminated in a bunch of whipping tentacles.

"The devils! The foul sea-devils!" muttered McLeod, seeing them for the first time. "So yon's them, is it? Oh, my heart is sore for Angus."

Ross vanished, and came up with his gun. Leaning over the rail, he took aim and sent a scatter of shot into the midst of the vile mass. At the sound, I think, more than the hail of lead, there was an agitated stirring, and with incredible rapidity the patches began to slither away. In a couple of minutes the neighbourhood of the lighthouse was free of them.

Alice came running up.

"A gannet," explained Ross hastily; "but I missed the old bird."

"I heard you fire. I couldn't think what was up."

"It's like to clear, ma'am," said McLeod quickly, "so you and the gentleman can be leaving us in the morn."

"Yes, we're going, Alice," I assured her. "We can't impose on our friends here any longer. And they want us to notify the Lighthouse Board to send another man right away."

"I think I'll be glad to go," said Alice, "though you have been wonderfully kind to us, Mr. Ross and Mr. McLeod."

"It's nothing," said Ross. "Common hospitality."

Such an evening! The eve of a criminal lying in the death-house awaiting the last summons! Three silent men about the card table, a wondering woman by our side—ears tense to catch the slightest sound, muscles taut to spring instantly from our hard wooden chairs; the air heavy with unspoken apprehension. We were in terror of—what?

And when finally we got to bed, it was not to sleep. The ticking of the clockwork was magnified to the stroke of some vast machine that drove spikes into my tortured brain. It seemed to me I could hear through the thick stone wall the stealthy flicker of these ghastly tentacles which could tear a man limb from limb, and so adhesive they could elevate those bloated bodies up the side of the lighthouse. What if they managed to reach the lantern, to break the glass and pour in upon us? I put my arm about the sleeping body of my dear one.

*

Ah, the devils! Once I found an octopus upon this shore. I killed it with rocks and tore it to shreds in my fury. Vilest of creatures, spawn of primeval corruption.

Can I write sanely now? I am telling myself I must. I must not give way to the fury which at times makes me leap and fling my arms wildly on the ribbed sand, shrieking my curses to the blast and the surge.

Let me try my pen once more.

The morning came. We rose. Ross moved silently among his pots and pans. We ate something—what, I can't remember; and then McLeod, orderly as ever, washed the pans and dishes and set them in their places. The fog had gone. The dawn was cold, grey, clear. There would be no danger in our trip, I felt.

We opened the door, and Ross looked about him anxiously. Then he nodded to me and we four set out on our way. We reached the steps and began to descend them. As we passed the crane, I noticed a box of tools had been torn from the fastenings and broken open. We reached the landing; I got aboard *The Sprite*. I hoisted her anchor, and McLeod held the aft mooring ready to let go. Ross shifted his gun to shake hands with us both. We shook hands with McLeod, then Alice scrambled past me and went forward. The waters washed about us, swelling and subsiding. There was no sign of danger.

And then I happened to look at the steps, and I heard someone— was it I or another devil-cry in a harsh screech of warning:

"Behind you—look—they come."

In one long undulating current the sea-devils poured down the steps. It was like a stream of turbulent water in which tossed the branches of submerged trees. Horrid, tentacled arms rose and fell.

They came on irresistibly. The two men turned to face them, and McLeod let fall the mooring rope. The wind crept into my sails.

Ross' gun went up. He fired, but he might as well have been armed with a child's pop gun.

The Sprite rocked. I felt the thud of heavy objects beneath her keel, and then in a twinkling the sea was alive. The landing and the sea alike were masses of scrambling things. I saw the two men on shore overwhelming by this blue-black wave of glistening slimy bodies.

The Sprite was moving. To attempt rescue was suicide.

Then abruptly one of the things reared itself out of the water. Its beastly eyes peered into mine, its obscene mouth gaped. Over the thwart of the boat its slimy suckers crept upon me. They leaped to my leg.

I shouted to Alice: "Loose that sheet!"

She made no reply, and I saw she had fainted. She lay on the thwart. I had but one glimpse which seared my brain—the flutter of her skirt—two appealing tentacled hands—a last impression of her unconscious face—her sliding body drawn over by a mass of tentacles.

I could not move, captured by this strain upon my leg. My eye fell on the axe I kept in the boat, and with a madman's fury I struck at the tentacles. I felt the clutch give, and, axe in hand, I stooped—and at that moment the boom swung... I felt a crushing blow on my head.

I opened my eyes to a watery sun. I was lying in the bottom of the boat, alone—alone. I raised myself on my elbow. I was in mid-ocean...

Once more my senses left me.

They tell me I was cast ashore here on this remote island close by Portugal. How I came, I know not. Better had I perished than sail like a ghost, like an automaton, unchallenged by any vessel, to live to drag out the weary years.

Ah devils, devils, you robbed me of all—of love, of hope, of reason. No, not all. What am I saying? Do I not sometimes see my

Alice? Does not her face, sweet and sad as I remember it last, hold out promise that some day we may be with each other?

My endless torture is finished. Words, words that I shall never read again. Can I read? I do not know. Yet I have written as though another held the pen, another spoke these words into my straining ear.

"There it is," said the young wireless operator. "If you can make anything of it, you're welcome."

"How did you fall heir to it?"

"We were wrecked off the coast of Portugal, and we managed to get ashore. The people did the best they could for us, got us the keys of the house of an old lady who was away. A barn of a place—and there hadn't been a fire in it for years. We were soaked to the skin. We tried to light a fire and nearly got smoked out, so we piled into bed. I didn't have dry clothes for days, and we were as uncomfortable as I ever want to be.

"However, a young fellow who spoke English came along. Son of a marquis, but a darned decent kid, and I got some clothes and he carried me off to stay with his family. I was there three weeks. Well, we got pretty friendly, and used to explore the neighbourhood. It was he who put me wise to The Solitary.

"Seems The Solitary was a crazy sort of guy who had been cast ashore a good many years before, and lived like a savage. The fishermen treated him well, though, and he never lacked food. He had died about a couple of weeks earlier, but his hut was still there.

"One day we had a look at it. Of course it was empty. He apparently had nothing but some old bottles and a battered pot or two. I was kicking at the floor of it when an old board flew up and I saw a tin can. Whatever made me dig it out, I don't know; but I did, and we found this manuscript in it. We had a rare old laugh over it, Emilio and me. The fellow must have been crazy. But it's in your line, so I thought you'd like it."

It took me some time to trace my clues, but I did eventually.

It seems that the tender of the Lighthouse Board carrying the relief man, oil, and provisions, was delayed several days. On arriving at the island—"The Country"—the crew were surprised to find no one to greet them, as was customary. They landed, and found the lighthouse empty, but all in order. In the kitchen everything was neatly put away.

There was nothing in the log to indicate excessive weather or accident. Only, the last entry had been made a number of days previous.

A search was made over the island, which is no more than five hundred by two hundred yards in extent, but no trace of the three missing keepers could be discovered. There were two landing places. That on the east was undisturbed. On the west a box of tools many feet above the sea had been torn from its fastenings.

Various theories were advanced in contemporary accounts, but to my mind none of them met the case. It was suggested an upheaval of the sea had swept away the keepers, but it seems to me most improbable all three could have come to their end in this way.

There was no reference made in any report as to finding anything in the lighthouse which might indicate the presence of strangers. Nor is there any mention in papers of the date of the disappearance of an American artist and his wife: but it may be this tragedy was overclouded by the mystery of the other.

And there the matter must rest, unless the unexpected happens, and from some far corner of the globe comes further verification of perhaps the most amazing story I have had the fortune to give to the public.

SEASHORE MACABRE:
A MOMENT'S EXPERIENCE

Hugh Walpole

At one point in "Seashore Macabre" (1933) the protagonist finds sand in his shoes, his eyes, and his throat. It is a familiar experience to anyone who has traipsed sand home after a day at the beach and found it impossible to be fully rid of the stuff. Hopefully other elements of this short but disturbing tale of a young boy's summertime excursion to the seaside are less common occurrences.

Sir Hugh Seymour Walpole (1884–1941) was a popular writer in the early decades of the twentieth century, though today he is certainly less famous than many of the writers who supported and praised his work—including Henry James, Virginia Woolf, Joseph Conrad and Ernest Hemingway. As is perhaps apt for a descendant of Horace Walpole—an originator of the Gothic tradition—Hugh Walpole wrote numerous pieces of horror fiction, most notably 1933's *All Souls' Night*, in which the present tale appeared, and edited at least one anthology of supernatural fiction, *A Second Century of Creepy Stories* (1937). Among Walpole's most touching weird tales are those—such as "Tarnhelm" and "The Little Ghost" (both in *All Souls' Night*)—that use the coast to explore, in understated ways, intimate and queer relations between men.

"Seashore Macabre: A Moment's Experience" takes place on a beach in Cumberland—a recurrent and much-loved setting in Walpole's writing (Glebeshire, another recurrent, and fictional, setting of Walpole's also features in *All Souls' Night*.) This is a delight-fully morbid tale with a strikingly odd climax and a few glancing references to Sigmund Freud that seem knowingly to anticipate—and undercut—a too prescriptive psychological reading of the narrative.

We had gone to our usual summer residence, a farm perched on the steep hill above Gosforth—Gosforth in Cumberland, where the Druid Cross is in the graveyard, so that foreigners come from the far ends of the earth to see it. For the rest the farm was hay and chickens' eggs, and wallflowers in hot dusty clusters under the narrow garden-wall, and the ducks walking into the kitchen, and Mrs. A—, the friendly, soft-hearted and deeply pessimistic farmer's wife, making cakes, hot and spicy, in the cavernous black oven.

But this incident, so clearly and sharply remembered, so symbolic, Mr. Freud perhaps would tell me, of all my older life, has nothing to do with the farm, except that it starts from there. It starts from there because on fine days we bicycled three miles into Seascale.

Seascale was the nearest seaside resort. It looked then as though one day it might become a true resort. It had long, lazy sands, a new golf course, a fine hotel, and there were little roads and lanes in and about that looked as though, with the slightest encouragement, they might become quite busy shop-haunted streets. Nevertheless, little roads and lanes now after thirty years they still are. Seascale has never taken that step upward into commercial prosperity that once perhaps was hoped for it. I myself am glad that it has not. It is the one place of my childhood that is not altered. The flat, passive sands are damp and wind-blown as they always were, the little station—sticky in the warm weather with a sort of sandy grit, damp in the wet weather like a soaked matchbox—stands just as it always did, as though with a rather stupid finger to its lip it were wondering whether it should go or stay.

No, not on the face of it a romantic place, Seascale—and yet to myself one of the romantic places of the world!

We bicycled—my father, my sister and I—while my mother and small brother were driven the three miles in a pony-trap. Then, if the weather permitted us, we spent the day on Seascale sands. We bathed in water that had always a chill on it quite special to itself, we ate ham sandwiches, hard-boiled eggs and gingerbreads under the shelter of the one small rock that the beach possessed (if that rock were not already occupied), and we read—my mother and father *The Egoist;* I—if priggish—*Le Rouge et le Noir,* if unpriggish, *Saracinesca.*

Now it happened that one day in the week was specially glorious to me; this was the day of my weekly pocket-money, threepence the amount, if not already owed for reasons of discipline, sin or back-answering. Now it also occurred that on the same day that I received my pocket-money was published the new number of a paper, yet I believe (and hope) in a flourishing condition—*The Weekly Telegraph.*

The Weekly Telegraph was my love and my dear. It cost, I think, only a penny. Its dry and rather yellow-tinted sheets (smelling of straw, liquorice and gunpowder, I fancy in reminiscence) held an extraordinary amount of matter, and especially they held the romantic short stories of Robert Murray Gilchrist, the serial narratives of young Mr. Phillips Oppenheim, and even, best of all as I remember it, *The Worldlings,* by Mr. Leonard Merrick. There were also "Country Notes," tinged deeply with Cumberland sights and sounds, jests, quips and oddities, ways of cleaning knives and forks, making pillow-slips and curing a child of the croup.

What I suppose I am trying to emphasise is the contrast of these happy simplicities with—well, reader (as Charlotte Brontë always said), be patient and you shall hear!

You can see me, small, spindle-shanked and wind-blown, while my family sat huddled beneath the one Seascale rock, struggling through the spidery sand to the little station, my threepenny piece damply clutched. It was, as I remember it, a day of bright, glittering sun and a high wind. I am at least certain of a general glitter in the heavens and fragments of burning sand about my eyes.

I fought my way up the slope, sand in my shoes, sand in my eyes, sand in my throat. I stood on the higher ground, rubbed the sand from my eyes and looked back to the distant plum-coloured hills where the Screes run down sheer to Wastwater and Gable rolls his shoulder. Then into the little station that burnt in the sun so that its paint sizzled. I asked for *The Weekly Telegraph*. I cannot remember what he was like who gave it to me, but I do know that I did not take two steps before I had opened the paper to see whether there were a Gilchrist "Peakland" story, all about My Lady Swarthmore and tinkling spinets and a room darkly hung with tapestries, and some fair child working a picture in delicate silks. Yes, there it was! The horn was blowing through Elf-land, the long slow sands below me were lit with mother-of-pearl, and there were mermaids near the shore. Mr. Oppenheim was also there—*A Prince of Swindlers*, Chap. XVII. "As he walked down the steps of the Hôtel Splendide, wondering whether he should try his luck at the Tables or no, Prince Serge..." I drew a deep breath of satisfaction, took a step out of the station and almost collided with the wickedest human being it has ever been my luck to behold. Now, wicked human beings are rare! I have, I think, never beheld another. The majority of us are fools with or without a little knavery. This old man was, although, as you will see, I never exchanged a word with him, really wicked—capable, I am sure, of real, fine, motiveless villainy like Iago.

He was a little man, bent in the back, wearing a rather floppy black hat and carrying an umbrella. He had, I remember, a sallow complexion, a hooked nose, and a wart on his chin. I say I remember, but indeed he is as vivid to me as though he were standing by my side at this moment—which in fact he may be for all I know to the contrary.

And now, how strange what followed! As I have said, I almost stumbled on him. He stood aside and looked at me, and *I* looked at him! His look as I recall it was cold, sneering and mean-faced. Then he turned on his heel and, waving his bulging umbrella in the air, walked down the road.

Why, of all things in the world, did I follow him? I cannot imagine. I was on the whole a timid child, a good deal of a coward. Moreover, I had in my hand my adored *Weekly Telegraph* and was longing to read in it. Nevertheless I followed him. Looking back across all those years it seems to me that a cloud passed over the sun as we walked along, that the walls of the houses shone with a less brilliant reflection, that a chill creeping little wind began to wander. That is doubtless imagination. What is true is that the little man walked without making any sound upon the road. He was wearing, I suppose, shoes soled in felt or something of the kind. What is also true is that I was drawn after him as though I were led by a string.

Now I have said that I knew him to be wicked. How did I know? Was it only the idlest fancy? At that time I had but a child's knowledge of the world, and wickedness was far from my experience. The nearest to wickedness that I had then reached perhaps was the sight of a schoolfellow who had pulled the wings from a fly, or the lustful anger in the eyes of a schoolmaster beating one of my companions. Well, this little old man with the umbrella had something of that about him. Cruelty and meanness? Are there any other sorts of wickedness? I am sure that this little man could be both cruel and mean.

Did he know that I was following him? He must have heard my step. He gave no sign. With his head forward, his back bent, waving his umbrella, so under the windy sun he pursued his way.

Beyond the little town we reached paths soft in sand and with stiff sea-grasses sprouting there. We approached the sea and I fancy that the wind increased in volume, began to blow a hurricane. My heart was beating with terror, a sort of sickly pleasure, an odd mixture of daring and foreboding.

The little man came to a cottage knee-deep in sand, on the very edge in fact of a dune that ran down to a sea where waves were flinging in a succession of fiery silver wheels. Although the sun shone so brilliantly, the cottage looked dark and chill. There was, as I remember it, no warmth here, and the wind tugged at my trouser-legs. The little man vanished into the cottage. Clutching my *Weekly Telegraph,* I followed. And then—how did I have the courage? What spell was laid upon me so that I did something utterly against my nature? Or was it that my true nature was for once permitted the light?

In any case I paused, my heart hammering the little cottage as still as a picture. Then—I turned the handle of the door and looked in.

What I saw was a decent-sized kitchen with a yawning black oven, dressers—but on them no plates; windows—but uncurtained. In a rocking-chair beside the fire sat an old man, the very spit of the old gentleman I had followed. The room was dark, for the windows were small; it was lit by candles and the candles were placed, two at one end of a trestle, two at another. And on the trestle lay a corpse.

I had never until that moment seen a dead person. This figure lay wrapped in white clothes; a white bandage was round his chin; his cheeks were waxen and yellow. So he lay. There was a silence, as there should be, of the grave itself. The corpse, as, with horror clutching my throat, I more persistently gazed, was that of an old man, the image again of the old boy with the umbrella, of the old boy in the chair. Nothing stirred. I could hear the solemn tick of a clock.

But, in my agitation, unknowing, I held the door open. A sudden gust of wind rushed past me, and instantly—most horrible of all my life's recollections!—everything sprang to life. The little man whom I had followed appeared at the head of the kitchen-stairs and, in the most dreadful way, he pointed his umbrella as though condemning me to instant death. The little man in the chair sprang out of his sleep, and I shudder now when I remember his loose eye with its pendulous lid and an awful toneless grin as he stepped towards me. But worst of all was the way in which the thin silver hair of the corpse began to blow and his grave-clothes to flutter.

The room was filled with the wind. Sand came blowing in. Everything was on the move; it seemed to me that the yellow-faced corpse raised his hand...

Screaming, I ran for my life. Stumbling, falling, bruising my knees, tearing my hands against the spiky grass, I frantically escaped.

A moment's experience—yes, but Mr. Freud might say—a lifetime's consequence.

A COAST-NIGHTMARE

Christina Rossetti

By way of conclusion, "A Coast-Nightmare" (1857) takes us away from any actual or tangible coastline of the British Isles and returns us to the weird and haunted dreamworlds with which this collection began. Christina Rossetti (1830–1894) is no stranger to fantastical geographies—perhaps most famously encountered in the lurid gothic visions of "Goblin Market" (1862). But where "Goblin Market" presents a narrative of erotically-charged fecundity, "A Coast-Nightmare" offers a blighted and lifeless prospect, a land of unripe crops and the drifting ghosts of humans and non-humans alike. Rossetti's nightmare vision of a shoreline strewn with "Blood-red seaweeds" that "drip along that coastland" proffers an unsettling encounter with a gore-streaked terrain; "The wordless secrets of death's deep" which the speaker discovers here are also framed in a way to implicitly connect the underworld or afterlife ("death's deep") with the watery depths the poem reflects on. Rossetti's poetry makes recurrent use of the sea and the shore as liminal regions, and here that liminality is both literal and psychological, and once more the "coastland" is a purgatorial space. Nor is it one which, once encountered, is easily forgotten: even on waking, the speaker finds themselves "hunt[ed]... like a nightmare".

"A Coast-Nightmare" has a slightly muddy publication history: the poem was first drafted as "A Nightmare" in September 1857. Part of it (the second stanza) was first published with variations as "A Castle-Builder's World" in 1885 in Rossetti's *Time Flies: A Reading Diary*; a longer fragment (based on a partial manuscript) was published in the posthumous *New Poems* (1896). A complete manuscript of the poem, with the title "A Coast-Nightmare", was auctioned in 1970, and published by H. B. de Groot in 1973.

I have a friend in ghostland—
Early found, ah me, how early lost!—
Blood-red seaweeds drip along that coastland
By the strong sea wrenched and tossed.
In every creek there slopes a dead man's islet,
And such an one in every bay;
All unripened in the unended twilight:
For there comes neither night nor day.

Unripe harvest there hath none to reap it
From the watery misty place;
Unripe vineyard there hath none to keep it
In unprofitable space.
Living flocks and herds are nowhere found there;
Only ghosts in flocks and shoals:
Indistinguished hazy ghosts surround there
Meteors whirling on their poles;
Indistinguished hazy ghosts abound there;
Troops, yea swarms, of dead men's souls.—

Have they towns to live in?—
They have towers and towns from sea to sea;
Of each town the gates are seven;
Of one of these each ghost is free.
Civilians, soldiers, seamen,
Of one town each ghost is free:

They are ghastly men those ghostly freemen:
Such a sight may you not see.—

How know you that your lover
Of death's tideless waters stoops to drink?—
Me by night doth mouldy darkness cover,
It makes me quake to think:
All night long I feel his presence hover
Thro' the darkness black as ink.

Without a voice he tells me
The wordless secrets of death's deep:
If I sleep, his trumpet voice compels me
To stalk forth in my sleep:
If I wake, he hunts me like a nightmare;
I feel my hair stand up, my body creep:
Without light I see a blasting sight there,
See a secret I must keep.

MORE TALES OF THE WEIRD TITLES
FROM BRITISH LIBRARY PUBLISHING

We welcome any suggestions, corrections or feedback you may have, and will aim to respond to all items addressed to the following:

The Editor (Tales of the Weird), British Library Publishing,
The British Library, 96 Euston Road, London NW1 2DB

We also welcome enquiries through our Twitter account, @BL_Publishing.